THE U.F.O. CASE

LIQUID COOL: THE CYBERPUNK DETECTIVE SERIES

From the Crazy Maniac Files
BOOK THREE

AUSTIN DRAGON

Published by Well-Tailored Books, California

The U.F.O. Case
Liquid Cool: The Cyberpunk Detective Series
From the Crazy Maniac Files (Book Three)

978-1-946590-18-3 (paperback)
978-1-946590-16-9 (ebook)

http://www.austindragon.com

Printed in the United States of America

CONTENTS

Introduction

There was my first "Crazy Maniac File." The storm of the century was coming to Metropolis, but so were the cyborg gangsters...after me. But none of them were a real match for the legend known as ***Classic Cyborg***.

Then came my second "File." One rainy afternoon, a real live samurai master, a suave gentleman wearing an expensive silk suit and slippers, strolled into my Liquid Cool office to retain my services—after he destroyed everything. He wanted to hire me not for himself, or his megacorp boss, but for a mysterious assassin known as ***The Digital Samurai.***

When you're a busy street detective working the high-tech, low-life mean streets of Metropolis, it's easy to get into the routine of solving a case, then moving on. In the world of private investigation, even after the dangerous cases with the potential to shoot you between the eyes with a laser blast, you close out and move onto the next one. I hadn't forgotten this particular case; I'd filed it away in a spare office of my mind.

But some cases were even "meaner" than my regular ones, the action more frantic, and the situations more deadly dangerous. These "Files" stood out because of said criminal crazy—or an even crazier client. I didn't have my full "crew" with me—PJ, Phishy, Run-Time, Wiz Gal, Quix, or The Mick. These files were usually just me with a minimal assist from outsiders, the equivalent of a cop going into a dank, dark warehouse full of multiple gun-happy bad guys without backup—also known as "being stupid."

My third Crazy Maniac File was in a category all by itself. The case was as close to a real horror show as I ever wanted to get. The "unidentified flying object" was the crazy maniac, and there was no place for any of us on the flight to go.

I cannot even imagine what it was like back in the Stone Age days, before hover-tech was invented. If you were on a plane and it malfunctioned, you went down with the "ship" and boom! No more you. They didn't even have the atmosphere stabilization tech we have today. All I was doing was minding my own business catching a flight on a new luxury airliner to the other Coast for a new case—a full-day meeting, then picking up a fat retainer. Instead, I—and all my fellow passengers—met *U.F.O.*, and I'm not talking about a flying saucer.

Why couldn't I have normal clients like every other detective mom-and-pop agency and corporate firm in Metropolis? Why did these crazy maniacs have to seek me out even when I'm forty thousand feet up in the air, relaxing, and not bothering anyone?

No gun, no parachute, no way out. No fun.

These were the cases *never* to tell the wife about, but I didn't even have that satisfaction.

Welcome to a Liquid Cool Sci-Fi "Horror" Mystery.

CHAPTER ONE

Cruz P.I.

The only center of the universe or reality that matters is the city.

I'd grown to love my glittering, neon-soaked supercity of Metropolis. But today, I'd be leaving her for a bit of an amazing little vacation to exotic points around the world and the boundaries of outer space.

My arrival at Metro Airport's *Shangri-La* Terminal, the newly opened, ultra-luxurious, multinational-sponsored super-structure, was ahead of schedule. The structure wasn't the largest in the airport city, but it certainly was unique—a shiny crystalline pyramid like Neo-Paris, the Middle East, or Mars colony. Now Metropolis had its own.

I'm Cruz. The president, CEO, COO, and detective-on-the-go of my own firm, the Liquid Cool Detective Agency. At that moment, I walked with an uncharacteristic spring in my step and a gleeful hum on my tongue. I couldn't remember the name of the tune. I'd soon be lounging first-class on my way to a real, much-needed vacation.

Though everyone simply called it Metro Airport, or Metro International, the full name was Metro International and Interspace Airport, and it was one of the largest travel hubs on the planet. Domestic and international air travel, peri-terrestrial space travel, and off-world spaceships to Up-Top all came through here.

Metro Airport's sky traffic could be seen from a hundred miles away and, by day, looked like the Earth was spitting out a steady flow of debris into the atmosphere and, at night, far into space. That debris was the millions of flights of hovercraft, hoverplanes, and space-jets going to their destinations, spiraling from the ground into the stratosphere, the exosphere, space, or to the moon and beyond. At night, the area looked like extraterrestrials were either invading or flying out for their next planetary conquest.

When I'd stepped out of my hovertaxi into a light drizzle without a care in the world, I didn't even need a hovertrolley—I was traveling that light. My trademark tan fedora was on my head and my tan slicker on my back as I pulled one long black suitcase on wheels behind me, strolling along in my extremely comfy aqua shoes on the black pavement.

The hovertaxi was courtesy of my best friend, Run-Time, who owned *Let It Ride Enterprises*. If it had to do with private transportation, Run-Time had a hand in it. His empire included all the top car washes, hovercar body shops, hovercar rental shops, and hovercycle rental shops, but it was his hovertaxicab and hoverlimousine services that made his company a staple of the supercity. But this time around, I wouldn't be seeing my friend.

Nor would I be seeing my one employee, PJ. My Neo-Paris born, ex-felon, champion boxer cyborg (her full street name was Punch Judy, get it?) would be holding down the Liquid Cool office while I was out of town. She was good at the office management stuff, which I don't think I fully appreciated when I first hired her. VP of Client Services was what she called herself these days, or was it COO? She changed titles like she changed her cigarettes and her haute couture designer clothes.

As I approached the main terminal, I had a weird feeling. On one hand, I was a man with a wife, two kids, and a classic hovervehicle, and I was going to miss them. On the other hand—I was glad to be getting away. My wife was the extrovert. I was the introvert, which means people, all people, wear you down after awhile, and you need that solo time. But no one tells you that when you're married with children, and co-cohabiting with those children for almost two decades! My wife, Dot (aka China Doll), and I were firmly of the same mind here: kids turn eighteen and out the door into their own place!

The real reason I was so sensitive about the subject was that our last family vacation—actually our first—turned out to be no vacation at all. It was a full-fledged murder case and civilians, including private detectives, were not allowed to investigate murders. But there we were on Jules Verne's Island—the ultimate exclusive, secluded, French-Caribbean resort and amusement park destination all to ourselves, except for a bunch of sci-fi writers—but no vacation. Just hiding, running, shooting, and explosions. Well, I did get paid. And Dot did get a lot of free clothes. And the kids did enjoy the island's amusement parks.

However, I still didn't get a vacation. When I first began my new career as a principal private detective, Run-Time had told me, "Bosses don't get vacations; they get an occasional break is all." He couldn't be more right.

I've had some big, high-profile cases in my relatively short career as a private detective working the "mean streets" of Metropolis. I had the big cases, which was what everyone remembered me for, but it was the small cases that kept the steady money coming in to pay the bills and became the "real world" of the business. Small meant boring. I liked boring. Big cases meant encounters with crazy maniacs—criminals, clients, and others. Also, lots of danger, running around, trying not to get shot, or getting shot. Humans, cyborgs, and occasional robots. But for my little "break," I was going to be flying in style, leaving my supercity behind for a little while.

I stopped just before entering the main terminal to turn around and take a final look at the Metropolis neon skyline. Flashing superskyscrapers reached into the dark rainy skies, some as tall as three hundred stories. The many lights of hovertraffic—hovercars, hovervans, hovercycles, and hovertaxis twenty to fifty feet above the ground—encircling it all. Hovertrucks had their own virtual lanes. Hoverbikers zipped wildly through all lanes. The red and blue sirens of a speeding police cruiser flashed in the distance. I was born and raised here; working and raising a family here. Metropolis was the largest supercity on planet Earth, a neon city overflowing with life in constant motion.

I turned back around and stepped into the new Shangri-La Terminal.

* * *

Three cases had brought me to the airport before—my Blade Gunner, Lunar Colony, and Biopunk Blues cases. The former was a good experience—I got to use my old hoverboarding skills—but the latter was the case where I was infected with a deadly virus by WHO (World Health Organization) bad guys. The Lunar Colony case was the first time I was ever off the planet, and I decided then that once was enough. I was a proud Earther and liked real gravity, real air, and a real atmosphere—all those little things we planet-centric types preferred. Technically, my family vacation-no vacation began here too, but, for me, the case didn't commence until our feet touched down on Jules Verne's Island.

Any terminal at Metro Airport was its own massive, sprawling self-contained city. There were lots of thick bay windows on the walls and ceilings, so that even inside, you could see all the rings of hovertraffic to and from its many terminals for departure and arrival. Metro Airport was a smaller but super concentrated version of the great Metropolis.

When I was last here, it was in the Asia Terminal, when the family and I thought we were going on a multi-country-hopping trip throughout Asia. Obviously, the wife and I were delusional. If it were just the two of us, then it would be great. But we had two hyperactive munchkins in tow. Now, Kat was well-behaved and a treat to manage. Cruz Jr.—also known as "ninja boy"—was a whole level of mischief. No wonder Dot and I were so easily tricked away from our Asian vacation for Jules Verne's Island, but it was the French Caribbean. Subconsciously, we knew we needed to stay at only one place if we wanted a real vacation, but without the murder and mayhem, of course.

Well, this time, it was a solo trip for me. My wife was known as China Doll by many. Her family and I called her by her real name—Dot. She was definitely more famous than me—second in command and consummate fashionista at Metropolis's premiere image and style salon, Eye Candy. For one week, she'd be taking care of the kids, but not alone. The Hellspawn—aka my parents-in-law—would be in my place too. Between my parents, Dot's parents, and PJ, Cruz Jr. and Kat would be speaking at least five languages by the time they were five years old. All I could speak was one, and I was damn proud of it!

I watched with a grin as other passengers around me frantically fast-walked or even ran past me with dozens of pieces of luggage stacked on hovercarts heading for check-in or elevators. However, I was in no rush at all as I strolled to the main golden doors (seriously, they were made of real gold) for the launch of the Falcon Express. It was the new peri-terrestrial flight for which the Shangri-La Terminal was built. I'd be a guest free of charge to be treated like a bona fide high-priced passenger. As my friend Run-Time would say, you know you've reached the heights of your profession when the clients pay your expenses to get you to do business with them. I liked these new heights, and my feet were still touching the ground in my comfy aqua shoes.

Good grief!

I came through the door and the press were everywhere. Crowds were gathered at a massive projection screen gawking at a live feed of the new Falcon Express sitting on the exterior runway ahead of boarding. I had forgotten how much of an event this was all supposed to be. The Falcon's owners clearly had spared no expense because they had bought off all the right people to have every media outlet, domestic and international, every channel, medium, and language to broadcast, promote, and evangelize for the company and the launch of its dazzling new hoverjet. Some of the reporters I knew by sight, and I knew many of them had never before worn a decent suit or dress in their lives.

They were everywhere recording their segments and interviewing people, with their camera people or camera drones following.

"Ladies and gentlemen of the press, the program will begin soon. Mr. Cosmo will be arriving shortly," said a thin young man in a shiny black suit.

As for the rest of the growing crowd, it couldn't just be passengers. More likely, looky-loos showing up to wherever the excitement was happening.

"Hey, Cruz."

Her voice was like the sound of a screwdriver scratching back and forth on the pristine paint job of my classic vehicle in an excruciating rendition of a heavy metal song I hated. Holly Live was the epitome of the media vulture, and, I guess, one of Metropolis's most famous investigative reporters.

"Ms. Holly Live," I said.

"What you workin' on?"

"I'm on vacation and not working on anything at all."

"Yes, I know you have a few more nickels to rub together these days, but don't tell me you'll actually be on the maiden flight of the Falcon Express?"

"Actually, I will."

"Even I couldn't swing that one. So what's the story, Cruz?"

"There's no story. A friend of a friend of a friend got me a complimentary flight. I'm going to be a mystery passenger. You know, like a mystery shopper."

"Cruz, I know what a mystery passenger is. Why do the corporate owners of the Falcon Express need a mystery passenger who happens to be a detective too?"

"Wait a minute. I'm not a detective here. I'm merely a citizen of Metropolis, a regular guy."

"Ha! You a regular guy? Cruz, you were never a regular guy, even when you were a nobody."

"Well, thanks for that bit of snobbery."

"In big leagues media, we tell it like it is. And, I smell a bit of deception."

"Of course, you do. Your fellow media vultures are all around you."

"I'll leave you alone on one condition."

"Leave me alone?"

"I won't broadcast that famous detective Cruz of Liquid Cool Detective Agency is on the maiden flight of the Falcon Express signaling—"

"Wait a minute! What are you doing? I'm a guest passenger."

"You were a guest on Jules Verne's Island, and look what happened there."

I was about to say something like: *But there was a case there.* And she would have said: *Yes, a dead body.* And I would have gotten flustered and said, *There's no dead body on the Falcon Express.* And she would have said: *Can I quote you?*

This was how media vultures worked. They'd turn nothing into something, or a big something, and get me kicked off the Falcon before I could even get to check-in.

"You have a good day, Ms. Holly Live." I gave her a big smile and walked away. I heard her yelling questions at me. "I can't hear you, Holly. What's that? You're secretly in love with me and want to tell the whole world? Oh, my, that's personal and profound, Holly."

"Whatever, Cruz!" she yelled as I quickly moved through the crowds for the check-in counters.

The media were truly dangerous. When in doubt, say nothing, or say all kinds of nonsense so that they couldn't make sense of anything and make them run away. I was very good at the latter.

Passing through the crowds, I noticed that people were waiting for something specific to happen, maybe the arrival of VIPs. I didn't care. I reached the ivory counters lined with gold and the smartly dressed, smiling male and female attendants behind it. I handed them my ticket.

"Mr. Cruz," one of the male attendants said as he scanned the ticket across the computer screen.

"One bag, sir?" asked another.

"Yes," I replied.

"We'll take that." Another male attendant opened up the counter to step out and take my long black suitcase on wheels.

"Thank you," I said.

"Mr. Cruz, you're all checked in," said a female attendant. "Just take the moving walkway to the waiting area. We'll be boarding all final passengers in about thirty minutes."

"Final? Am I late?"

"Not at all, sir. Boarding is done in stages. You actually arrived ahead of time," she said.

"Great."

"This is for you."

She handed me a swanky silver bag, along with my ticket. My very own Falcon Express swag bag. "You won't need your ticket again, sir," she said. "Just board when the announcement is made."

"Thank you."

I smiled, and they smiled. I turned. I stopped smiling. Holly Live was right there.

"You didn't let me finish, Cruz. My feelings are hurt."

"You don't have feelings, Holly."

"Ha ha. Yes, I've never heard that one before. Cruz, you are one of those people in the universe that...how should I say it...attracts trouble."

"What? No, I don't."

"Yes, you do."

"No, I don't. I mind my business. I can't help it if crazy maniacs run into me."

"Don't feel bad about it. If it wasn't the case, no one would find you interesting in the least way."

"Holly, what do you want? I have a flight to catch."

"I want to hire you."

"What?"

"If something interesting and newsworthy happens aboard the Falcon—"

"Nothing will happen."

"But if something does. I—my station, will be happy to compensate you for the scoop."

"Compensate?"

"Yes, Cruz, that means money. Nothing happens, you don't see me. Something does, and there's a payday in it for you. You don't even have to do any detecting. Come on, Cruz. We've helped each other out before."

"I bet I'll fall asleep the whole trip."

"Yes, but just in case. Nothing happens, then nothing. But if there is something, you'll be our inside-man, our eyes and eyes aboard. Besides, I'll owe you and you can cash in that favor whenever you need to."

"Sure, Holly. I'll do it."

"Deal. I'll let you catch your flight, while I have my work to do."

I watched Holly return to the crowds around the projection screen. She glanced back at me a couple of times, but I was confident I wouldn't run into her again. But I had to be sure.

I stepped back to the counter where the four smiling attendants quietly watched me. "Please tell me that that reporter will not be on the Falcon Express."

"Sir, neither she, nor any reporter like her, will be on the Falcon Express."

I reached out and shook the man's hand. "Long Live the Falcon Express."

The attendants laughed.

#

I liked the retro-tech of a moving walkway, which were far more common when my grandparents were kids. My Pops would say that something was new, then old, disappeared, then came back as new again. The platform moved passengers quickly, but comfortably, throughout the terminal. I think I preferred it to hovertrolleys, only because it wasn't the norm.

Quite some time ago, I had gotten Premium Check-In for the entire family. I had to go through all kinds of government background checks and pay a hefty fee, but we loved it. We could bypass the congested lines of people at the regular check-in counters. But you couldn't bypass security. However, as I got off my stop from the moving walkway to the spacious waiting area, I noticed that I hadn't passed under even one scanning arch or been through a single checkpoint. From the massive bay windows, we could see the Falcon Express with our own eyes sitting on the tarmac. I'd never seen a hovercraft like it ever before. It looked like it was part plane with the pilot's cockpit section shaped like a bird's beak, and part ocean liner with at least seven passenger decks. The Falcon wasn't the tallest or biggest hoverjet ever. It was, however, the longest, most expensive, most luxurious hovercraft ever built. If you weren't rich, famous, or married or family to either of those groups, you wouldn't be traveling on it anytime soon. Clearly, they couldn't allow passengers aboard without a single security scan.

"Sir, is there a problem?" a voice called to me.

I turned to see the Information Counter manned by three attendants.

I walked to the counter. "I've been to Metro Airport a few times, but it looks like we'll be boarding soon, and

I haven't been security scanned once. I've practically walked from the street to here without so much as someone wanding me."

"Carrying any knives, guns, or other illegal weapons, sir?" she asked.

"Of course, not."

She smiled. "Thanks for your watchfulness, sir. The entire terminal is a scanning arch."

"Really?"

"The main entrance is one, the section from luggage check-in to the transport walkways is another, this area is another, and the tube before you step onto the Falcon Express is another."

I felt relieved. "So, you keep the scary security guards hidden away."

"Yes, sir. We want our passengers to have a no-pressure, idyllic experience from when they enter the terminal to when they take their seats aboard the Falcon Express."

"Thanks for that."

"You're that detective, aren't you?" asked another attendant.

Shhh! I gestured with my index figure over my mouth. They all smiled.

"Enjoy your trip aboard the Falcon Express," one of them said.

"I certainly will. And I can't wait to fly. It's a new engine system, right? I've built hover-engines myself, as a hobby."

"The Falcon Express is the first hoverplane to use the new sky-walker model design."

I nodded. "In ancient times, their only hover-technology were aircraft called helicopters and VTOL planes—vertical take-off and landing—which were like a hybrid of helicopters and planes. These sky-walker engines incorporate new anti-grav technology. Basically, eliminating the whole...crashing thing. This is a big deal. Everyone is going to be using this tech."

"Mr. Cruz, you know more about the Falcon Express than we seem to in those regards."

"I'm certainly going to have a great flight," I said with a big smile.

When I was a kid in middle school, I'd found the shell in a junkyard that over the next few years I turned into my bright red classic Ford Pony, which I drove to this day. An expensive, sky-worthy muscle hovercar, I built spare part by spare part. Today, I felt like I did the day I finished building my Pony and took it out for its own maiden flight. I couldn't wait to step onto the new Falcon Express. For now, I'd sit and relax with my fellow co-passengers.

This flight was going to be so much fun!

(Yes, yes, I know. I should never have said that.)

18.

CHAPTER TWO

Chief Hub, Metro PD

I'd been in pre-boarding VIP lounges before, but the Shangri-La Lounge had to be in a class by itself. We had a secluded area so just us privileged first-flight passengers didn't have to co-mingle with any "mere mortals." The seats were big enough for a family of six to sit in comfortably. I was enveloped by my chair and didn't know if my body was meant to sit, recline, or sink into it. Each seat had a voice-activated entertainment center for music, TV shows, movies, news, white noise, or religious sermons with headphones you didn't need to wear. It simply beamed the sound right into your ears and no one else outside your little zone. While other VIP lounges had vending machines for cold and hot food and drinks, we had real chefs—and we hadn't even boarded yet!

Normally, I'd use my time in the waiting area to read or people-watch, but I wasn't kidding when I said the lounge chair and me had become one and I couldn't see anything beyond the display screen in front of my face. Some action movie was playing but I was uncharacteristically not interested. I had to get to my feet, but was having difficulty.

"Sir, the chair is voice-command, too. All you have to do is say, 'Raise me to my feet,'" one of those Information Counter attendants said, standing not too far from me.

I noticed some teenage girl in a mink coat and leather skirt watching me from her seat across from me. "Like this," she said. "Raise me out of the chair." The chair literally lifted her up to her feet. "Amazing what technology can do these days. You do know about technology."

Finally, I managed to respond. "No one likes a smart-ass, kid," I said. "And I'm far more tech-savvy than you."

"I doubt that, old man."

"I...am...not...an old man."

"I...am...not...a kid."

"Do you drive?"

"Yes."

"No, you don't."

"I have my learner's license, but who needs that when I have my own personal driver."

"Of course, you do."

I had no idea how I got sucked into the meaningless conversation. Was this what I had to look forward to from a future Kat? I sure hoped not. It was already too late for Cruz Jr. The brief moments he granted his mother and me his presence when not being a teleporting ninja. The attendant was still standing there. I thanked her, and she strolled back to her counter.

"Well, look at this," the girl said.

I turned, and the teenager was holding up her mobile phone and my smiling face on the screen.

"Are you like one of those people who's smart in one area, but a dummy in others? You can build a hovercar, but can't figure out a smart chair. Like Einstein couldn't do basic math."

"That's a myth. Albert Einstein could do basic math fine. Are you going to be on the Falcon Express?"

"What do you think, Detective?"

"I think your parents think you're as annoying as I do, which is why you're bothering me rather than sitting with them. Bye."

I won't repeat what she said back to me, but it wasn't very ladylike. It was part of the job—kids seeking me out to pester me. It was like people driving out to Old Penn to see the Amish. They did it but never could tell you why, other than they saw them on TV. We detectives were on TV too, unfortunately, and people had all sorts of ideas in their heads about us. Most of which was very far from the truth.

After the useless conversation ended, I made my way to the bay window to get a closer look at the Falcon Express. The silver plane was huge. Seven-story, "double-decker" style passenger section, a pointed front cockpit section shaped like the head of a majestic falcon, two hover-turbine wings each on either side, a large fin on the roof on the plane with its own hover-turbine, and an elongated tail with multi-sectioned stabilizers and rudders. The entire body of the plane had an aerodynamic design. Emblazoned in gold across its fuselage was its name.

The truth was that my best friend, Run-Time, was supposed to be the "mystery passenger," but his high-level meetings overseas had been extended. After the gazillions of dollars the new airline must have spent on the plane from inception to R & D to construction and launch, it was interesting that they were still doing market and customer surveys. Run-Time recommended me to take his place, and it so happened that its first maiden flight was to the Coast where I had to meet a new client. Perfect timing all around. I'd never been on the maiden voyage of anything before. The Falcon Express was supposed to be making history with the flight using its new engines.

From my vantage point, I could see the plane rolling to the boarding tube. We'd be going aboard soon. Outside on the tarmac, crowds of reporters followed a group that had to be members of the airline's board of directors and senior staff. They were holding a press conference right in front of the plane.

"Ladies and gentlemen, the Falcon Express will begin boarding all final passengers. Please make your way to the departure gate at this time," said an overhead voice.

I turned, and there was a valet with my suitcase. "I'll take this aboard for you, sir, and the on-board flight staff will have it taken to your cabin, if you so choose."

"Cabin?"

"Yes, sir."

"We get cabins?"

"Yes, sir. All passengers have complimentary sleeping cabins. But most of the trip will be in the main passenger area for you to enjoy the flight, meals, and entertainment."

"This is all a bit fancier than I expected."

"Only the best for guests flying the Falcon Express."

* * *

We got the first call to begin boarding. I still couldn't believe I had my own luggage valet, but I saw that everyone had one too, and most had more than one. For the first time, I got to look around at the people who would be my fellow passengers on the flight. There were more than one hundred of us after a quick count. I never dressed shabbily, but I was clearly the odd-man out among the crowd. The others were wearing clothes and jewelry more expensive than my Pony.

We all waited in an imaginary line to one side of the check-in counters, like we were about to run a marathon. I'd be fine, but the exquisite dress everyone else had on wouldn't allow for any more exertion than a slow walk. Even before being a detective, I never understood the sense of wearing clothes too fragile, clingy, or expensive to allow you to dive to the ground for cover or run at a second's notice whenever needed. We did, after all, live in Metropolis, where laser gun battles and other mayhem weren't unheard of. I wore clothes that allowed me to run, hide, or fight, whichever made the most sense or whichever I was in the mood for at the time.

My wife, as a professional stylist, would have been able to give me a full rundown of the dress and accouterments of this crowd. Mink, fur, and reptile-skinned coats. Tons of expensive rings and jewelry. Mostly dark clothes—blacks and dark grays—but also lots of colors—scarfs, gloves, shoes, belts—to stand out. No slickers, multi-colored or spiky hair, or half-naked presenting in this set. I'd be the first to say it: they looked good. "Camera ready," as my wife would say. I noticed that bratty teenage girl throwing me a dirty look. So, she would be aboard too. I ignored her.

I wondered if there were any cyborgs amongst them. I was used to the bold, brass, gaudy cyborgs—lots of metal. But I had a case where my uber-rich client had the side of his hand and forearm fitted with blades for chopping...people. I learned of it when he killed his criminal son in front of a whole crowd of hostages and me. Long story, short, it was a burglary gone wrong in so many ways for the bad guys. However, I wouldn't be thinking about that or any other cases on this trip.

The giant golden doors to the boarding tube opened, and we got the signal. Get aboard the Falcon Express!

The tube was about two stories up from the ground and, except for the actual walkway, was made of some kind of thick, clear glass. Below us were two more tube walkways, each with its own boarding entrance. Three different passenger levels all boarding at the same time. As we walked to the plane, or the walkway did the walking for us, we all noticed that we were now the center of attention as the media on the tarmac filmed us and waved. All of us got a kick out of it. The tube was wide enough for four people to comfortably stand shoulder-to-shoulder. At the entrance to the actual plane, one male and one female uniformed flight attendant greeted us. I don't know how, but they greeted everyone by their name while no one had to show a ticket.

The luggage valet called us guests rather than passengers. As we all finally got aboard and looked around, it seemed like we were in the lobby of some vintage hotel or one of those ancient railways made obsolete with hovertravel. Other planes had a commercial and first-class section. On the Falcon Express, commercial was first-class! Single travelers had their own seating pods, and those travelers of two or more had their pods clustered together. The Falcon Express had a maximum passenger capacity of two thousand. By no means the largest capacity of a hoverplane, but none I'd ever seen had this kind of luxury.

I wasn't the only one who thought they'd hit the jackpot as we were directed to our seats. When I sat down at my pod, in a super-plush leather seat, my eyes caught the controls on the armrest. Were we going to need a class to learn all the features of our pod? Like a first-class section, there was only one other person across from me—a slim young woman who gave off that "leave me alone" vibe, which was fine with me. First, she sat, reached into her jacket for what looked to be a physical ticket, made a face, and abruptly went back down the aisle. I guess she didn't like my aftershave.

Behind me were two other single pods. As I looked down to the back of the plane, the layouts were all us single travelers first, then couples, then families. Nice. The kids would be as far away from me as possible. The only kids I liked were my own.

"Cruz."

I heard his voice but couldn't believe I was hearing it.

Standing in the aisle was Chief Hub. What was the head of the Metropolis Police Department—the largest police force on the planet, with five hundred thousand-plus officers—doing on my plane?

The six-foot tall, musclebound, dark hair, thick-mustached, veteran officer in a business suit stared at me with a look of shock. He probably had less than ten percent body fat. He did far more exercise than I was ever willing to do. For me, never start any exercise you can't do at age one hundred. I'd seen it before, people doing all these super-exercises with toned, tight physiques—they stop, then blow up like a balloon.

"Chief," I said. "What are you doing here?"

"I was about to ask the same thing."

"Don't tell me you're a passenger too."

"I am. Both of us here for the maiden voyage of the Falcon Express. I didn't see you come aboard. Where do they have you?"

"I'm in first class. We board first."

So even the Falcon had its class distinctions. First-class was at the back of the plane.

"What a small world it is."

"Cruz, can I talk to you privately?"

The chief usually responded to my lightheartedness well, but this wasn't one of those times. He led me down the aisle toward a quiet area between sections. We were outside the lavatories.

"Cruz, why are you on this plane?"

"I'm taking a flight to the Coast."

"I didn't see your name on the itinerary. When did this happen?"

"Chief, it was a gift. Run-Time was supposed to be here. He couldn't make it due to business, so I'm here in his place."

I could see the realization come over his face. "Run-Time," Hub said.

"Yes. I'm doing him a favor and he's doing me a bigger favor. This plane is amazing."

"Cruz, I don't want you to take this the wrong way, but how much would we need to pay you to leave this plane right now and catch another flight?"

"What? Leave? Why?"

"Cruz, trouble has a tendency to follow you."

"You're the second person today to say that. That's not true. How many cases have I had already? A very, very, very small percentage of them would fall into the 'trouble finding me' category."

"How much?"

"Why are people trying to pay me off? Chief, I'm staying on this flight, period. I'll be sitting in my seat, minding my own business, as usual. Are you expecting one of the passengers to transform into a crazy maniac and pull out a plasma machine-gun from thin air? No. This is going to be a fun and quiet flight. Since you're asking me questions, why are you here?"

"Vacation."

"Chief, if you're going to lie to me, at least put some effort into it. Okay, I'll let you vacation back there in first-class, and I'll return to my what-I-thought-was-first-class pod. Chief, you're the top cop of the Metro Police Department, right aboard the Falcon Express. I feel super-safe already."

I left the chief right there and walked back to my seat. I never looked back, but I could sense he was still watching me. I had rarely seen the chief worried. The last time actually was when we both were close to being gunned down by the entire Animal Farm Crime Syndicate. But that was my first major case. What was he so worried about? There wasn't a single person aboard this big new-age hoverplane that I had any concern about, not even the teen-age brat. We were all perfectly safe—safer than safe, even.

CHAPTER THREE

Captain Pilot (Voice Only)

With its double-decker-style floor design, or deck in the case of planes and ships, the Falcon Express had a simple staircase in the center before the lavatories, between regular and first-class, connecting one level with the next. Before I got too comfortable in my pod chair, I wanted to at least familiarize myself with my area and my fellow passengers. Looking over the balcony, I saw a real golden spiral staircase. I could see that there were two more decks below, but I knew there were at least two more.

As I returned to my seat, the Falcon's interior reminded me of great retro-vintage craftsmanship. Designed to look like the high-society ages of the past, but elegant and exquisite in every way. Where the wall met the ceiling at the top, there was a foot of dark mahogany trim, and the same where the wall touched the ground. The ceiling lights gave off a nice glow, but an equally nice added touch was the golden candle-holders about six and a half feet up on the walls. For the moment, none of their authentic-looking candles were lit. High-class travel, high-class surroundings, high-class comfort.

As we passengers got settled, the details of the craft's interior came more into focus. I was an extremely observant person by nature, and the Falcon was definitely made for people like me. The ceiling and walls were actually holo-screens, so who knew what images would be displayed in the course of our trip.

"Did you see the bathrooms?" one of the nearby passengers said to me.

"Bathrooms?" I asked.

"The toilet."

"What about it?"

"You gotta go see it."

"I'm not big into toilets. In and out is how I like it."

He grinned. "You gotta go look."

Against my better judgment, I played along. Back to the bathrooms I went, where I had chatted with the chief. Just my luck the male bathroom was unoccupied. I stepped in expecting to see a spacious but simple toilet and urinal set-up. Was I wrong. What I saw was this thing—I'd never seen one before, so at first, I didn't know what I was looking at. It was some kind of plastic-looking giant contraption.

"Do you desire the toilet or urinal?" the contraption said.

I ran from the room.

* * *

At some point I'd have to deal with the bathroom situation, but not for the moment. When I returned to my seating pod, I looked down the aisle to see more passengers boarding, so I'd been in the first wave after the real first-class, still unseen, passengers.

I focused my attention out my window, but I was on the side not facing the airport terminal. All I saw was tarmac. I had to lean forward to get a glimpse of the forward wing; the Falcon Express had two massive wings on each side.

Dozens of luggage valets streamed down the aisles for the exit. We all heard the closing of the boarding doors with the final passengers on and at their seats. The A/C came on automatically. I turned to look out the window again to see a lone reporter quickly snapping more pictures of the plane before running back to wherever he came from. Flying on hoverplanes never bothered me. How could it? Being on the illegal hovercar amateur race circuit in my youth would have cured any apprehension about flying, if I ever had any fear. Hover-tech had transformed Man from a land species to a flying one, just without the feathered wings.

The flight attendants appeared, dispersing to different sections of the plane. I assumed they came down from the level above using the craft's elevators. They all looked like models, male and female. How much working out must one do to have zero body fat? Their uniforms looked like they were originally in liquid form and poured onto their bodies. Men in super-pressed white shirts with black ties and black pants with gold pinstripes, women in super-pressed white blouses with gold pinstriped black dresses. The black shoes they wore were so expensive they glowed.

My section was assigned four flight attendants—two men and two women. As of now, the airline was going to get a five-star rating from me for customer service. They personally introduced themselves to each of us. I'd never had that kind of service before. When I traveled on planes, they'd throw a bag of peanuts at you if you were in economy or stick a glass of booze in your hand if first-class. But on this flight, even their permanent smiles didn't seem fake. They loved their jobs, all right, and I'm sure they had a compensation package to make them love it a whole lot.

All passengers were seated, and all the attendants were standing quietly together. We were waiting for something. As I scanned all the passengers I could see from my seat, I thought what an attractive and classy bunch we were. And, other than me, rich. This was going to be a very satisfying flight. I might even snag a few future clients too.

"Good evening, ladies and gentlemen. This is your captain." His voice boomed over the plane's overhead. "My name is Trace Dash. Sitting next to me in the cockpit is my co-pilot and first officer, Jomar Hacker. Between the two of us, we have fifty years of flying experience, so you're in good hands. The press is calling this the pre-maiden flight and you, our advance flyers, but let me cut out all that and tell it to you straight. You are the first-ever passengers to fly on the state-of-the-art Falcon Express. Don't let anyone tell you otherwise. You are Neil Armstrong, not Buzz Aldrin or whoever the seventy-thousandth person was on the moon. You're the first, ladies and gentlemen. Give yourself a round of applause."

Well, of course, the passengers clapped. People always like to give themselves applause. With my contrarian nature, I didn't care so much for being first.

I cared about being on the Falcon. First, last, it didn't matter. I was here.

"We will be taking off shortly and we'll be lifting off ahead of schedule by a whopping five minutes. The Falcon Express is a one-of-a kind craft. It's the only commercial passenger hovercraft on Earth designed to travel in the sky, on the water, underwater, and in space. For this flight, you're going to experience all four of those mediums. We won't be flying around the Earth's circumference, as will become the standard flight path for the Falcon Express in the future. What we will be doing is hitting two states, two countries, two oceans, and outer space."

I felt it myself. We were all like kids in a candy store in Christmas Town. We looked at each with giddy smiles.

"But before we depart, ladies and gentlemen," the captain continued, "you're in for a special treat, if you can look at our special projectors on the wall. We have someone who wishes to see you off."

The attendants, on cue, pointed our attention to where we needed to look. I had seen the man before, but I said so before and I said so again when his big head appeared on the plane's holo-wall—the man looked like an alien. I mean, like a real one from another galaxy.

CHAPTER FOUR

Carnegie Cosmo, Owner of the Falcon Express

"Good evening, ladies and gentlemen. My name is Carnegie Cosmo, and I'm the President, CEO, and inventor of Fortress Enterprises. The Falcon Express was my brainchild twenty years ago, merely a sketch on a piece of paper. Through years of hard work, sweat, sleepless nights, an army of engineers, and a ton of investors, you sit comfortably in that dream become reality. Thank you for sharing my dream with me. You are aboard the best hoverplane ever created by humans with the best pilot, crew, and staff I could find on Earth, and no expense was spared. Enjoy your flight to the fullest and tell family, friends, and strangers, you were there on the first flight with many, many more to come. God Bless and Safe Journeys."

Trillionaires usually didn't hesitate when it came to cosmetic surgery to correct any defects. The man had a huge forehead. Maybe he was going for the brainiac look, but with his dark tan, bright green eyes (brighter than even Chief Hub's), balding at the top, but bushy hair on the sides, he did remind me of an extraterrestrial. Also, he never blinked. I didn't trust people who didn't blink, but I pushed all that out of my judgmental mind. I was here to enjoy myself, not profile people looking for criminals or other crazy maniacs.

I knew Carnegie Cosmo's entire life story. Basically, he started out as a neo-hippie born to a single mom who became a self-made trillionaire working in the high-tech transportation, robotics, and energy system industries. Very few people on Earth or Up-Top literally started with nothing and became one of the richest people at the top. Lots of wealthy people claimed to be self-made millionaires, billionaires, and trillionaires, but when you did a little bit of digging, you'd see that they came from a rich family to start off with. Or, as the Average Joe and Jane would say: a pretty damn significant head start. With Cosmo, the rags-to-riches fable was all true. Regardless, you had to admire that kind of drive, creativity, luck, and I'm sure, ruthlessness. To get those heights of wealth, you needed all those traits and the right people around you.

We could feel the hoverplane slowly moving. I looked out my window and saw that we were rolling around. And there he was, Mr. Cosmo himself waving at us. With that big forehead I could spot him a mile away. Surrounding him were all the press and a ton of other people. They were waving, and some of the passengers aboard were waving back.

I sat back in my seating pod, content with the fact that we'd be in the air soon, the fasten seat belts sign would be off, and I'd be free to move about the cabin to explore. Cruz Jr. and Kat would have loved this. Maybe, I could see if I could get family guest tickets for the next time.

CHAPTER FIVE

The Flight Crew

We were like the attendees to a big theatrical production play only the part where all the actors come out on the stage was how it started. On the closest holo-screen walls, we watched as the broadcast begun.

The first man had a thin mustache above his lips, and his black-and-white suit with gold at the edges reminded me of a movie mogul. "Ladies and gentlemen, I am Chief Steward Apex, and I am responsible for all interior activities aboard the Falcon Express and with flight crew, ensuring that you receive excellent service at all times.

"Let me introduce the rest of the flight staff."

The screen cut off, and all our eyes went to another man who appeared in the center of the four flight attendants, similarly dressed as Apex.

"Ladies and gentlemen, I am Mr. Java, your deck manager. I will oversee your time here on this level, aided by"—he pointed at the two female attendants first—"Ms. Proxie, Ms. Zenobia, Mr. Polo, and Mr. Marquee. They will directly attend to your needs while you're here on the passenger deck. We, of the Falcon Express, firmly believe in the simple, guest-first, old-fashioned human service that technology can never replace.

"Later tonight, after dinner, you will meet our cabin stewards who will attend to all those using your individual cabins on the sleeping deck, but of course, if you wish, you're more than welcome to sleep in your main pod seats.

"We will be lifting off shortly, and when we're in the air, we will begin serving refreshments. But later..."

Mr. Apex reappeared on the screens. "Yes, Mr. Java. Later, I will personally give First Deck a tour of all the sections awaiting you on the Falcon Express. Our first-class restaurant with a full bar, our on-board full-body workout gymnasium, hover-exercise bike room, onboard jogging course, steam room, swimming pools, tennis courts, VR game room, and onboard casino complete with poker rooms.

"We are truly a palace in the sky and, as our captain stated earlier, you will be the first to experience travel at a new level of high comfort. The Falcon Express will be the sought-after standard in the luxury, high-end travel industry courtesy of Mr. Carnegie Cosmo."

"Thank you, Mr. Apex. We look forward to the tour, and while you wait remember that you sit in the most advanced pod chairs ever devised. The entertainment center gives you access to a full book, music, and movie depository. The communication system allows you to call anywhere in the world or off-world. Also, take advantage of the chair's many heating and massage functions.

"Before I go, let's get a peek at our two pilots."

Two faces appeared on the holo-wall and screens, on either side of Apex, wearing their captain's caps. Apex disappeared and the men's images grew in size, complete with flashing yellow letters with their names under their now waving images. Captains Trace Dash and First Officer Jomar Hacker. It felt like we were in a sports stadium, and the franchise was showing off its star players, complete with the oh-so-white smiling teeth.

They disappeared and Apex reappeared. "Enjoy your flight, ladies and gentlemen, on what will become the Legendary Falcon Express."

Finally, they were done. I could stomach a bit of corporate advertising and promotional talk, but not much. However, they did stop just before you got to the point of wanting to check the net or put on the headphones for music.

"Any questions?" one of the female attendants asked.

I had no idea why that passenger near me looked at me with a wicked grin. He motioned at me with his chin. I shook my head vigorously.

"Can you tell us about that contraption in the bathrooms?" a woman asked behind us.

Everyone laughed. We were all thinking the same thing.

"Thank you for asking," the attendant replied. "That is our new 'sentient lavatories.'"

The passenger laughter was even louder.

"Sentient?" the woman passenger said. "I don't want my toilet to be sentient. All I want from it is to sit there and flush when I'm done."

The laughter grew louder. A couple of passengers were laughing so loud I thought they might have heart attacks. So, the impeccable Falcon Express wasn't perfect on everything. I didn't expect their "sentient lavatories" to survive past this maiden voyage. Actually, I had no idea what they even meant by "sentient" and I didn't want to know, or why they'd think people would want their toilets talking to them. When I got to my cabin later that day, I was going to tell my cabin steward to get me a regular toilet. To quote my Pops, "Sometimes people get so technologically advanced that they bypass 'advanced' and reach back to 'stupid' again."

* * *

Being a private detective was a profession even more dangerous than being a police officer. They had body armor, wicked guns, and backup. A private detective's best asset would always be a keen sense of observation. The ability to size up a situation in an instant, see when something was out of place, see that shadow in the alley that ducked away just before you stepped forward. A quick eye could save your life. Knowing how to capitalize on that quick eye could make for a very successful detective in the business.

Everybody had assigned seats. Though I pretended I didn't, I noticed that the little guy who was seated directly behind me was gone, and a big brawny guy in a sparkling light blue suit was in his place. Everyone else around me seemed to be the original occupants. Was this Chief Hub's doing? But why? Well, if someone wanted to watch me lounge in my pod chair sipping silk coffee, be my guest. I had more important things to observe.

The Falcon Express was about to take off!

Hover-technology had revolutionized commuting on Earth. It was like the ancient days when there was the land-bound automobile, which the rich already had, but it was Henry Ford that put it in reach of the masses, and he changed the world. The rich had hovercraft for decades, then the government had hovertrains and hoverbuses, but when everyone got it, that's when everyone said that humans had finally arrived "in the future."

But all that was centuries ago. Hover-tech hadn't made any real strides until now. The Falcon Express had the next generation "sky-walker" hover-engine, or likely more than one for sure. On the amateur hovercar circuit, I had seen my share of crashes. In each case, vehicles and occupants "returned to the surface," often in a gut-wrenching crash of metal and bodies or a full-on explosion. Hover-engines only worked when they were on. Otherwise, we were slaves to the same gravity as everything else. The "sky-walker" would change that. As long as it was on, its "hover-field" could not be disengaged, unless the craft was near the ground. The engines were synced to geo-positioning satellites at all times. I followed the news myself when Carnegie Cosmo announced at a major press conference years ago that the Falcon Express was "un-crashable."

Naysayers balked at the bold claim, but no one could find a flaw in the engineering. With global government agencies and the media satisfied, Cosmo was able to fund his entire enterprise with private investors in less than a year.

One could hear the engine revving as it glided down the runway. All of us were at our individual windows looking out. I had no expertise with large hover-engines used in planes, but some of the illegal hovertrucks on the amateur circuit had hover-engines rated for planes. I listened and realized that whatever the revving was, it was not the sky-walker engines. Sky-walker engines were silent. I was sure of it. Maybe the revving sound was for show. Megacorporations were known for gimmicks, if they could increase brand awareness and the bottom line.

We officially took off. The Falcon Express ascended fast, but it was a nice, steady incline up. Soon, and I do mean in minutes, the massive structural monstrosity known as Metro Airport was a mere dot on the ground, and soon after, so was the great supercity of Metropolis. We were high in the sky and into the clouds.

* * *

We were free to move about the plane, but no one was going anywhere. Our section flight attendants appeared with their hovercarts stocked with refreshments and drinks. I didn't even listen to what flight attendants Ms. Zenobia and Mr. Marquee were saying. It all looked good, and I took one of everything. Never had caviar before. I already had my coffee, but they coaxed me into taking some yellow, fizzy soda–something. It tasted great, and the bubbles continued bubbling in your stomach even after you drank it down.

We Falcon Express passengers were totally, completely, and fully content. One hand with food, another hand with a drink, face staring, transfixed, out the side window watching the sky. It was still daylight, but you could see the dots of flashing multicolored neon lights of the megacities. Metropolis was the only true supercity in this hemisphere.

We'd been in the air for about fifteen minutes. "Ladies and gentlemen, let's make our way to your tour by Mr. Java," one of the flight attendants said, and all of us passengers erupted in applause.

The attendants gathered our entire section at the back between our area and the real "first class" section in the back, which was closed by a velvet partition.

"What's back there?" a female passenger asked.

"That is a private party, ma'am," Ms. Proxie replied.

"Investors," Mr. Polo added with a smile.

That shut down any further curiosity from the passengers.

We all entered elevators, with one attendant taking a different group.

All of us got a pleasant surprise when the elevator went down and then abruptly moved vertically away from the front of the plane. The doors opened, and I swear I was in a scene from some museum or vintage movie. There was Mr. Apex in person to greet us and show off the restaurant and recreation deck.

"Welcome, ladies and gentlemen, to your grand tour of the Falcon Express," he said.

Now, the man did tell us what he was going to show us, but he actually should have warned us. Personally, I was overwhelmed. Everything was so beautiful that I'd feel apprehensive about using anything. The gym seemed larger than the one I went to in my town of Rabbit City. The hover-exercise bike room looked like it was for Olympic athletes, definitely not us. The steam room wasn't a steam room; it was an Asian-Russian amusement park of steam, polished rocks, and waterfalls. The swimming pools had water so clear you had to stare at it for a long time to be sure that was actually water in it. One of the passengers finally just walked over to it, bent down, and put his hand to touch the water. The tennis courts and VR game rooms were huge. We were on a two-day flight, not settling in for a twenty-year stay in our own biosphere.

The casino did get our attention because it was more down-to-earth. And when we saw the poker rooms, we already knew that quite a few of the passengers would be walled up in there for a few hours.

"Now for the best," Mr. Apex said.

We all knew he meant the restaurant and bar. It seemed we had to walk a mile to get to it, but when we did, the chief chef, sous chef, and the entire cooking staff were lined up to greet us—all dressed in pure white attire. The chief chef made it a point to let us know that the restaurant was always open and it was always "all you could eat."

Then we followed Mr. Apex to the bar area, where the entire bartender staff waited. They didn't wear jackets but wore the same dress attire as the flight attendants.

The bar also looked like it was pulled straight from the past, maybe the Old Chicago speakeasy times with red mahogany walls, ceiling, and floor, but lots of gold trimming. The bar stools absolutely looked like they were taken out of a museum. Classy, fun music, and ever-flowing drinks.

"Shall we have them serve you a drink to take back to your seats?" Apex asked.

Did he really think anyone would say "no"?

In centuries past, luxury trains and ocean liners catered to the rich, the famous, royalty, politicians, mobsters, and spies. All were whisked away from normal life to one of complete self-indulgence. If this was the kind of service that the Falcon Express would have on a routine basis, they'd be swimming in money forever, and not just from the uber-wealthy. The masses would save up for their once-in-a-lifetime Falcon Express family trip. But between Earth, Lunar Colony, and Mars, that wasn't going to be a problem. Flights were going to be sold out in advance every year.

CHAPTER SIX

The Peanut Gallery

When I got back to my seat, I wanted to do the same thing every one of my fellow passengers wanted to do even with drinks in hand—sleep. Our senses were on overload, but I'm sure that was all part of the Falcon Express plan. I looked at my watch—nearly two hours gone, just like that. Fastest two hours I'd ever spent. It felt like only thirty minutes. I was in the presence of time-consuming masters. If we passengers weren't careful, we'd find ourselves with only thirty minutes left in the flight without any chance for any steam bath or poker. I bet our private cabins were a whole new level of heavenly bliss, complete with "sentient" beds. I'm onto your game, Mr. Cosmo.

At this point, my body had sunk into my pod chair and my eyelids were feeling quite heavy. I never slept on planes, but the Falcon Express was no ordinary plane. I remembered what the captain had said: We'll be hitting two states, two countries, two oceans, and outer space. If I didn't take a nap now, I'd regret it.

"Do it while you can," the male passenger said as he returned to his pod chair across from me. He looked to be about my age, meaning older than college but younger than middle age. He had shoulder-length dark hair and wore all black, but it was a very expensive suit, like most of the people on the flight, except for me. As he sat, he grabbed a plastic pill container from his pocket.

"Are you okay?" I asked him. I had noticed that he looked a bit wobbly from the first time I'd seen him walk aboard.

"You're going to think this strange, but...I'm afraid of flying."

I smiled. "Don't you think you're in the wrong place?" I remarked.

"We all have our phobias to conquer."

"I know about those."

"What was your poison?"

"Good ol' germophobia."

"How did you beat it?"

"Sex," I said without hesitation.

The man laughed as he downed his pills and took a swallow from his glass. "Wish it was as easy for me. All I can do is keep flying and popping the pills. I'll beat it."

"Of course, you will," I said.

"Willpower." He leaned back in his chair. "We'll speak when I return to the living."

"Don't sleep too long. You don't want to miss the sights."

"I've already seen them. I'm here for the flight. I care a lot about this flight. I should, as one of the original investors." He sunk into his pod chair, and he was already asleep.

I glanced down at my armchair controls. If the modern hovercar had them, so would this pod chair. I found the sleep alarm. I set it to a thirty-minute countdown, then I reclined back with my eyes closed. That's all the time I needed for a quick nap.

An investor, huh? They wouldn't have one investor out among the masses by himself. So who was in the closed-off first-class section in the back, the same section where my "buddy" Chief Hub was?

I was falling asleep myself. I could worry about it later.

The alarm worked on the same tech as the entire entertainment system. The annoying sound beamed right into my ears. I shut it off and stood to do a series of stretches to fully wake.

I already knew that the Falcon Express wasn't at full capacity, but as I looked around the plane, the lights a bit dimmer, there was hardly anyone in sight. My sleeping, pill-popping investor friend was still fast asleep, but we were the only two at the front of our section. However, in the middle section that included pods for couples, there were a few people, and in the rear family area, a few more.

Ms. Zenobia appeared, pushing a hovercart to me.

"Where is everyone?" I asked.

"Mr. Apex did give you the tour for a reason, sir. The Falcon Express is to be fully experienced. There's plenty of time to sleep."

"I missed the speech, didn't I?"

"You did, sir. You looked so content where you were that we couldn't bear to disturb you. But you can't leave now, we are about to see our first scheduled site."

"Which one?"

"Space."

"We see space every day, and I've been on one peri-terrestrial flight already."

She smiled. "Not like this."

In the meantime, I contemplated watching a movie. From my fancy entertainment console, I scrolled vertically and horizontally through the featured selections. There was a lot of horror. I never understood the allure of the genre. My advice: Do Not Watch Scary Movies on Half-Empty Planes. But this was the soon-to-be Legendary Falcon Express. I couldn't do something so mundane as watching a movie.

I decided to take full advantage of the phrase: You're free to move about the plane. All my fellow passengers had returned from wherever they were. I didn't think anyone was doing any exercising in the gym, pool, or tennis courts, went for a jog, or went for a little sit-down in the steam room. So that left the restaurant and bar, emphasize bar, and the casino. Kids and teens lived for VR, so that's where they were, probably calling their friends from around the world to join them.

"A detective. How interesting," said the man, who I stopped by to visit.

"What do you do?" I asked. "Don't tell me you're another investor of this fine hover-palace."

"I wish. That actually would be the wife. She's the money-maker in the household. I'm an evolutionary biologist."

"Really? What inspired you to do that?" I asked.

"They have made a million versions by now, but I was hooked by the movie Planet of the Apes. I read Island of Dr. Moreau a million times too."

"So, you were inspired by talking monkeys?"

He gave me a look, wondering if I was making fun of him.

"I should go now," I said.

His wife returned to the seating. They exchanged looks, and soon, she was giving me a very unfriendly stare.

One of the female passengers had a red bag in her lap, and one didn't have to be a detective to know what was in it.

"What's in the bag?" I asked with a smile.

She grinned and opened it up. "Muffin the Great." The rat-dog, better groomed than I'd ever be, popped out. Some kind of Pomeranian or chihuahua. I had a bear-trap of a mind for thousands of criminal mugshots and cases, but couldn't remember the difference between two rat-dogs.

After I finished making the rounds, I slowly walked back to my seat. My eyes were locked on the big, brawny man sitting behind me, who was not the original passenger. He had a mane of thick black hair and a perfectly groomed mustache and beard. He tried so hard not to look at me that he finally just turned to stare out the window. Why was I being watched on my one, once-in-a-lifetime vacation aboard the maiden voyage of what was soon to be called the legendary Falcon Express?

The layout of the Falcon Express was simple—three columns of seating from the front to the rear—window seats, aisle seats, window seats. But the plane's windows were big enough that even those sitting in the center had their pick as to which window they wanted to look out of.

We were no longer in the Earth's atmosphere. My investor passenger friend across from me was waking up, as if on cue, to see for himself. But there was something else that appeared as if on cue—two screaming little kids running down the aisle with their mother chasing after them.

"We're in space, Mommie!"

"If you two do not stop this instant, the only thing in space you'll see is one scary BEM pulling you through the glass."

I had no idea what a BEM was, but the two brats froze where they were, which happened to be right next to me. The mother reached them and grabbed both boys.

"BEM?" I asked. "I have two little ones too. Anything to help me make them behave, especially my Cruz Jr., I'll take, parent to parent."

"Not even your Cruz Jr. is anything like my two demons here."

"Who's this BEM?"

"Bug-Eyed Monster. Use their overactive imaginations to your benefit."

"Mommie, what is over-active magination?" one asked.

"Yes, Mommie. What is it?" the other asked.

"I'll get them out of here," the mother said and dragged them away.

A BEM would be unlikely to be a good deterrent for Cruz Jr., who fancied himself a teleporting ninja and had the mischievous skills to match thanks to too many hours of inappropriate children's anime TV.

Our attention returned to the windows. I don't know how they managed it, but our mouths hung open as we beheld a lunar eclipse—and a meteor shower. The meteors came out of the darkness of space and swarmed around the plane, passing from the right side of the other. Everyone on my side of the plane, including me, jumped out of our seats and walked or ran to the left side of the plane. The meteors fell to Earth, brilliantly burning up in the atmosphere. The plane erupted in applause again.

"That was amazing," one passenger said.

"Wow."

That was a sample of passenger comments for a good ten minutes as people settled back in their seats and the gossiping began.

"Ladies and gentlemen," the captain's voice came from overhead. "I didn't want to spoil the event with any commentary from me. You saw it yourself. We actually planned to make the lunar eclipse the show, but I think a real meteor shower passing by us and burning up in our planet's atmosphere tops even that.

"As many of you know, all the Space Station Colonies and Lunar Colony are fully protected by a battery of anti-meteor guns. However, this time they let a few small ones by for us to see and enjoy.

"The show isn't over. We'll descend from here, and don't be alarmed by what you see, but we're going to be diving, so to speak, through the center of three storm fronts in the Asia–Africa corridor. Enjoy, ladies and gentlemen."

The left side of the plane was wondering if they needed to get to their feet again, and my right side was thinking the same, and the center aisle passengers were laughing at the both of us. For the first time, I was feeling the real power of those sky–walker engines right in my gut as the Falcon Express descended back to planet Earth.

* * *

We were all glad that Captain Dash had warned us. As we made our descent, the dark storm clouds did look quite ominous, but the center of it all was as clear as could be.

"Ladies and gentlemen, we'll be leveling off in ten minutes," the captain's voice announced on the overhead.

When the Falcon Express leveled off, the attendants appeared with their hovercarts of food and drink. I wasn't the only one making the rounds and visiting fellow passengers. Everyone was doing it now. Before I could even stand up, two passengers popped over to my seat.

"You're the detective," one man said.

"I am."

Both men slapped my pod chair, and another chair sprung up from the floor. The men sat with their drinks sloshing around in their glasses, but then I noticed one of them had nothing but water in his.

"What do you two do?" I asked.

"I'm a pilot. And don't bother with the 'if something happens to our pilots, I can fly for them' joke. Heard it forever. Actually, I'm a military pilot. Don't fly these big passenger craft."

I looked at the other man with the water in his gin glass.

"I'm a mental sherpa," he said.

"Counselor or therapist?" I asked.

"Very good," his friend said. "Most people can't reason anything out these days."

"Well, I know what a sherpa is, so a mental one."

"I help people guide themselves through their own minds to achieve greater enlightenment."

"Is this done with talking or drugs?" I asked.

The sherpa chuckled. "Deep meditation outside in nature with only my voice as the tether. One must make the journey for oneself."

"Sounds like a lot of work."

Boom!

The three of us looked at each other. None of us wanted to say anything, but then some of our fellow passengers in the aisle walked to us.

"What was that?" my sleeping pill investor friend asked.

"What?" I asked.

"That noise."

"We didn't hear anything," I said.

"Sounded like something hit us," he said.

"Hit the plane?" I smiled. "There's nothing up here but us and the Falcon Express."

My investor friend stepped closer to our window and looked out. We caught ourselves doing the same thing.

"Nothing," I said. "Oh, how rude of me. He's one of the investors."

Immediately, the two men forgot everything and stood to shake the man's hand. It took less than ten seconds for them to completely forget the incident.

Something made me turn around.

The big, brawny man sitting behind me was gone. I stuck my head out into the aisle just to catch the back of him open the partition and disappear into the first-class section way at the back. The lights were very dim and the partition was quickly closed.

As far as I could tell from making my rounds and mingling, half the passengers were actual investors for the Falcon Express. Some were there from the very beginning when all Carnegie Cosmo had was a drawing on a tablet. They were the founders and were responsible for the lion's share of the project's seed and launch capital. Others joined when Capitol Street whispered to everyone that the Falcon Express was indeed the next big thing. They were investors for the subsequent funding rounds. The returns would not be as big as the founders', but they would be massive enough.

But if only half were investors, then the rest of the passengers were normals like me. I was surprised by how many people actually knew who I was. Being famous in a supercity like Metropolis was a relative term. It meant at most less than one percent of the city's population had heard of you once. Publicists and marketers said that people had to hear your name at least seven times for you to register in their brains as anything more than a fleeting afterthought, never to be considered again.

What the non-investors all had in common was they were connected in some way to the uber-wealthy investor class, and that's what I found interesting. How? Family, friends, occupations, or other connections? That's how I spent my time meeting my fellow passengers.

One guy was a real professional poker player and he had already fleeced people of their money in the plane's poker rooms while I was taking my thirty-minute nap. It was his son who was the investor, who stood by his father as enraptured by the father's poker tournament stories as I was. He'd even gone to Mars for their big annual poker tournaments, winning the grand prize once and coming in second another. I didn't know much about poker, but I did know that a grand prize would net the winner millions of dollars.

Just my luck, I came across a trio who knew and hated me. I could feel the negative energies, but I was in an uncharacteristically gregarious mood.

"I can tell by the looks that you know me," I said as I stopped at their pod of seats.

"Yes, Mr. Cruz," one of them said. "I don't suppose you have too many clients from Movie Town."

"Oh."

"Yes, oh."

"Actor, director, or producer?" I asked.

"Studio producer until you came along."

As you became a seasoned detective and the string of cases successfully solved grew, your list of friends grew too, but so did your list of enemies. To this day, I still wasn't a favorite of Movie Town because of my NeuroDancer case. Lots of villains almost did me in, or tried to. This villainess came very close to succeeding.

"It's not my fault. Two actors tried to kill me," I said defensively.

"One of the highest-grossing action stars and one of the most beloved movie legends."

"Yeah, I saw their movies too, but they tried to kill me."

"And you killed them."

"And those actors' union thugs were engaged in real violence against me. Killing, violence, and corruption is a no-no in my book."

"Corruption? Funny you would say that with all the police thugs you're friends with."

"I am friends with no thugs of any profession, and I would remind you that all the corrupt cops I ever came across I dealt with, too, as you well know. It was on the news."

"Give him a break," said his friend sitting next to him. "Those Movie-Town studio and union bosses were stealing from us, money from our salaries, you know."

"Yeah, I know. But look how long it's taking for Movie Town to get back on its feet. He got practically the whole damn studio system arrested."

I leaned down to him. "Sounds like someone's in line to be running their own movie studio, then."

The irritable man looked at me for a second, then his eyes darted around. Then he looked at me again. I nodded at him.

"I need to make some calls." The man jumped up from his seat.

His two friends laughed. "You go do what you need to, Mr. Movie Mogul," the second man said.

"Now, if I see him making movies, I want my cameo," I said.

"You got it," the man said.

I learned that none of them invested in the Falcon Express, but all had spouses who did.

The next group I spent time with was a retired realtor who was making even more money as a day trader. He had done high-end residential and commercial but now worked the Up-Top financial markets. His five sons ran their own investment firms whose portfolio included the Falcon Express.

Another man was an executive recruiter who specialized in the space pharmaceutical and life sciences industries. He found and hired people for these firms all day long, and got to travel the world.

"My office is whatever city I happen to be in," he said.

"You mean whatever swanky, high-end hotel you can book your suite in," I said.

"You should take your detective firm global and you can do the same."

"Metropolis is plenty global enough for me. I've lived there all my life, and there are still parts of it I've never even driven over."

The other members of our little chat groups were a Reiki healer, a professional bodybuilder, and a celebrated musician who played the classical and opera circuit. We were joined by one of their daughters who was a laser tattoo artist. All of them were spouses, siblings, or children of Falcon Express investors. I enjoyed my time with them the most because after we quickly got through the occupations and the "where you from" small talk, we had a great conversation about life and family in general. Lots of jokes but lots of good advice, especially from the bodybuilder guy who had ten kids. Whoa! He didn't compete anymore, but he looked like it and demonstrated for all of us by wiggling his pecs under his shirt for us.

I now realized the genius of the Falcon Express. It wasn't the fancy sky-walker engines or the amazing global destinations that were going to make it a success. It was what we were doing now. The ability to meet and talk with interesting, successful people from different professions and from around the world. It reminded me of the ancient days of land-bound trains and pleasure cruise ships. Meeting new people was the draw, otherwise you could remain in your own residence forever with your eyes and ears glued to your VR console. Virtual reality would always come in second place to real life for as long as human beings existed in the universe.

"Ladies and gentlemen, lunch will be served soon," said one of the flight attendants on the overhead.

Lunch? They were always feeding us. I started to reconsider my earlier dismissal of the plane's gym and sports facilities. I was going to be fat after my flight on the Falcon Express.

* * *

The hovercarts that the flight attendants pushed down the aisles were twice the size of the previous ones, and the aroma made it impossible to think about anything but the mouth-watering food choices that awaited you.

This time I sat in the family section with none other than the bratty teenage girl in a mink coat and leather skirt and her parents, who were both founding investors. The father actually knew one of my previous corporate clients and the mother had been to Eye Candy Image Salon—my wife's job—with its staff of makeup artists, hairdressers, manicurists, pedicurists, skincare techs, tattoo artists, wardrobe stylists, and even dressers to assemble their wardrobe.

She described the specialist who did her hair, face, and nails.

"That's my wife, all right," I said.

"What a small world," the mother said.

"You may have won my parents over, but I still don't like you," the daughter said. "What's with wearing a hat when you're inside a plane?"

"I am not wearing a hat. It's called a fedora and eat your food," I said.

Both my wife and I felt that the more choices any eatery had, the lesser the quality because they couldn't master any specific cuisine. I'm sure her mind would have been changed as mine had after enjoying my first Falcon Express lunch. All around me was French, Moroccan, Israeli, Italian, Mexican, Brazilian, Japanese, Scottish, American, Caribbean, and more. All of it looked and smelled good. All of it tasted amazing from the looks on the faces of my fellow passengers. The menu was truly global, and from the comments, all of it was cooked as if by a master chef from that specific region.

Ms. Proxie reached us again for another pass.

"I'll have some more kombucha," the teenage daughter said.

I frowned.

"Why the face? It has great health benefits."

"People my age and your parents' age have to worry about health benefits, not you. At your age, you can eat twice your body weight and still lose weight."

"That's not true. I work out."

"You're on the Falcon Express. Live a little," I said.

She looked at her parents, and a wicked grin came over her face. "Okay, Detective. Miss, what alcoholic beverage goes well with my lunch?"

"Miss, I'll have another of what I had, and you can give me a glass, a small glass, to share," her father said.

"Very good, sir," Ms. Proxie said.

"Yes!" the daughter said, raising her arms in triumph as if she came in first in a relay race.

"What was he having?" I asked in a whisper.

"Japanese whiskey," she whispered back.

"Now we're talking."

"Okay, Detective, you won me over."

"Yes!" I said, arms raised in triumph.

* * *

I remained with the one family, and the one sitting across from us—all of them bankers—joined us. We talked and laughed for a good two hours, like most of the section of our plane.

I stood a few times to look toward my seat. My brawny watcher still hadn't returned to the seat behind me.

Okay, I'll admit it. I had an ulterior motive in joining the family section, and it wasn't to get a decade's head-start on dealing with teenagers. Dot and I still weren't convinced we'd survive the pre-teen years with Cruz Jr. No, I wanted to be closer to the closed-off first-class section. Not once in all those hours was that partition ever opened. It was strange. I'd been on flights before and you always got a chance to glance into the first-class section, if you weren't lucky enough to be there. Chief Hub was back there, and so was Mr. Brawny Watcher.

It was happening again. I could feel it, but I refused to have another vacation taken from me and become something else. I refused. This was the maiden voyage of the legendary Falcon Express. If they wanted to close off the first-class section to the rest of us, that was fine. It wasn't illegal. I had all my fellow passengers to keep me company.

The teenage girl had been joined by a few other teenagers—one female and one male. "What are you doing over there?" she asked me.

"Let's play a game," I said.

That got her attention.

"What?" she asked.

"Let's see if we can figure out who's the air marshal aboard."

That got all the parents' attention around us.

CHAPTER SEVEN

Stephen Strata, Plane Manager

I had to hand it to the Falcon Express. They spaced everything out perfectly. We got to see Earth from space along with a lunar eclipse and meteor shower. We maneuvered through three storm fronts to fly above a calm but turbulent Pacific Ocean.

"Ladies and gentlemen, this is your captain. We do have a treat for you. We're over the western Pacific Ocean, the Oceanian region to be specific."

Like most non-traveling Metropolitans, the only places I knew of were Australia Prime and Fiji, though I was certain that most of my fellow passengers had been in the region before.

"We've been to space, we're here at our first ocean stop, and as for the first country, it will be many.

"First Melanesia, the region of thousands of islands that includes the countries of Vanuatu, the Solomon

Islands, Papua New Guinea, Maluku, Timor Leste, New Caledonia, and the famous Fiji. Then Micronesia, another region of a couple thousand islands. Finally, Polynesia, the region of more than a thousand islands too, including Samoa, Tonga, the Cook Islands, French Polynesia, and New Zealand."

I looked around and saw I wasn't the only one with a map pulled up on my personal entertainment screen.

"This can't be right," I said to myself. "Hawaii is so close to Australia and New Zealand?"

"You're thinking of a map. Earth isn't a map, it's a globe. They are that close." I was being lectured to by a fellow passenger.

"The treat, ladies and gentlemen, is we've added an impromptu stop for everyone to stretch their legs and get some tropical island shopping done."

Again, the plane erupted in applause.

"Ladies and gentlemen, I will turn it over to another key member of the Falcon Express who has joined our maiden flight. I give you Dr. Stephen Strata. His title with the company is plane manager, but he's much, much more that. He's the man who literally oversaw the very construction of this fine craft."

A face appeared on the plane's holo-wall, and he was dressed as exquisitely as Mr. Apex and Java.

"Hello, everyone," Strata said. "Firstly, never call me doctor. I'm a builder. Thank you for joining this special flight. The captain was not exaggerating. I am honored to have overseen the construction of this fine plane from stem to stern—all the mechanics, electrics, and hydraulics, down to every seal and bolt.

"There are many things that make the Falcon Express a one-of-a-kind in the world of advanced hoverplanes. First, it is much more than a hoverplane with the ability to travel in the air or in the vacuum of space, on the reverse, underwater and even over water like a hydrofoil with its adaptable landing gear. Next, the Falcon Express is second to none when it comes to onboard amenities, and you've already gotten a personal tour from our chief steward, Mr. Apex. Lastly, my own pride and joy, is our revolutionary "sky-walker" engine system. No other corporate or government hoverplane on Earth possesses these engines, but one day they will be the standard. You've read the stories and seen them on the news. They make any airborne hovercraft 'uncrashable.' They create a protective energy field around the craft that's synced with its computer brain to monitor speed and altitude. It never disengages until safe to do. I am proud to say that I was even part of the original R&D teams so many years ago when Mr. Cosmo found us.

"What do we have next for you? When we land, I'm going to do something I rarely ever get to do. I'm going to fly you. I'll be your tour guide from island to island. We'll disembark, board our chartered hoverbus, and get all your shopping done to get you back in your seats. We'll start the shopping extravaganza on world-famous Fiji."

The plane applauded again, but not me.

* * *

The Falcon Express vertically landed on the tropical island of Fiji, which wasn't on our original itinerary. We landed, and our section's four flight attendants led everyone from their seats to disembark.

I'd met or seen everyone on our deck, but only when I stepped off the plane, did I see the passengers from the other two decks. The maiden flight may have been less than full capacity, but there were more than a thousand people waiting as a mob on the ground. We could see not one but three large hoverbuses gliding toward us in the sunny sky.

The Falcon Express seemed bigger than the airport itself. In fact, the airport was by no means meant for any craft of our size. There were police and fire personnel in the distance. We all also glimpsed crowds in the distance and stopped hovercars, kept just outside the airport perimeter fencing. Fiji did have a main airport, but this wasn't it.

A smiling Strata appeared at the top of the plane's steps to walk down to join us. He was moving through the crowd and shaking hands with the men and doing that European kiss on each cheek for the women.

Then both Mr. Apex, the chief steward, and Mr. Java, the deck manager, appeared. There was another man and woman with them, which I assumed were the deck managers for the other two decks. They all came down to the ground to join us.

"Mr. Strata," Mr. Apex said. "I wouldn't hear of you being a hoverbus tour guide. Our deck managers will take charge."

"No bother, sir."

"We'll do it," Mr. Java said. "We want to do it. We don't get out enough."

"Very well," Strata said. "I'll use the time wisely to catch up on reports. Mr. Cosmo wants minute-by-minute updates."

"Don't we know it," Apex said.

Besides our four flight attendants, there were dozens more. They all took their stations at the three hoverbuses once they landed. Passengers were ushered aboard quickly, then the flight attendants, and finally the deck managers. A smiling Strata waved as the hoverbuses lifted off into the sky. When the hoverbuses were mere dots, he ran to the plane's steps and raced up like he was on fire. His smile was gone.

I was literally hiding under the plane, resting on one knee.

I noticed Chief Hub wasn't among the passengers. I wondered if anyone from first class on the first deck had left.

* * *

I stepped onto the Falcon Express with not a soul around. No staff. No security. The fact that I had disappeared from the rest of the passengers without anyone noticing spoke volumes. This was not a bunch of amateurs, so why were they acting like one?

"Excuse me," a voice said as I reached the first deck.

Stephen Strata stood there in the aisle with a look of shock on his face. I walked right to him.

"What's going on?" I asked him point-blank.

"What do you mean? Who are you?"

"I'm a passenger."

"Why aren't you with the others?"

"I came to fly the Falcon Express, not shop in Fiji. I can do that on my own time."

"I'm sorry if you feel inconvenienced, but it was decided."

"How long will this shopping take? Over a thousand passengers. You plan to visit how many islands? How long do you suppose something like that will take?"

I could see the man sweating. "You're going to have to leave right now and join them."

"No. I'm staying right here. I'll stay in my seat and watch a movie or two, because we both know they won't be back until dark. Go do whatever you were going to do."

I walked past him and headed to my seat. Strata watched me nervously, but I wasn't looking back at him. I was looking past him. The partition to the first-class section was closed. They were still aboard. Who was back there? What was going on?

When I reached my seat, I planted myself down in my pod in a huff.

CHAPTER EIGHT

Four Words I Really Didn't Need to Hear (Or Is It Five?)

As I sat at my seat brooding, a realization came over me. The chief was absolutely right. I should have listened and stepped back off the plane, but he knew I wouldn't listen to him. I felt something wasn't quite normal. He wasn't in a Hawaiian shirt, so he wasn't on vacation. He was working. Cops did VIP security all the time, but not chiefs of entire city departments. Besides, why would Carnegie Cosmo want to hire government police for the Falcon Express when there were far greater options in terms of corporate samurai or cyborg soldiers?

Cruz Jr. wasn't the only one. Adults had overactive imaginations too, and mine was racing. I hadn't seen Strata at all. No one came near me, even though I was half-expecting someone to show up. The passengers were gone but not the plane's non-flight staff and crew. What I did notice in the corner of my eye was that something was going on outside the plane. I turned my head once to catch a fleeting glimpse. Why were maintenance hoverpods buzzing around the plane? Was that why they came up with their "impromptu" shopping excursion for the passengers?

And there was the mysterious, secluded first-class on my deck. I leaned into the aisle from my chair and looked to the back of the plane. The partition was open! Unlike the rest of the plane, the lights were off, and I could see the glow of the lights of the individual seating pods. I didn't see anyone, but that didn't mean I wasn't being watched.

Now my eyes looked up, and I scanned the walls and ceilings. This time I wasn't interested in the Falcon's exquisite interior craftsmanship. These days if you could see a surveillance camera, it was because they wanted you to. Visible surveillance cameras were a crime deterrent. Hidden ones were for real surveillance. There was not a doubt in my mind that I was being monitored.

As I sat there thinking, I remembered that loud bang that the two passengers and I heard. Maybe we shouldn't have ignored it and pretended not even to hear it. In an instant, the magic was gone. The

Legendary Falcon Express was anything but to me. I wanted off before something else happened. However, that wasn't going to happen.

I stood and opened the overhead compartment. Small, medium, and large. Large blanket was the choice. I grabbed it, covered myself, and planted myself back in my seat as I reclined. I'd stay put for the duration of the flight. I'd pretend to sleep, but I knew that wasn't going to happen either.

It was just as I said to Strata. It was night by the time everyone returned to the plane. A normal person would have been pissed, but I just pretended to be on a stakeout. Instead of sitting in a hovercar, watching and waiting for hours, I was balled up in a luxury chair pod under a blanket. An hour? Strata was either a liar or a dummy. Everyone was gone for three hours. In addition to being dark outside, it was pouring rain.

There was not a sound on the plane while I waited all those hours, except for one notable time. I could hear multiple voices arguing in the back from the mysterious first-class. It went on for about ten minutes, then abruptly stopped, or they closed the partition again.

My eyes were closed and my back was to the aisle but I felt a presence. I quickly turned over, and there they were. Two little munchkins wearing some kind of scary-looking tribal masks with mean eyes and jagged, ragged pointed teeth painted on the mask.

"Boo!" they said in unison, raising their hands and lunging at me.

I stared at them without blinking. They stared back at me, realizing their amusement was at an end.

"You're no fun," one of them said.

"My kids tell me the same thing."

"You two get back here now!" their mother screamed from behind us.

The kids dashed away. I leaned over to watch them race down the aisle back to their waiting mother. I immediately noticed the number of boxes and bags in her hands. All the passengers were back from their "shopping trip." Down the aisle, they came from the elevators loaded up with wet shopping bags. I remembered the days in elementary and middle school when they took us kids on field trips to the many local museums. The teacher could barely manage to keep control of thirty of us. The Falcon Express crew unleashed a thousand people onto the streets of Fiji.

"Where were you?" asked my sleeping pill investor friend returning to his seat across from me, loaded up with four big bags.

"Not feeling very well," I said. "Been fighting off a stomach bug for a few days."

"You missed a great time," he said. "I didn't want to do any shopping myself, but why not take advantage of it? Got all my holiday gifts taken care of for the year. You missed the street musicians. They were quite good."

"Next time," I said. "I'll be ready for our next off-plane trip. Can all those bags fit in the overhead compartments?"

"Not a chance, but they told us that the flight attendants would help us tag everything, and they'd transport it to the baggage hold for us."

"Sounds like a plan."

Sounded stupid. It meant that we'd be another hour at the least before take-off.

The flight attendant, Ms. Proxie, weaved her way through passengers down the aisle to where we were. She handed my friend clip-on tags for his bags.

"I'll tape them up," he said to her.

She turned to me and walked over. "Mr. Cruz, we missed you. Are you okay?"

"I'm fine."

"You shouldn't have broken off from the rest of the passengers and remained aboard alone."

"Were you able to do whatever it was you needed to do?" I asked.

"Pardon me."

"You wanted to get everyone off the plane for a number of hours so no one could see what you were doing. Were you able to do whatever it was you needed to do?"

She stared at me for quite a while, not knowing what to say or do.

"All done," my passenger friend said.

She snapped out of it and turned to him. "Umm. Uhh. Just follow me, sir. We'll load up another hovertrolley at the end of the aisle."

She walked by and he followed, oblivious to our conversation. Other passengers followed suit. At the other end of the aisle was the flight attendant, Mr. Polo, with the hovertrolley.

Again, I was right. One hour and ten minutes of delay.

"Ladies and gentlemen, this is your captain. We're going to be lifting off in a moment, so I ask you to get seated and strapped in. We'll be in the air in no time and on our way to our next national stop, which will be the pyramids of Egypt."

"Don't they have pyramids on Mars, too?" I heard a passenger ask aloud.

"No, they don't," her husband answered.

"They do. Big casino and amusement park. It's called Pyramids of Mars," another passenger said.

"To avoid the brunt of the storm, we'll fly the long way around," the captain said, continuing. "But we'll be there by lunchtime."

He definitely was taking the long, long way there. I may not have been a hoverplane pilot, but I knew something about flying. Who cares about storms? A hoverplane that could fly into space or dive and fly through the sea had absolutely no restrictions at all. They could fly above or under the storm and be at the pyramids of Egypt long before lunch time.

I was clearly getting annoyed. Again, I reclined my seat, and this time, I would be sleeping. Maybe I could drift off and get up at lunch time to avoid any more deception. The Falcon Express would not be getting a favorable review from me on Trusted Reviews, the bible of Average Joe and Jane reviews about businesses.

* * *

We were skyborne in minutes, and once the plane leveled off, I could hear the bustling of passengers leaving their seats for the recreation deck or the sleeping cabins on the sleeper deck. I never opened my eyes. I simply listened to the voices and other sounds. Besides myself there were about a dozen other people remaining in their seats at different points. I did feel a presence a couple of times, but I never looked. Likely, one of the flight attendants making their rounds or someone checking up on me specifically. I wondered what the crew was saying about me in private.

My mind went to that loud thud as if something had hit the plane when I was talking with the military pilot and the mental sherpa. The fact was that air-travel was far, far safer than local hovercar commuting by miles. In fact, I couldn't even remember when the last hoverplane had crashed. I doubt anyone could, because it just didn't happen, which is why the whole "uncrashable" Falcon Express hype didn't appeal to me. It was also kind of ballsy, considering the Titanic was supposed to be "unsinkable." But I guess they reasoned that the disaster was centuries ago, was not taught in school, and no movie was made about it in the last fifty years, so no one would make the connection.

I was fascinated by the Falcon Express sky-walker engine for what it would do to revolutionize hovercar safety. An uncrashable hoverplane—so what? Even before hover-technology came into existence, airplane travel was safer than pre-hovercars rolling around the ground on rubber wheels at crazy speeds. An uncrashable hovercar. That had my full attention, and everyone else's. That was where Carnegie Cosmo was going to possibly make himself the richest person in the solar system. The patent to the sky-walker engines was the next "big thing."

I was interested in the Falcon Express for the craftsmanship in its construction, its retro-vintage aesthetic, and a reminder of a classier, simpler time. Well, I was interested in the Falcon Express until now. I was seriously contemplating bailing on the flight when we got to Egypt. The problem was, could I get to the Coast in time for my client meeting? But we were already way behind schedule, which I noticed that Captain Dash neglected to mention, as if everything was normal. Maybe no one else knew something was not quite right with this flight, but I did.

Sleep. Get some sleep, real sleep, and I'd awake and could re-evaluate the situation.

The words.

At first, I thought I was dreaming, or daydreaming. I couldn't possibly have heard what I heard. On Earth, there were things you just didn't say—ever. You never said "I have a bomb" on a plane. You never said "Fire!" in a crowded theater, when there was none, and even if it was real, you didn't say it. You never said "Gun" in a school. No, I was dreaming.

"Didn't anyone hear me?" the same male voice called out. He was sitting on my side of the plane, about three seats behind me.

I had officially entered my own horror show on a plane with a crew possibly up to no good. I pulled the blanket from my body and opened my eyes. The vacation was over, if it ever was a vacation.

"There's a man outside."

We were forty thousand feet in the air, traveling at over seven hundred miles an hour, and that's what the man said out loud.

CHAPTER NINE

The Man Who Cried...

I rose from my seat like a demon, ready to unleash death rays from my very eyes upon all who vexed me. My gaze locked on the man who uttered the four words (or was it five?). I could see that he held his breath and was terrified as he stared back at me, probably wondering what I was going to do.

The lights were dim in the section, and there were still only about a dozen of us on the deck. Everyone else was either seated or standing watching the man, then me. They probably wondered if the man was playing a prank or was crazy. They were wondering what I was going to do too.

I marched out of my seat to the man. He leaned back away from me. My eyes did peer out the window to see what there was to see in the night sky and pouring rain.

The man was seated right at one of the wings. I shook my head.

"Get up," I yelled.

"What? Why?" he asked.

He was one of the few passengers I hadn't had a chance to chat with when I made my rounds earlier in the day.

"We're not in the mood for any games," I said.

"Games? I'm not playing games. There was..."

"A man outside? Let me guess. He was running around on the wing."

"Actually, he landed on the wing and was staring at me."

"Only you?"

"I'm the only one looking out the window on this side."

"Tens of thousands of feet in the sky, going hundreds of miles an hour?"

"I saw what I saw."

"Where is this naked man, then?"

"I didn't say he was naked."

"Did he have fur or was he wearing a black dress suit?"

"You don't have to mock me. I saw what I saw."

"You are going to move from where you are to one of the aisle seats now!" I said.

"No! You can't tell me what to do. You have no authority."

I looked at the other passengers nearby. "Ladies and gentlemen, we're going to take a vote. All in favor of moving crazy man from the window seat to an aisle seat raise your hand."

Thirteen hands raised, some immediately.

"It's settled. Move!" I said.

"You can't do this."

"Listen to what he's saying," a passenger yelled at him. "I was looking out the window too, and I didn't see anything. You're a liar trying to scare us."

"Scare you? I'm scared. I'm the one who saw it."

"You saw nothing!" the same passenger yelled at him.

"But I did," the man said with almost a whimper. The man was actually starting to cry.

"Come on," I said. "Aisle seat now."

With his head down, the man relented and let me lead him to an aisle seat.

"If anyone returns to the seat, have them see me. You are to sit here, be quiet, and behave yourself."

"There was a man outside, you'll see."

"I'm not going to see anything. I'm going to sleep, and so are you. Why are you being mean?"

"Mean?" he asked, confused.

"This is the Legendary Falcon Express, and look what you're doing. Scaring passengers. What if kids were here? Why are you trying to ruin our flight in such a mean and cold way? Pranks are for kids, not grown adults. You should be ashamed of yourself."

"I'm not going to be treated this way. If you don't want me here, I'm going to leave and go to the sleeper deck."

"Even better," I said.

The man got up from the seat, holding back tears (for real), and stormed away for the elevators.

"Good. We can get some sleep," said another passenger.

"Everyone," I said, "he's either crazy, drunk, or bored and trying to get attention. He saw no such thing despite what he said."

I saw him first, then the other passengers. Crying Man was coming back down the aisle with two of the flight attendants—Ms. Zenobia and Mr. Polo.

"I saw him out there," Crying Man said to them, pointing outside the right of the plane.

"Please ignore him," I said. "He's making stuff up."

"I'm not. I saw what I saw!"

"We banished him to the sleeper deck, and I think that's where he should go," I said.

"You are making a very serious allegation," Mr. Polo said to Crying Man. "I'm going to have to insist that you leave the deck and go either to the restaurant—not the bar—or the sleeping deck. I'm going to have to also insist that you do not repeat your story to any other passenger, or you could be prosecuted by the company."

"Prosecuted?"

"False claims of the nature you've spoken can only incite terror and panic. You can be fully prosecuted and, if convicted, it will result in both imprisonment and hefty fines. Do I make myself clear, sir? Unlike you, we are not making up stories. Do you understand?" Polo asked him.

"I understand," Crying Man said, his head lowered.

"Ladies and gentlemen," Ms. Zenobia began, "can you also please vacate the section for at least an hour?"

"Why?" a passenger asked.

"Despite the obviously false story, we are obligated to follow a protocol," she answered. "Please go to the restaurant or spend the night in your sleeping cabin. You'll be able to return in an hour."

"I'll go to the restaurant instead, then," Crying Man said and stormed off again.

We all waited until he got in the elevator this time and was gone. All of us remaining passengers were now gathered together as we walked to the elevator. I glanced back and both attendants were watching us go, or were they watching me?

"Ladies and gentlemen, the same applies to all of you. Do not repeat what that man said to anyone. We mustn't ruin the flight for our fellow passengers," Polo said.

The elevator returned and we all stepped in.

* * *

The passengers already in the plane's restaurant and bar knew something was wrong when we appeared from the elevators. The atmosphere of the place went from festive and full of laughter to a complete zero as people suspected something was up and stopped talking and eating. All eyes were on us as we made it to the tables. Of course, no one was sitting with Crying Man.

I found a seat by myself where I could keep an eye on him. My eleven other fellow passengers were gathered at one table, whispering amongst themselves and glancing over at Crying Man.

"What happened?" It was my investor friend.

"Nothing important," I replied. "Just someone trying to scare people with an inappropriate joke."

Around us, there were quite a few passengers I didn't recognize. No doubt from the other two decks. The start of a commotion made me turn my attention back to the crying man. I couldn't believe what I was seeing—the beginnings of a brawl between four of the male passengers and the crying man.

"Wait a minute," I said, jumping up from my seat. "There's no fighting on the Falcon Express. What's wrong with all of you?" I stood between them and the crying man. "What exactly is trying to beat him up going to accomplish?"

"We want him to admit his lies!" one of the four men said to me. I did recognize them, or their type. High-rolling investors. The kind who expected to be in control at all times, and if things didn't go their way, they weren't beyond a little violence.

"Don't worry, he will. You're investors. You think Carnegie Cosmo is going to allow this guy to besmirch the maiden voyage of the Falcon Express? The lawyers will have him in court faster than Superman can get to Krypton."

The four men chuckled. That satisfied them. Sued by lawyers. I was speaking their language.

As they backed off, I led Crying Man to another table. Suddenly, another passenger joined us as we sat.

"Thanks for that," the new man said to me. He patted Crying Man on the shoulder. "You'll be okay."

"No one believes me."

"Forget about it," his friend said back to him.

"You two talk while I visit the bathroom. Just sit and relax and I'll be back," I said as I got up from the table.

I headed through the restaurant and bar, but I wasn't going to a bathroom with "sentient" toilets.

* * *

I didn't just know a little bit about the Falcon Express. I knew the plane's complete schematics. I had to thank my best friend Run-Time for securing that information for me, who, incidentally, was also one of the late-stage investors. I'm fascinated by schematics. Maybe they reminded me of the days when I built my Ford Pony in high school. I liked studying them, almost as much as I liked memorizing criminal mugshots and reading criminal case reports.

My recent hobby was about to come in handy. The elevators weren't the only way to get from the restaurant and bar back to the passenger decks. I made a hard right just before the restrooms, cut through a part of the kitchen—the staff were too busy with cooking and joking around to notice me—and I was out a side door.

I found myself in the long staff corridor that ran the entire length of the plane. Some real exercise at last. I bolted through the carpeted, empty corridor as fast as my legs would carry me. Passengers weren't allowed in the corridor, so I wanted to get to my destination before any plane staff or crew could see me. There was only one question that my schematics wouldn't show me.

I reached a door. No lock or key-code panel on it, just a latch to pull and enter. I did and hurried up one short staircase to reach the bottom of the three passenger decks. I casually stepped onto the spiral staircase and made my way up. Like my own deck, the third deck had few passengers. Lights were dim, and those few passengers I saw were either sleeping in their seats, listening to music, or watching a movie. It was the same for the second deck.

The voices from the first deck were not loud, but I could hear them as I slowly came up the staircase.

"We have to do something," one male voice said.

"What do you want us to do?" a female voice asked.

"We have a doctor aboard."

"To do what."

"Poison him. Then we can confine him without suspicion."

"No, we have sleeping pills and tranquilizers for emergencies. We put them in his drink, and that will put him out for the entire flight."

"What about the other man?" another male voice asked.

"Keep them all below with everyone else. We just need to keep them away from the windows," said another female voice.

"The man who saw it is with another man," a third male voice said.

"Then him too," said the first male voice.

"Did you see him?" the second female voice asked.

"No," the new male voice said.

"Then where is he? We'll have to get them back to their seats temporarily. We'll deal with Mr. Cruz first, then Mr. Sym, then Mr. Mortran."

I wasn't going to push my luck. The five of them could have started down the spiral staircase at any moment and seen me. I slowly double-backed as quietly as possible. Fortunately, no one spotted me.

* * *

I returned to the table in the restaurant section. Crying Man and his friend were seated where I left them but had a small plate of calamari and drinks in front of them.

"That was a long time," Crying Man's friend said to me. "We thought maybe you got swallowed up by their new-age toilet or something a bit more embarrassing."

"Not this time," I said. "I do have a question, though."

"Sure."

"Your names wouldn't by any chance be Mortran and Sym?"

They looked at each other. The Crying Man didn't say anything, but his friend did.

"Yes, I'm Mortran," the crying man's friend said. "How did you know our names?"

I sat back in my chair to collect myself. I'd heard all four of my first deck flight attendants—Ms. Proxie, Ms. Zenobia, Mr. Polo, Mr. Marquee—and the plane manager, Mr. Strata, plotting to poison the three of us. Shouldn't the attendants have been handing out peanuts to the passengers? Shouldn't Mr. Strata have been walking around the plane, polishing every shiny surface and admiring his construction? But poison? Murder aboard the Falcon Express?

What the hell did I get myself into on this plane?

The feeling grew in my gut that Chief Hub was so right. I should have turned around and never come aboard. And I'd been wrong about something else. This flight was not going to be any fun, not even close.

CHAPTER TEN

Four Other Words I Didn't Need to Hear (Or Is It Eight?)

The flight attendants and the plane manager weren't just liars. They were straight-out crazy maniacs. If they were capable of poisoning us, what else were they capable of? The Falcon Express had psychopaths as flight attendants handing out peanuts and poison. I had a strong urge to parachute from the plane right then and there. The two small problems were, I had no parachute and didn't know how to skydive.

More importantly, this all meant that Mr. Sym did see a man outside. But what did that even mean? How? What man could be outside a plane forty thousand feet up and traveling at over seven hundred miles an hour?

Mortran and Sym hadn't taken their eyes off me while I sat there thinking and rubbing my forehead.

"Don't ask," I said. "If I told you everything I know, then you'd be fighting the panic too." I calmed myself and looked at them straight. "The three of us will become good, very good friends on this flight. Listen to me very carefully. Number one. The three of us are going to relocate to the couples' section. I'll take one window seat, Mr. Sym the other. You, Mr. Mortran, will take the aisle seat, but while we watch out the window, you'll swivel your seat around and watch the attendants like a robot."

"What?" he asked. Both men were confused.

"Number two. Under no circumstances are you to drink anything from the flight attendants. Canned or bottled, unopened, only."

"What?" Mortran said again.

"Number three. Don't sleep."

"You need to tell us what's going on," Mortran said with his eyes squinted.

I leaned toward him. "Mr. Sym did see a man outside."

* * *

Mr. Mortran led our trio back to our top-floor passenger deck. I took up the rear with Mr. Sym in the middle. I was expecting one or more of our flight attendants to be watching for us, which is why I didn't lead us out of the elevator.

None of our assigned four attendants were anywhere to be seen. In fact, now that I thought about it, it was another sign that something wasn't right. No airline would leave a section or deck without staff. It was unheard of on any airline, even the smallest one. Safety was the primary reason; liability was the other. Also, just basic customer service. Even if there was only one passenger in the section, an attendant would be on hand to bring over a cup of coffee or alcoholic beverage, or pull down a pillow from the overhead.

While the section was dimly lit, we could see that more than a few of our fellow passengers had returned too. All of them were in window seats, and all were glued to their windows. So, word had spread that someone had seen a man outside the plane.

We still managed to find open windows on either side of the plane. All three of us took our "stations." Sym was on the other side of the plane, I was on the right side, and Mortran sat down in an aisle seat and swiveled around. There was a ceiling light above him. He stood and turned it off. No one could see him now.

Staring out a window for hours was no problem for me. I was the stake-out king. I'd been on stake-out for days on end, watching and waiting for suspects on a case. I wish I could say it was a skill I learned being a private detective, but it was courtesy of the days when I was a true OCD headcase. Someone scratched my vehicle, and I was determined to find out who, even if I had to watch and wait for the miscreant for a whole month. All that was behind me now, but I was still the stake-out king.

Out the window was nothing. Rain and darkness and one of the plane's wings covered with navigation lights. I could think while I did my surveillance. The inconsistencies and strangeness of this flight kept growing. There was a police officer aboard, but I didn't know if that was necessarily a good thing. Also, I couldn't believe that drugging passengers was part of the Falcon Express training class for the flight crew. What was going on? I had a puzzle where not one of the pieces seemed to go together.

I heard coughing. Was that Mortran? I turned just to see a hovercart stop opposite me. A smiling face of Mr. Polo hung above me. My eyes noticed that Ms. Zenobia was in the other aisle with her hovercart near Mr. Sym.

Once again, I rose like a menacing animal. Polo's confidence washed away from his face and was replaced by uneasiness.

"Listen good, you maniac. I was listening to you and your fellow conspirators," I said.

A look of shock came over his face.

"You won't be poisoning me, drugging me, or anything else tonight. I may not have a gun to shoot you, but we can find out if I can beat you to death in this aisle. The news is going to have a great story about the Falcon Express."

"Zen!" he called out.

Polo pulled his food and refreshment hovercart away as he quickly backed away from me. I could see Ms. Zenobia holding a cup in one hand and a coffee decanter in the other.

"Put it down. We're leaving," he said to her.

She set them back on her hovercart and pushed them back down the aisle to follow. Sym was looking at me with teared-up eyes. The man was terrified.

I noticed a shadowy shape from Mortran's area. He stepped out of the shadows and walked to me with a look of utter anger. "Are you going to tell us what's happening or not?" he asked.

I shook my head. "What you suspect is a far safer way to be than what I suspect."

"What happened when we were shopping on Fiji?" he asked me.

"The question is: why did our plane land at an airport too small for any kind of craft its size, for a stop that was by no means planned?"

His eyes darted around. "Are we in danger?"

"Mr. Mortran, change of plans. You keep Mr. Sym with you at all times."

"What about you?"

"I'll follow your lead, turn off the light above me, and try to get some sleep. I have a feeling I'll need it."

"But we're looking out the windows."

"I didn't say I'd be closing my eyes."

"You're a peculiar individual, Cruz."

"I've been called worse."

"I bet you have. I hope I'm not going to be an investor aboard a hoverplane that has a disastrous end on its maiden flight."

"You and me both."

I was going to sleep for real because I didn't need to watch for any "man outside." There were plenty of passengers doing the work for me on both sides of the plane. Faces resting on windows, watching for some kind of gremlin of a man, either out of curiosity or fear.

With my light above me off, I sat in a cone of darkness. I didn't expect to see any of our four flight attendant maniacs sneaking up on us. What concerned me was what they were going to do now, knowing we knew what they had been planning to do to us. Likely I had made a mistake by telling them, but there was no undoing it.

At least an hour. I tried to sleep, or at least take another nap, but my mind was racing. I felt trapped. I felt confused. None of this made any sense. The actions of everyone on board, except for the passengers, made no sense at all.

Never had I been startled as I had by the simple turning on of a light. My hat was pulled just a tad down my forehead, so none of them saw clearly just how much they scared me. In the aisle around me was not one, but a bunch of passengers. I pulled my hat back.

"Mister," began one of the female passengers, "there is a man outside."

"On the wing," said her husband.

I remembered them—a family of major investors. Behind them were their twenty-something kids. They didn't have a humorous bone anywhere in their bodies. They were serious as a heart attack and business all the time. But tonight, as much as they tried to hide it, the five of them were terrified.

CHAPTER ELEVEN

Jomar Hacker, Co-Pilot and Human Jack o' Lantern

The investor family pointed to one of the plane's windows behind us, but this time on the left side. I rose from my seat and noticed more passengers had returned. All eyes were on me.

They led me to the window, and, of course, Mr. Sym was already there.

"I told you I saw what I saw," he said.

"No one here doubts you anymore," I said.

"What does this mean?" the family patriarch asked, nervously looking at me. "What do we do? We need to land immediately?"

Despite all our advancements—hovertech, androids, robots, off-world colonies, and opposable thumbs—we humans were still skittish mammals who acted like every other lesser animal in the face of fear.

"Sir, you are absolutely correct. Let's get it done," I said.

"Where are the flight attendants?" the family matriarch said. "Where are they? We've barely seen them this flight at all."

"People," one of the passengers called out.

We looked at the passenger who called out first and saw he was staring down the aisle. A lone man stood there, and all of us, even me, were frozen. The good news was he was wearing a pilot uniform. He had the lean muscle mass and bearing of a law enforcement or military type. The bad news was his eyes were glowing like flashlights. I'd seen it before. It was a popular practice among street gangs—bionic eyes with enhancements such as glowing like the high beams of a hovercar. Was the Falcon Express being more liberal in their hiring practices than the average megacorp? But I was hardly one to talk. I had an ex-felon as my sole employee. Smartest decision I ever made—a cyborg secretary who could punch three-hundred-pound villains through walls. Too bad she wasn't here now. Too bad I didn't have my omega-gun, or I'd be pointing it at the man with the glowing eyes as he approached us.

I stepped toward him, and my fellow passengers were more than happy to let me take point.

"Hello," I greeted. "Which pilot are you?"

The man "turned off" his eyes.

"Cute trick," I said. "Should we get the kiddies from the rec deck for the full performance?"

"Jomar Hacker, First Officer and co-pilot of the Falcon Express," he said. "For your information, I was born blind. Surely, you agree that's an undesirable condition for a pilot."

"Did you come to tell us we won't be doing our two states, two countries, and two oceans after all? Or did you come to tell us about the man outside the plane? Did we forget to let one of the passengers back in before you closed the doors in your haste to depart from your fake Fiji shopping excursion?" I asked in the most insufferable tone possible.

"I'm going to have to insist that you all move to the sleeping deck."

"We're going to have to insist that your land this hoverjet right now," I said.

"I need you to comply," Mr. Hacker said.

"Didn't you hear what the man said?" the investor patriarch said. "We need to land."

"Didn't you hear us tell you that there's a man outside?" Sym asked loudly.

"Save your breath," I said. "He already knows. Is that what all these games have been for?" I asked Hacker.

"Ladies and gentlemen, please move to the sleeping deck."

"No," I said. Other passengers repeated the same refusal.

"We invested in this plane. You can't treat us this way. We demand answers," Mortran yelled.

"Land this plane!" another passenger said.

Hacker watched us with unflinching resolve. "Ladies and gentlemen, if you don't comply, we will have to make you comply."

That only made us passengers angry.

"Make us!" one shouted.

"I pay your salary!"

"Who's we? You said 'we will make us comply'? We only see you," another asked.

"Me, as in us!"

There she was. The slim woman who was going to sit across from me when we first boarded, had abruptly left, and hadn't been seen until now. In her hand, pointing at all of us, was a very big gun.

"The air marshal finally arrives," I said.

CHAPTER TWELVE

Air Marshall Punk

"The first officer of this plane gave you a direct order," she said. "I need you all to vacate this deck and go to the sleeping deck until further notice."

She was in the same black pants suit, but her footwear was a pair of black jungle boots. A passenger wearing military footwear? She had been wearing closed heels before.

"Shoot me!" the investor matriarch said. "Shoot us and see what happens."

"Maybe you should lower your gun," I said to her. "Mr. Hacker introduced himself. What about you?"

"I am Deca Punk, assigned air marshal of the Falcon Express."

"Punk" was not as uncommon a last name in modern day as one might think. The last name was like Smith. I'd met many Punks and, of course, punks.

"Punk? So Punk," I said. "I thought you left because you didn't like my after-shave, but you were just afraid I might figure out who you were."

"I know all about you, Mr. Cruz."

"Now I know who has a gun aboard."

"Mr. Cruz, trying to take an air marshal's weapon would be a fatal mistake," she said.

"Not you," I said. "Remember. There's a man outside."

"There is no man outside, Mr. Cruz."

"How many of us need to see this man before you stop playing games with us?"

"Ladies and gentlemen, follow me to the elevators," Hacker said to all of us.

Air Marshal Punk stepped out of the aisle to behind a seat but kept her gun pointing at us.

Now, I was angry and walked right up to her. "I know a bit about airplane protocols when it comes to air marshals. Your weapon's not permissible aboard a passenger plane, even for you, and pointing it at passengers who clearly are not a threat is completely illegal. We could land this plane and have you arrested, Marshal Punk."

"All true, Mr. Cruz. Except in the case of an emergency and/or approved by a senior police authority."

Chief Hub. That's who she meant. I knew that, but none of my fellow passengers did.

"What emergency?" a passenger asked.

"The man outside!" Sym yelled.

"Follow me, ladies and gentlemen," Hacker told us and started to the elevators.

"Yes, light the way for us, First Officer," I said.

We all followed him with the air marshal watching us closely, gun in hand.

"Are we prisoners?" a passenger asked.

"You are guests, sir," Hacker replied.

"Guests with a gun to our backs," another said.

"No, ma'am." Hacker pressed the button and the elevator door opened. "Ladies and gentlemen, trust us. That's all I ask. Trust us. Wait in your cabins until you receive further instructions."

We filed into the elevator. Hacker reached in and pressed a button. He stood in the aisle with the air marshal at his side. Finally, she lowered her gun.

"The cabin steward is waiting," he said as the doors closed.

"Just another great day flying the legendary Falcon Express," I said back to him.

"The only thing legendary will be the lawsuit we file against them," the investor patriarch said.

CHAPTER THIRTEEN

Carl Cursor, Cabin Steward

"**G**ood evening, ladies and gentlemen! My name's Mr. Theodore Cursor. I'm the chief steward of the Falcon Express, and I'll be looking after you. Step lively!"

If we hadn't just had a gun pointed at us, we might have all been taken in by the man's charm and exuberance. He was dressed in a golden suit and cap. On either side of him, several stewards in white suits and caps stood shoulder to shoulder in a line.

They were all smiling. None of us were.

"Let's get you all to your own private cabin so you get a great night's rest," Mr. Cursor said.

"What if we're not tired?" one of us asked.

"What if we don't want to sleep?" another asked.

Mr. Cursor laughed. "I was told you might say that. But I am a persuasive man. Besides, you've never had a real sleep until your body has graced a bed on the Falcon Express. But wait, here comes Mr. Vala. Everyone keep to the wall."

Like most people, I'd heard of sleepwalkers, but had never seen one in real life. Here came a bald, middle-aged man in pajamas strolling down the corridor. His eyes had a glassy look, as if in a trance. We all thought the same thing—zombie, but he was snoring. We all looked at each other as he passed us.

Mr. Cursor also had his back to the wall but directed one of his stewards to gently steer the man back around. The steward walked ahead of the man to return him to his cabin.

"What was that?" a passenger asked.

"What's wrong with him?" another asked.

"That was a sleepwalker, ma'am," Cursor answered. "Those of us who've been in the hospitality business awhile come across it from time to time."

"Guess his body didn't like to be graced by a Falcon Express bed," I said.

Cursor chuckled but ignored me. "You'll all be deep in a heavenly sleep as soon as your head touches your pillow. Let's go take a look at your home away from home for tonight."

We all looked at each other, but we followed the man.

"Can we make a call?" Mortran asked.

"Of course, sir," Cursor replied.

Who was he fooling? No one aboard this plane would be able to call anyone. We might get the phone and it might dial out, but I'd bet no connection would be made. Even I didn't need to be like our champion poker player aboard to know not to take those odds.

For a moment we were all reminded of the majesty and museum-like quality of the plane. The corridor had plush deep purple carpet, the walls were white with gold trim at the top, bottom and down the center, and the ceiling was a mirror with the lights running down the center and ends.

"First-class sleepers ahead," Cursor announced.

We reached a section where the doors to the cabins were open. Cursor was right. They were small but swanky. The plush white beds were literally floating above the ground. I wondered if the beds were "sentient" too. There were cabins for singles and those for couples.

"Don't be shy, ladies and gentlemen, step right in. Any empty cabin is yours for the night. Once claimed, our computers will automatically assign the cabin to you alone for the rest of the flight. My staff and I will be on hand at all times.

"Too bad the flight attendants don't have your same work ethic," a passenger said. "We haven't seen them for hours."

We all reluctantly entered cabins. I wasn't the only one who noticed that while Mr. Cursor was all smiles, his legion of staff was not. They seemed more like Japanese oshiya, or pushers, the frumpy, maniacal attendants who shoved passengers into packed hovertrains. In fact, new tourists to Japan purposely used their public hovertrains to see them or get personally "pushed" into a passenger car. Here we were being led to our cabin and watched like robot hawks until our doors were closed.

With my door closed, I stood in my cabin. I wasn't even going to sit on the bed, or rest my hat on the side table and dresser. My ear was pressed against the door, listening carefully for every sound to be heard in the corridor. I'd wait until everyone was settled into their cabins and the stewards were gone.

As I waited, only one thought rang in my head: How the hell did I get off this plane?

Not too long after, there was a knock at my door. I opened it slowly. There was Mortran, Sym, and a few others.

"Good," I said. "Saved me from having to find you. We need to get everyone else."

"To do what?" one of them asked.
"We're taking over this plane," I said.

CHAPTER FOURTEEN

More Useless Banter with the Peanut Gallery

As a detective, you were used to having meetings anywhere—in a seedy hotel lobby, a half-flooded alleyway, up in a hovertaxi, down in a dark parking lot, wherever. Sym and Mortran stood across from me in the sleeping deck corridor, but all along the wall on both sides were the passengers who'd also been pulled into this weird affair, and quite a few more.

"Sym," I began. "Simply tell us exactly what you saw. Try to be as detailed as you can."

He looked down at the carpeted floor for recall. "I was doing what I always do. That's why I take the window seat on a plane. I like to watch the clouds. I find it soothing. But then I saw him. I couldn't believe it. He startled me even. At first, I thought that a scuba diver had fallen from some other plane above us, but that didn't make sense. There was no plane above us, and he was floating. He was flying."

"What did he look like?" a passenger asked.

"How do you know it was a 'he'?" another asked.

"It was a man," Sym confirmed. "The suit reminded me of a scuba suit. It was skin-tight, but with ridges. He had those scuba face-things over your eyes, but I didn't see eyes. More like it was a mini, rectangular TV screen over them. He watched me as he hovered in the air. Then he...flew away."

"Flew?" I asked. "Was he wearing anything on his back? A jetpack?"

"No, I didn't see anything, or remember that. I was in shock. I couldn't believe it. I didn't want to call out to anyone, but I had to. We could've been in danger. I knew people would think I was crazy or making things up, but I had to say something."

"You did the right thing," Mortran said.

I looked at the investor family who was next to me on my side of the corridor. The patriarch nodded. "That's what we saw."

"Yes," confirmed the matriarch.

"But that's impossible," a passenger said. "How high are we, and how fast?"

"We're forty thousand feet up and flying at least seven hundred miles per hour," I said.

"Then how could he fly alongside us?" the passenger asked. "I thought the 'man outside' was on the plane. He's saying he was flying alongside it."

I, too, thought the same thing, which made things a lot scarier. It was impossible, but if Sym had truly seen that, then the impossible had become possible. I turned to the investor family. "Was the man flying alongside the plane too?"

The couple shook their heads. "He was on the plane," the wife said. "On the wing, then jumped off."

"Flew off," the husband said.

"Jumped or flew off," she said.

"No, jetpack?" I asked.

"What jetpack on Earth or Mars or anywhere in space colonies would allow the wearer to keep pace with a hoverplane in flight? No," the husband said.

I looked at the kids. "Did you see him?"

"We only saw him as he was jumping and disappeared below the plane," one of the sons replied.

"Mr. Mortran, you're one of the investors," I said.

"Second stage," he said.

"My mind can't help thinking. Is there any scenario, however remote, that would make Mr. Carnegie Cosmo want the Falcon Express venture to fail intentionally?"

There were gasps from everyone gathered, followed by chatter. Mortran himself was also taken aback.

"You mean crash? Absolutely not! I've known Carnegie for the better part of two decades. He's tough and tenacious but not ruthless and certainly not corrupt, or psychopathic. It's unthinkable what you're suggesting. I'd believe many things before that."

"What then? I'm at a loss. The crew and staff are also involved," I said.

"Involved how?" Mortran asked.

The chatter erupted in one consensus: Land the plane.

"How?" a passenger asked.

"We have to make them," I said.

"How?" a passenger asked me.

"I told you already. Take over the plane," I said.

They all looked at me incredulously—again.

"We heard you. We just didn't believe it," one said.

"That can't be done," said another.

"Can something like that even be done?" another asked. "We're passengers."

"I hesitated to tell you this, but I guess I should." I recited my encounter overhearing our section flight attendants and the plane manager plotting to poison, or drug, Sym, Mortran, and me.

Now people were panicking.

"I don't believe you," Mortran said, point-blank. "They'd never do such a thing. What do you think this is? This is a luxury airliner. They're hired from a pool of the most seasoned, respected, and tenured aircraft staff in the world and off-world. The airline doesn't hire convicts from a street corner or alley that you frequent in your detective work. No offense."

"None taken," I said. "But it doesn't change that I heard what I heard. Just like your friend Sym saw what he saw, and now he has company."

I could see in people's faces that some doubted me too.

"I do agree with Mr. Mortran that their behavior and what I heard makes no sense whatsoever. It is completely out-of-character. But does everyone agree that this isn't fun anymore and landing this plane is the best course of action?"

Everyone nodded or voiced their approval.

"Then we must act," I said.

"What about the mid-air crash sound?" a voice said.

Everyone turned to the man. It was the ex-military pilot with his friend the mental sherpa, next to him.

"What?" a few passengers next to him asked.

"My friend and I were chatting with the detective when we heard this thunderous sound. Something hit the plane in mid-air."

"We're going to crash," a passenger said in a panic.

"We're going to die," said another.

"No, we're not," Mortran yelled at them. He looked at me. "Why didn't you say something then?"

I looked at the military pilot and his friend, then sighed. "We...I just wanted to ignore it. I didn't want to prove what people say about me."

"Bad things follow you?" a passenger said.

"No," I said. "Why say that? Things happen. But I make bad things go away. But I don't want to go looking for them either."

"The three of you hid what you heard," Mortran said disapprovingly.

"Could something have fallen off the plane?" a passenger asked.

"Oh God," said a passenger who looked like he was about to faint, his wife holding him up.

"It was the man outside!" Sym yelled.

"Okay, no more talk," I said. "We need to act and get this plane landed." Even I was nervous as hell. The plane was supposedly equipped with state-of-the-art sky-walker engines, but I was no longer willing to bet my life, or the others, that they would work as advertised. It was just that kind of day for us. This was a very big hoverplane.

"How?" a passenger asked again.

"We'll capture all four flight attendants on our deck."

"My God," someone said.

"Capture?" another asked.

"How else do we force them to land? The pilot cockpit has more fortification than Fort Knox. We'll never get into it."

"What about the air marshal?" someone asked.

"I'll take care of Punk," I replied.

"How? She's armed. You're not."

"Never you mind. I'll handle her. I've done this before. You all get the flight attendants. We'll rush them, all at once."

"This is madness," a passenger said.

"So is falling out of the sky," I said.

Mortran folded his arms and wasn't budging. "Make the case to us, Mr. Cruz, the detective. We do what you suggest, and we'll all be arrested and hauled off to court, in front of a judge, facing multiple felonies. That means long jail sentences. I have small children that I'd at least like to see grow up, and having a felony doesn't do much for someone in my line of business, which is getting other people to give me large amounts of money. My career, and I'm sure yours, would come to an abrupt end."

I was up to the challenge. "One. The Metropolis Chief of Police is on this plane and hasn't left the first-class section since we took off. In fact, none of us have seen anyone from back there."

"He's aboard?" Mortran asked.

"Two. Our friend, the military pilot turned investor, has told you about the mysterious crash sound that on any other plane would have caused the flight crew and staff to acknowledge and do something about. As passengers, if we ignore it, it's one thing. As crew, that is quite another, very dangerous matter.

"Three. We made an unscheduled—that's what it was, no matter how well they play-acted—stop in Fiji at an airport that is not made for a plane of this size. That is not allowed, but we did it. It was an emergency landing, no matter how much they pretended it was a happy treat for us, and was not to do some shopping. No, they did it to get everyone off the plane, except for the first class on our deck.

"Four. I stayed behind on the plane. Our friendly plane manager was in a panic. They were checking the plane. Why wouldn't they tell us why? Why didn't we just stay in Fiji? We were landed and safe. Why did we fly off again?

"Five. The Man Outside. Seen now by more than one person.

"Six. The poison plot of our friendly flight attendants that I overheard.

"Seven. The behavior of the flight attendants in general. What flight have you ever been on where the flight staff completely disappears and leaves the deck unattended, only to show up to stuff us with food and drink? Where are they hiding?

"Eight. No air marshal points a gun at passengers like that. None. With permission or not. She's no air marshal.

"Nine. They can say what they want. We are being confined to this sleeping deck to keep us away from the passenger deck, and the windows. I'm done."

Everyone stared at me, overwhelmed.

"Ten." It was one of the teenagers, the trio. "We've been flying in circles for the last two hours," the boy said.

"Circles?" a passenger asked.

"How do you know?" I asked.

The boy held up a handheld device. It was one of the older GPS models, which was why it worked.

"Eleven," I said. "Our mobile devices are being jammed."

"What?"

Everyone, in unison, grabbed their mobile phones, pads, and computer tablets. After a quick moment, they all looked at me. They were scared, but ready.

"Let's do it," Mortran said.

CHAPTER FIFTEEN

The Taking of the Falcon Express

I peeked out the door into the long-restricted corridor. Two cabin stewards were on guard at the very door to the passenger decks above. They were tall, lanky, and young. No problem.

Out the door, I came without my hat or jacket, my shirt collar up, and sporting dark glasses. I approached them laughing to myself hysterically, bobbing around as if drunker than drunk.

"Sir! Sir!" they yelled. "This is a restricted corridor."

I whirled around with my crazy laughter and sauntered back the way I came. They ran to me.

I can only imagine what went through their minds. Reaching me at the door I came from, and immediately being besieged and grabbed by dozens of people spilling out into the corridor like straight out of a zombie movie. The stewards yelled and tried to run, but it was way too late. My passenger warriors captured their prey, holding them down to the floor.

With my hat returned to its proper place on my head, collar down, and shades gone, I led my "passenger army" back down the corridors. We expected that the evil flight crew would reason that if we disobeyed and came back from the sleeping deck, we'd return via the elevator. They'd have people stationed at the elevators on all three decks. But did they know I knew about the private passenger corridor?

We were about to find out.

Through the door I went and immediately raced up the spiral staircase. My plan was to come up behind them with my army backing me up.

I reached the top of the spiral staircase onto the first deck, and there was the Big Brawny Guy staring right at me, as if he was personally waiting for me alone. I rushed him.

He was good. With both arms, he deflected me into one of the seats. I turned to take him on and only had a split second to protect my chest. The man karate-kicked me in the chest with enough force to send me flying down the aisle. If his legs were bionic, I'd be dead. Luckily, my arms kept him from bruising or even breaking ribs in my chest, but they were throbbing with pain. I didn't care. Just as I was about to rush him again, I let out a scream that anyone who heard would swear I was being viciously murdered. The only reason I was rushing a guy who clearly was a professional fighter and better than me was that my passenger army was almost upon him, and he didn't know they were about to pounce. But they stopped in their tracks when I yelled out.

I looked down. My foot was under attack by that woman's evil dog called Muffin. It had my right ankle in a vice grip with its little piranha teeth, looking at me with literally glowing red eyes and growling. What was it with this plane with mammals and bionic eyes?

The creature was crushing the life out of my ankle in its jaw. The Brawny Guy rushed me. I was not about to be kicked by him again. He was six feet and a half of solid muscles with long, powerful legs. He assumed that I was incapacitated by the dog. He was wrong.

I didn't want to hurt Muffin, even though I do hate rat-dogs, but Muffin was hurting me—a lot. I'd practiced the move many times in the gym. I was not a professional fighter, but working the streets of Metropolis, you'd better know how to fight. Some days at the gym, I made the move flawlessly; on bad days, I almost fell flat on my butt, looking like an uncoordinated mess to all observers. This one moment was a good day.

When you do a roadhouse kick flawlessly, it's truly a beautiful thing to behold. I whipped around and struck

Mr. Brawny with my Muffin leg. I caught him in the jaw, and everyone heard his lower jaw teeth knock into the upper jaw. His head jerked back as he tumbled to the floor backward, and, on the way down, hit the side of a seat.

Muffin, the evil rat–dog, was knocked out cold. Lying on the floor like a dead rodent, complete with all fours pointing to heaven.

"Muffin!" I heard his female owner yell just as I was about to direct my useless passenger army to subdue the brawny man.

She came up the aisle like a mad screaming banshee with something sharp in her right hand, raised and ready to stab me. But she was not what I was focused on. Right behind, running just as fast, was Air Marshal Deca Punk, if she was a marshal, with her gun raised and ready to shoot me.

Stressful situations can negatively affect anyone, including me. When I told my fellow passengers I'd "handle her" even though I had no weapon myself, it wasn't hubris, it was reckless at best, but more likely laughably foolish. I'd never go after a perp into a dark alley without a gun. All the normal rules, like air marshals can't shoot innocent passengers on a plane, didn't apply here on the Falcon Express. Though I had to admit trying to "take over the plane" wasn't exactly innocent behavior, and might warrant a bit of gunplay in our direction.

However, if my useless passenger "army" had their act together, they would have taken them both out of commission. I felt like we were storming the beaches of Normandy. I jumped out of the boat and advanced forward with my laser machine gun in hand, but my fellow passenger warriors jumped out only to hide behind the boat, leaving me all by myself to take on the enemy. Both attackers were almost upon me.

I know every dog-lover on Earth and Up-Top, including Mars, would hate me until the end of time for what I did, but the threat was Punk, not Dog Mom. I just needed to get Dog Mom out of the way. I snatched up and threw her unconscious dog at her face. The look on the woman's face was of utter shock as she dropped whatever the hell was in her hand and lunged out to catch her "baby."

It gave me the time I needed to scoop up her knife weapon, which I realized as soon as I touched it was nothing more than a very long cigarette holder— useless. Punk tried to get around her one way; I went around the dog mom, the other way.

What Punk did next confirmed she was no law enforcement. She stopped, picked up the dog mom, and threw her out of the way into some seats. Her gun was pointed squarely at me. She wasn't giving me any chance to attack or retreat. Unless there was divine intervention, I was about to get shot.

What happened next I could remember with vivid detail, as it was all in slow motion. The terror of what occurred turned everyone on the plane into children wanting to run home to our mommies. People witnessed terrifying events in slow motion because fear pumped so much adrenaline throughout their bodies. You froze. You were along for the ride as whatever happened to you took place, and you would be able to perceive every second as it transpired.

We were suddenly weightless and realized that the plane had suddenly and violently dropped. My entire body crashed against the ceiling of the plane. I had to give her her due. Punk attempted to flip her body to hit the ceiling feet-first. She almost did it, but she didn't quite complete the rotation fast enough and hit her knees first.

I crashed back to the ground hard. The plane had leveled off again. It was like my ears had been turned off and then back on, because all of a sudden, a flood of yells from passengers on the deck overwhelmed me. Dog Mom had her unconscious Muffin in her arms to keep the dog shielded, but she didn't protect herself from impact. Now both she and the dog were unconscious.

There was one and only one thing on my mind.

Punk crashed to the ground and rolled over to face me. She received a stab to her gun hand for her trouble. Dog Mom's cigarette holder doubled as a switch blade. These rich people were as bad as the street gangs. Maybe Dog Mom used it against Cat Moms. Punk yelled out and let go of her gun.

All of us felt it. The plane flew as if unstable and out-of-control. We were holding on to whatever we could grab or had to fight to stay on our feet. The plane was drifting up and down, and side to side.

I glared at Punk, as she sat on the floor, holding her bloody gun hand.

"I have the gun now," I snarled and pointed it at her as I held on to a seat with my free hand.

"Cruz!" a passenger called out behind me.

I turned and shot him. The brawny watcher guy dropped to the floor, gripping his bloody shoulder and bruised face. He wasn't going anywhere.

"Good. Those who need to be bleeding are."

But Punk wasn't giving me the "I'll kill you" dirty looks anymore. She was looking out the window. I was looking out the window. Everyone else was too. When would this horror show end?

CHAPTER SIXTEEN

Wing Nut, the Ultimate Crazy Maniac

In the space of probably not more than fifteen minutes, there was a brawl on a luxury hoverplane, an attempted stabbing, an actual stabbing, a gunshot, and a plane dropping so violently that is slammed passengers into the ceiling and back down again. In any other universe, only one of those things was needed to classify the maiden flight of the Falcon Express a disaster of historical proportions to be followed by people going to jail, people never working again, and a megacorp going out of business. But the Horror Express wasn't done with us yet. I began to believe that the hoverplane itself was sentient, and evil, and determined to bring us all to the point of a fear-induced heart attack.

Sym's "Man" was there for me and everyone else on the deck to see out the plane's left-side window. The flying man did look like a scuba diver in a dark, bluish, greenish-ridged skin suit. The single-window mask over its eyes had a silver reflective lining. His hands and feet looked translucent. I looked closely for it, but there was no sign of any jetpack or modified rocketpack on his back. How could this man fly over seven hundred miles per hour at this height to effortlessly keep up with a hoverplane? We couldn't create evil flying Supermen yet, or skintight suits with superpowers. Was he an android of some kind? That was the only logical explanation I could come up with.

He walked on the plane's wing and jumped to a section above one of the engines. Fortunately, they were well-encased. Since I knew about engines, I knew the housing for the sky-walker engine could take a direct rocket attack and remain unscathed. The Wing Nut (as I called him after this incident) leaned down and began to pound the wing. Then his pounding grew in speed and intensity, then crescendoed to an outright wild and explosive frenzy. It was as if he meant to pound the wing right off the hoverplane. We all held our breaths.

"What is he doing?" one passenger yelled.

"He has to stop!" another said.

"Do something! We have to do something!" another yelled.

I gripped the gun in my hand. The idea popped into my mind, but there was no possible way to do it. The Wing Nut may be able to flaunt the rules of physics, but I couldn't. Suddenly, he dove and disappeared. Everyone jumped, and some screamed out again.

"Where did he go?" someone asked.

"We're going to die!" a passenger said.

"No, we're not!" Mortran yelled.

Something made me turn my view to the opposite side of the plane. The Wing Nut flew up into view, vertically hovering above the wing. He flew closer. I felt he was staring directly at me through his eye mask. Then he waved.

He jumped up and away he flew over the plane.

Passengers ran to windows everywhere to see him again. But he was gone. Eyes began to turn to me. I felt sick. This was one of those times when I didn't want to be the leader.

I surveyed our captives. Air Marshal Punk was on her feet, holding her bloodied hand, but she was surrounded by passengers, ready to pounce if she tried to run or attack us. Brawny Man was on the floor but had sat up to see our Man Outside. Near the elevators, all four of our flight attendants were surrounded by my passenger warriors, so they wouldn't be doing any poisoning or plotting.

"Sym, I have a job for you. Take two of our fellow passengers with you. Hurry. Before our Wing Nut friend comes back."

"He doesn't have to come back," the ex-military pilot passenger said. "He's outside on the plane doing God knows what."

"Why won't they land?" someone screamed.

"Hold that thought," I said. "We're going to get the answer to that question in a moment."

CHAPTER SEVENTEEN

Don't Make the Passengers Angry

Mutiny on the Falcon Express? That's what it had come to.

"Are we prisoners?" Punk asked us, as we gathered the four flight attendants, Brawny Man, and our air marshal all together around one of the empty family pod seats. They'd be watched closely.

I sent Sym with two passengers to the other two decks. We had to communicate with all the passengers on the plane. Since I was the man with the gun, the first deck was where I'd remain.

However, we really didn't need to send anyone to the other decks. Frightened passengers began coming up on their own, as well as other first deck passengers from the rec and sleeping decks. Passengers in fine suits or dresses; passengers in nightgowns or pajamas and slippers.

People yelled questions, and my own passenger warriors did their best to answer them.

"Where are the flight attendants on your decks?" I asked.

"They're keeping everyone calm," a new passenger answered.

"What's going on up here?" another asked.

"The other flight attendants don't know anything," Mr. Polo yelled at me.

"You had your chance to talk. Keep quiet. You're the underlings. We want to talk to those in charge." I looked at my own warriors. "Get every one of the other flight attendants here. We're not taking any chances," I directed.

"Leave them alone!" Polo and the other flight attendants yelled. A couple of them tried to stand to their feet and were abruptly pushed back down to the floor.

"What do you mean, get them here?" a passenger asked me.

"Go back to your deck, grab them, and lead them here so we can watch them in one place," I replied.

The new passengers looked at me incredulously.

"Are you crazy?" one said.

"He is. They all are," Deca Punk said.

I looked at my own passenger warriors. "Take care of it."

A group of my passenger warriors moved quickly, as if we hijacked planes all the time. Hijack. I can't even remember the last time I used the word or thought of it. There was no way to sugarcoat what we were doing. Mortran glanced at me a couple of times. He was probably thinking the same thing. We all could potentially be in very big trouble. But nothing compared to the trouble the Falcon Express was in. The mutineers were the Falcon's own uber-wealthy investors.

I heard loud talking from the passenger deck below us.

"What's happening?" I asked.

One of the teenagers popped up from the spiral staircase. "The guy who first saw the man outside the plane. He's giving a speech. He's telling them what's going on."

"I'm glad someone knows what's going on," I said.

I don't know what Sym said to the other passengers, but they started to trickle up the staircase. Angry faces had replaced the fear. They crowded onto our deck, glaring at our four flight attendants, Punk, and the brawny guy.

The elevator arrived and as soon as it opened, there was loud shouting. Passengers pushed flight attendants we hadn't seen before out and led them to us.

"Stop this!" a new female flight attendant said.

"Are you all mad? You're hijacking a plane," a male one said. "Did you forget that the plane dropped twenty feet?"

"Then why hasn't our pilot spoken to us on the overhead?" I asked him as he was placed with our 'captives.'"

He thought about that for a moment and realized he had no answer.

More passengers came up the staircase. More passengers came from the elevator.

I knelt in front of the four first-deck flight attendants. "Who's in the first-class section?" I asked them.

None of them answered.

"Don't make me ask you again," I said.

"Or what?" Punk asked.

"You are all going to prison for a very long time," Brawny Man yelled out.

"What's your name?" I asked him. "I can't call you Brawny Man or The Man I Shot in the Shoulder all the time."

"Remember it good. Kojo."

"I'll remember. I remember everyone I shoot. Maybe I'll get to shoot you again."

People screamed or yelled out. The Falcon Express dropped again, though not as far or violently.

"Enough of this!" I said as I rose to my feet. "The answer to all this has always been the same place. The people in the first-class section."

"We need to land the plane!" a woman yelled.

"Land the plane!" someone else called out.

"Land the plane! Land the plane!" erupted from every passenger on our deck, and we could hear the chants from the decks below too.

No longer were we the Legendary Falcon Express. It was "the plane," and we all wanted to be on the ground and as far away from it as possible

"Yes, let's make them do that right now."

I moved through everyone crowding the deck and marched through the aisle, past the elevators and restrooms, to that closed partition.

As if on cue, it opened, and there stood a lone Chief Hub. He looked at me, shaking his head. "Cruz," he muttered, and noticed the weapon in my hand. "Your detective license doesn't authorize you to possess any kind of firearm on a flight, private, commercial, or otherwise."

"Chief, don't take this the wrong way. I've saved your life, and you've saved mine. But if you don't get out of my way, I'll shoot you."

CHAPTER EIGHTEEN

The People at the Back of the Plane

The chief had the good sense to step aside. I don't think he'd ever seen me truly angry before. When he first opened the partition, all I saw was him. But now I was on the other side and scanned the aisle and the rest of the interior. Immediately at the front were two rows of facing seats, then a wall of compartments. There was another partition ahead, maybe ten feet away. So, the first-class section had another first-class section?

I stopped in my tracks. I'd passed a few rows of empty seats on either side, then reached a cul-de-sac area. I'd imagine it was the flight attendant station, but there were no attendants. Several corporate samurai soldiers, dressed in shiny black suits and bright white shirts, stared at me in wait. They filed out and took positions across the aisle in front of me to block my path to the back of the section. The only good thing was none of them looked Japanese. The Japanese had the best samurai soldiers only because they'd been at it longer than any other country. The Russians were good, as were Americans, Chinese, Jamaicans, and Brazilians. Every megacorporation of note in every nation on the planet had them. For the layperson, "good" was a relative term. They carried samurai swords, and even the worst of them could slice you in half. Five of the ones in front of me held their katanas raised in front of them; the sixth had his hands behind him, which was the most worrying. That meant he was likely carrying throwing daggers or shurikens. He could embed a dozen of them into me before I could blink.

"Maybe you should come back here and sit down," I heard Hub say from behind me.

I was going no farther unless they wanted me to.

"Sure, Chief."

I returned and we sat across from each other.

"Cruz, I told you not to come on this plane."

"If I didn't, would I have read the next day about the crash of the Falcon Express? Metro Police losing their longest serving chief of police. And I just know that sometime in the future, I'd be in trouble, and you wouldn't be there to save me, so I'd be dead too. My wife would then find you in the afterlife and kick your ass and mine in the grave. Does that answer your question?"

He leaned into the aisle. "Apex! Java! Strata! Where are you?" he yelled.

Outside the section, the aisle was packed with passengers watching us closely and listening to every word. Hub didn't hear a response and leaned back.

"You caused exactly the situation we were fighting to avoid."

"And what was that, Chief?"

"I should have barred you from the plane."

"Why didn't you then?"

"We all make mistakes."

"I should have marched back here the very first moment my suspicions said something was very wrong with this plane."

"What a damn mess you've caused!"

"Me? Do I need to recount all the things you, your criminal flight attendants, that Mr. Koji, the not-a-real air marshal, and the rest of the revered Falcon Express staff and crew have done?" I jumped up from my seat. "What's wrong with you? You're trying to get me and the passengers on this plane killed! I have a family! I have a wife and two little kids!"

Hub turned red, exploding with his own anger, and jumped up from his seat. "I have a wife and seven kids and twenty grandkids and two great-grandkids. Don't talk to me about getting killed! I have a family too!"

We stood there glaring at each other, fuming. We really wanted to knock each other's heads off our necks.

"Why would you do this? Why won't you land the plane? Land the plane!" I yelled.

Suddenly the loud chants from the passengers began again. "Land the plane! Land the plane!"

The senior flight staff pushed through the crowd of passengers. I watched the men stop at the entrance to the first class. Hub turned to see who I was looking at.

"Get in here!" he yelled at the three men.

Apex, Java, and Strata stepped into the section. Apex and Java may have looked impeccably dressed before, but now they looked like they had slept all night in their clothes. Strata looked even worse—clothes disheveled, messed up hair, spots that looked like mechanical fluid all over his jacket and pants. What had he been doing? Was he playing mechanic?

"Should we close the partition?" Apex asked.

"What do you think, genius?" Hub asked him sarcastically.

"Probably not."

"Probably not is the right answer unless you want to be taken away by the passengers too."

The rally began again: "Land the plane! Land the plane!"

Hub angrily pointed at me. "You created this mess. Get your fellow passengers under control."

"Land the plane then," I said.

Hub leaned close enough so that we were literally almost eye to eye. "We can't," he said.

I couldn't believe what he said. Why? "Land it now, or you'll have a real mess," I said. "We already have the attendants and the cabin stewards. I swear, we'll do whatever we have to."

"Take us hostage?" he asked, mockingly.

"Call it whatever you want. No one cares about me. But you have a plane full of very, very rich people who have more connections than we'll ever have, and the money to put you in jail and make your life into a living hell for the rest of your life. Land the plane!"

I saw my fellow passengers gesturing to something behind me. I instinctively thought the samurai soldiers were about to attack me. I turned with my gun hand, ready to fire, and stopped.

"Chief Hub, it would appear our original plan in regards to Mr. Cruz has failed completely," the man said. "We have, in fact, caused the very result we sought to avoid."

"Yes," I heard Hub acknowledge.

"We should have brought him in and told him what has been happening from the start, before we lifted off from Metro International."

"Yes. I know that now."

I had seen the man before, and my mind was racing to remember who he was. I remembered. My gun arm dropped to its side.

"Oh my God!" I said to myself, but loud enough for all to hear.

The dots were connecting in my mind. The other passengers and I couldn't figure out the "why." The behavior of flight crew and staff. The impromptu landing in Fiji. Hub's behavior. The Wing Nut. What Hub just said to me, that they couldn't land. I didn't know the details yet, but I realized what that "why" was then and there, staring at the man and monarch to a nation. In the universe of the average Joe and Jane, there was only one true horror situation above all others— terrorism!

CHAPTER NINETEEN

The King

"Is the Falcon Express under the control of terrorists?" I asked the man point-blank. I could hear the gasps from the passengers listening in the aisle outside the first class.

He walked right to me and extended his hand. "King Bahamut of the Saud Monarchy."

Shiny dark suit, white silk shirt, and combat boots. All the corporate samurai soldiers wore black combat boots too. Maybe it was the official footwear of the desert supercity of Saud. I shook his hand.

"You can secure your firearm," he said.

"Technically, it's not mine."

"No, it belongs to my head of security, but since you had the skill to take it from her, it is yours. We may live off-world, but my people adhere to the same values we've followed for thousands of years. You win a man's sword in battle; it belongs to you. The proverb also applies to women of the blade—or gun."

"Your head of security. Explains the combat boots."

The king smiled. "Shall we discuss this terrible affair?"

"I really would appreciate answers, sir."

"Then we should be quick about getting them to you. We don't have much time."

"That, sir, I wish you didn't say."

"What's happening, Mr. Cruz?" a passenger yelled.

The king didn't miss a beat. He walked from the first class into the crowd of passengers. Some recognized him, others only knew he was important. He raised his hands until all eyes were on him. The senior flight staff, Mr. Apex, Java, and Strata, stood behind him, and the corporate samurai soldiers, without swords or guns in hand, stood behind them.

"Ladies and gentlemen, I will not deceive you. We are all in the gravest danger. What we ask is for your patience. I will be blunt. We cannot land because if we attempt to do so, the unknown enemy, literally flying around us, threatens to take down and crash the Falcon Express."

The gasps were muted. He told them what we already suspected. The fact that he told them the truth gave him credibility.

"Please turn to our flight crew and senior staff. They are truly here to help you. All their actions from the time you boarded were to that end. We must all enter into a pact to survive. Return to your decks and seats but maintain your watchfulness. We will devise the plan to defeat our enemies and land this plane safely."

He did the kingly thing and calmed the masses. I had to close the deal.

I stepped out from the first-class section to the front where the king was. "We'll keep you informed, but you must help. Designate a person, one for each deck, to be the one who keeps us informed too. Watch the windows. Watch for that flying man outside. Most of us have seen him now."

"Also, ladies and gentlemen, stay seated with your seat belts fastened for your safety," Apex said. "Our pilot is the best, but he's doing the best he can. I can't promise the plane won't drop again."

Everyone just stood there looking at each other.

"People, let's move." It was Sym.

Other passengers joined in, and finally, people began moving to their seats, the elevators, or the spiral staircase.

"What about them?" a passenger asked from the group guarding all the flight attendants, Punk, and Kojo.

"I'll take charge of them," Mr. Java said, stepping toward them.

"Thank you, Mr. Cruz," the king said to me. "Let us have our talk before it returns."

\#

As I followed the king down the aisle deeper into the first-class section, it was even more luxurious than the rest of the plane. The Falcon's first-class interior had even greater craftsmanship. The foot of dark mahogany trim touched the wall and the ground shimmered like liquid. The mirrored ceiling lights had a warm glow, and the walls had even larger golden candle holders about six and a half feet up on the walls, each with yellow wax candles. For a moment, I felt the magic of the Falcon Express again. But in a flash, the feeling was gone.

The king's quarters were a private section of the first class. He opened another partition, and it was like a business office and a single flat all in one. The ceiling and walls were holo-screens. The walls displayed a busy market and commercial street complete with people on the ground and hovertraffic in a day sky. It was probably a live feed from a street in his supercity.

From one of the tables, a blue surface light came on and a holographic picture was projected up into the air in a V-shaped form. First appeared a woman wearing a gold head scarf to match her business suit with a black pinstriped line of what appeared to be diamonds from top to bottom. Then flashed a tall young man in a white military dress uniform, then another young man, a third and fourth, then a younger female, and finally the youngest of the group, a girl who couldn't be more than seventeen. The images disappeared and the holo-projector automatically turned off.

"My beautiful family," the king said.

"My wife and I have two," I said.

"Take a seat, Mr. Cruz."

Now the leather-like chairs were even more plush than the chair pod in the rest of the hoverplane.

The nation of Saud was an extremely wealthy one of the Arabian Peninsula in Western Asia, and one of the largest in the Arab world. Its supercity of the same name was not as large as Metropolis, but it was close. But while Metropolis's buildings were old, Saud's were newer. Megaskyscrapers were always being rebuilt and refitted.

"Why is it that you said terrorism when you first recognized me?" he asked as he sat too.

"You've been plagued by them before. I remembered it and seeing you in the news."

"Sad. To have my face connected to the average person by news of a dark week in my country some ten years ago. Yes, my region of Earth is blessed in many ways, and cursed in others. Namely, those who believe it should be the historical base of their evil."

"It was the only thing that explained the behavior and all the different things I've observed on this plane."

"Chief Hub and I did indeed make a great mistake in not seeking your counsel at the beginning."

"I'm on vacation, sir. At least, I thought I was. I thought I had the great fortune of being a part of hover-travel history."

"Sadly, the history we might make is not what any of us intended."

"Sir, I'm a street detective. I doubt I can be of any help with this situation, though I will help any way I can."

"I wish to hire you, Mr. Cruz."

"Excuse me?"

"I'm sure working in your profession that you have some sense of the security measures a man in my position has to undertake at all times. My itinerary for any given day is meticulously planned weeks, or even months in advance. For the Falcon Express, it was years in advance.

"Mr. Cruz, the Falcon Express is being held for ransom. We received their first message while we were boarding all non-first-class passengers. There was no possibility that we'd delay a flight of this magnitude, planned years in advance. The decision was made to take off."

"They wanted you to delay the flight?"

"Yes, but I believe, and know now, that they expected and wanted us to depart as normal because their true plans hinged on it. Then they sent the second ransom demand, and to prove they were serious, informed us that they had killed our air marshal. We verified that it was true, but we were already in the sky."

"How could they know who the air marshal for your plane was? Aren't they assigned at the last minute? Neither the flight nor the air marshal knows who's assigned and where they're assigned."

"How indeed. I will have you speak to Chief Hub and the rest of the flight crew and staff, each of whom will inform you of specific details."

"What is the ransom demand, sir?"

"Money, the release of prisoners, and relinquishing my throne."

"Money is a given."

"And no concern for mine. What they consider a king's ransom even is well within our threshold of financial pain."

"The other two are the problem, sir?"

"And impossible. The prisoners they want me to release are terrorists of the darkest psychopathic and unbalanced breed. They'd threaten my nation, the planet, and the off-world colonies. I can't stress it enough. They must never see the light of day outside our prisons. They live only so as to not make them martyrs. If they were ever released, the political fallout to my nation would be catastrophic, as my nation's justice system did the work theirs were too afraid to do. The relinquishing of my throne is an interesting demand since they undoubtedly know how Saud Monarchy works."

"You suspect your own government is involved?"

The king smiled again. "I have chosen my detective wisely."

"I'm flattered, sir, but I don't think I can do much to help."

"Nevertheless, consider yourself hired at double your normal fees. It would be no different than me hiring Chief Hub. He is the government law enforcement consultant aboard. You would be the civilian consultant. In my position, one can never have too much competent assistance."

I said no more. "What of the Wing Nut?"

"Interesting nickname."

"Flying man would be too...common."

"U.F.O."

"Excuse me, sir?"

"The terrorist group behind all this. They call themselves U.F.O."

* * *

"What does the U.F.O. stand for, sir?"

"Depends on whom you ask. They have many names in English and Arabic. However, 'unidentified flying object' is not one of them. 'Unidentified Freedom Order' is their most common name. I believe there is no real organization. Only a patchwork of disparate actors with differing agendas who've come together for this one purpose. They appeared on the scene only a few years ago. Many threats but no action of any kind, until now. An act that no other criminal entity could ever hope to accomplish, but they have, which is why I believe them not to be a new organization but one that has been around for a very long time. Only the name is new."

"When I asked if your own government might be involved, you smiled."

"My nation had always believed monarchies to be the best form of government for the modern age. A clear line of authority. No doubt who is in charge. However, the downside is that for any ambitious enough to want that role for himself, a monarchy has only one option for replacing the leader—death—and to end the line of succession—the dissolution of the monarchy."

"A very dangerous way to live, if you don't mind me saying so, sir."

"I agree completely, but this has been our way for thousands of years. People seem to like it. The real people, not the perpetual malcontents and outsiders."

The king's onboard quarters had more than a business office. He took me to a large ivory desk, and with a push of a button, a full bank of surveillance camera displays rose.

"Ordinarily, this would not be on the Falcon Express, but it was an added security measure for my safety."

"I'm sure presidents, prime ministers, and celebrities will do the same," I said.

I assumed that the plane did have advanced surveillance. Then I noticed that one of the feeds had a full view of the same restricted corridor I used and my passenger army.

"You saw me?" I asked. "Saw us?"

"I did," he said, chuckling under his breath.

"Why didn't you do anything?"

"Do what? Besides, it was for my security and the plane's staff to contend with. Not my affair. I was still under the illusion that we could get control of the situation."

"You mean me."

"Yes. Besides, it showed me you had familiarized yourself fully with all areas of the Falcon Express and possessed the know-how to access its private sections. You showed continued initiative in an affair you were placed in without your consent."

"This is what I wanted to show you." He pointed to one screen.

The camera POV was on the inside of one side of the plane facing the other. The Wing Nut flew past one side of the plane.

"No jetpack of any kind," I said.

"No, there isn't, and the aerial maneuvers he's been making shouldn't be possible at this altitude and speed, with any type of propulsion pack."

"A military exo-skeleton suit? Up-Top has a lot of tech that we don't have."

"I'd be privy to any military or corporate combat suit of that kind. The Space Colonies and Mars do have technology we don't have, but not this."

"I'm thinking an android then."

"Yes, or an android suit controlled remotely."

"But he'd have to be close by. Another hoverplane?"

"Possibly, but our choices of action are limited. The threat from these people is very real. They can bring the entire plane down. We must bide our time until we can formulate a plan. As my representatives negotiate with these terrorists, they give us some time, a few hours at most. This is our calm before the storm. Ultimately, we must deal with our flying man outside our plane—neutralize him."

Neutralize? I needed to get home to the wife and kids. I'd always been very legal-conscious in my work, but not this time. The Wing Nut was preventing us from safely landing the hoverplane, but I was prepared to do anything to remove that obstacle. The beauty was that I'd have the full backing of no less than a king, a chief of police, and a plane full of people.

"In Metropolis, we speak a bit more bluntly, sir. We need to kill him."

"In my part of the world, we are blunt people too. But I am royalty. We have to throw in the requisite euphemisms to keep up appearances. We, however, speak the same language.

"Mr. Cruz, you are about to learn a great many details of this terrible affair. Some of these details—and I fully appreciate you're a professional and understand discretion—must not be disclosed yet, even among the passengers you've befriended."

"What about these details, sir?"

"You may find them quite shocking."

CHAPTER TWENTY

All the King's Men

The king said this was our "calm before the storm" time. After my Classic Cyborg case, which literally took place just as our "storm of the century" was rolling into Metropolis, I hated that phrase. Further, unlike that case, we were forty thousand feet up in the air, not safe on terra firma.

Chief Hub had been hired by Carnegie Cosmo as a chief security consultant to oversee all related matters while the plane was in Metropolis. He was the perfect choice, of course. Who better to watch for, identify, and stop any with evil intent while in Earth's largest supercity?

The Chief filled me in on his year-long involvement in the run-up to the maiden voyage. Incredibly, he was only supposed to be a passenger too, courtesy of the king. Then the ransom demand came in.

"How could they find out who the air marshal is?" I asked.

We were sitting in our same seats in the front of the first-class section, but the partition was closed. Our previous little mutual outburst was already a distant memory. My Pops told me that only true friends could yell at each other one moment, then go out for cerveza the next.

"I'd say it was impossible, but it clearly isn't if they did it," he replied. "There will be an exhaustive review of the Marshal Service's procedures. They'll find out how it was done and all directly and indirectly responsible. You can be certain of that."

"How did you find out the real marshal was killed?"

"Marshals arrive hours before the flight. He didn't show up two hours before departure, as is procedure, and the Service had already called him a dozen times with no answer on any of his mobiles, and no callback from him. At that point, the protocol was to send agents to wherever he might be, starting with his residence. They found him."

"How was it done?"

"Laser blast, point-blank in the head at close range."

"The king said the first ransom came when the non-first class was boarding, which was what prompted your greeting."

"Ransom demand came in with the general threat and to postpone departure. Then there you were, stepping onto the plane."

"I was as surprised to see you."

"The second message came later about the marshal, once we were in the air. Also, only they could have known the details about how he was murdered."

"Or they could have intercepted the report from the agents or the coroner."

Hub shook his head. "There was another detail not shared that they knew. They tattooed the man. Initials U.F.O."

"I see, and Ms. Deca Punk became the air marshal."

"Mrs., and yes. She's been the king's head of security for five years. The previous head of security was her father."

"Who's the other man, Kojo? One of the king's security?"

"Part of the king's elite corporate samurai soldier detail. We thought, foolishly, that we'd have him keep an eye on you. Now, he lies on the floor with a gunshot wound. What if you punctured the hull of the plane?"

"Chief, you've seen me shoot before. Not likely."

"Possibly."

"He's not very good at inconspicuous surveillance, is he?"

"I don't suppose he was."

"Chief, what do you want me to do? I should ask: what are we going to do?"

"We've been instructed to keep the plane in the air until the ransom is paid and their other demands are strung out as long as possible, until we find a solution. If we don't comply, Flying Man will bring down the entire plane."

"Can he really do that?"

"Yes, he can. I'll take you to the cockpit myself and have you talk to the pilots. As to what I want you to do? Do what you do. You've established yourselves as the passengers' ringleader. This situation may get a whole lot worse before it gets better. We'll need all the help we can get to manage everyone. I've been in many panic situations, and people can become extremely dangerous. Panicked people are very dangerous people. We have to keep them as calm as humanly possible while we deal with all this."

"Have the pilots called in help?"

"Yes, Cruz. We did that already too. Two military jets were dispatched."

"What?"

"The jets reached us in no time."

"What happened?"

"You, and I believe a couple of fellow passengers, heard what happened. Flying Man shot something at one jet, blowing its engines. The loud thud you heard—"

"Like we hit something."

"We did hit something, or it hit us. It was the pilot ejecting from his jet. We hit him as he came down. Flying Man can bring down this plane."

* * *

I sat there stunned. The king did warn me I'd be shocked. The chief continued his story. The jet that Wing Nut attacked dropped back to the Earth and exploded in a ball of fire when it hit the ground. Fortunately, it was an uninhabited area. The unconscious jet pilot did survive, though he broke both of his legs on impact. The second jet was immediately recalled to its military base.

"Chief, you're telling me there was an aerial battle outside the plane, while all of us were enjoying the flight, the tour, and refreshments."

"Ignorance is bliss, isn't it?"

"What are we going to do?"

"We, nothing. The corporate samurai soldiers and I are devising a plan to deal with the situation."

"Then what do you want me to do besides babysit the passengers?"

"That's plenty for the moment. We tried to keep this from everyone, but since they insisted on knowing, they know. You just keep them calm. I don't have the time to deal with them."

"No, I don't want you to deal with the passengers either. Deal with the terrorists." I noticed the Chief's reticence, as if he wanted to say more. "Do you disagree with the king?" I asked.

"It could be real terrorists or those wanting us to believe they are terrorists."

"Chief, what do you know?"

"You're not the only one who has hunches."

"What do you know, Chief?"

"Stay with the passengers, but I may need your gun-hand before this is all over."

"Wow. Are you hiring me to be a backup officer?"

"Absolutely not. I'm a consultant. You're a consultant. Neither one of us are in our real job. Our only job is getting this plane to the ground with all aboard alive."

"Sounds like a good plan to me."

"We'll talk to the senior flight staff, then the pilot."

"May I ask a simple question, Chief?"

"Go."

"I do appreciate this respite, but is someone keeping an eye on our flying friend?"

"At all times. The entire flight crew and staff have been taking shifts on watch."

"Explains why our flight attendants were so absent from the deck."

"Don't be too hard on them. They were trained in school to handle terrorist situations, but what simulation could prepare a person for this? And none of them had flying men buzzing around a speeding hoverplane in mid-air."

"Not the kind of legendary start we were all hoping for for the Falcon Express."

"No."

Hub stood from his seat. I did the same.

"The main pilot is Mr. Dash?"

"Yes."

"I'll be speaking to him and Mr. Hacker, with the bionic high-beam eyes."

"Hacker mostly."

"Mostly? Why not hardly? Chief, what are you not telling me about the plane's chief pilot."

"Let's move to the cockpit."

* * *

Panic does make people dangerous, and stupid. The one and last time I ever drove my Ford Pony to the scarce farm areas outside Metropolis—I can't even remember why I was there—I was landing my vehicle in a field and this giant cow (or was it a bull?) came out of nowhere. Clearly, the animal was terrified of a hunk of red metal descending from the sky with its high beams on but instead of running away, it charged me! The Falcon Express had panicked and caused far more trouble for themselves in the process by trying to hide things from us passengers. But if I were in their place, what would I have done? Likely, not something too far different from what they did, though the plotting of drugging passengers was a bit much.

I was bracing myself for more shocking revelations in the Falcon Express cockpit. The chief opened the partition of the first class but there stood Mr. Apex, Java, and Strata, and they were looking at me.

"Chief, we need to speak with Mr. Cruz," Mr. Strata said.

"I need to take him to the cockpit."

"We'll only be a minute," Mr. Java said.

Chief Hub looked at them, then back at me.

"Follow us, Mr. Cruz," Java said.

Hub watched the three men lead me away from the first-class section. I followed but then wondered where they were going. Ahead of us, I could see all passengers were back in their seats. A few of them noticed me and watched.

"I'm not going in there," I said, when I realized where our meeting was about to be held.

"Why not?" Java asked. "It's a private meeting place."

"I don't want to be anywhere near those so-called sentient toilets."

The three managed to laugh a bit despite their stressed-out demeanor.

"They are already a thing of the past," Mr. Apex said.

Java held the door open, and I peeked in. No sentient toilet, just the regular kind.

"How did you do that?" I asked.

"It was a simple marketing exercise to see how the public responded," Apex answered. "We had both models on hand. Maintenance replaced them when Mr. Java was doing our tour."

"Smooth," I said.

Java entered and gestured me in. I felt like I was back in high school, where such meetings were common. I followed, but Apex and Strata stayed outside the door.

"Mr. Java can speak for us," Apex said.

The door closed, and there I was, standing in one of the plane's bathrooms. It was, of course, larger and more elegant than any plane bathroom I'd ever been in, but that didn't change what it was.

"We need to hire you, Mr. Cruz," Java said.

"What?"

"Hire you."

"How can you hire me? I'm a passenger."

"But a detective."

"A detective your Mr. Strata was plotting with your flight attendants to poison."

"They were never going to do that. The plan was to drug you for an extended time."

"So, you know what they were doing?"

"We were desperate."

"No excuse."

"The terrorists threatened to down the entire plane. And one of them is flying around the plane as we speak. Who knows what he's doing out there? We need to hire you."

"Why?"

"We believe they have an accomplice aboard."

"What?" He could see the shock on my face. "Have you told the Chief?"

"We want you to handle it."

"Why? You have the chief of police of the largest supercity aboard this plane, and you won't tell him. Have you told the king?"

"No."

"Why not? You don't think the accomplice is one of them?"

"No, of course not, but we have to be cautious. If we tell them, then they will have to act. If they tell others, one of them could be the accomplice. We can't take the chance. We need an outsider."

"Why do you believe there's an accomplice aboard?"

"More than a few of the staff noticed when we were airborne. Then when we landed in Fiji because we had to check for any damage to the plane—the terrorists gave us permission..."

"The incident with the two jets."

"Yes, it was a full-scale laser battle."

"Laser battle?"

"When you get to the cockpit, they'll fill you in."

"Are you telling me the chief gave me only a piece of the story?"

"They'll tell you, but we have to find the accomplice."

"What did this accomplice do?"

"Sabotaged the plane."

"How?"

"The Falcon Express has countless security and defense systems."

"Defense systems? What does that mean?"

"External surveillance camera nodes for one. That's why we had to land. We couldn't see if there was any damage from our surveillance displays in the cockpit. They were disabled. We are completely blind. We can't see anything outside on the plane."

"Defense systems? You told me about security surveillance, now tell me about the defense."

Java hesitated, but he knew I wouldn't let it go. "For strictly emergency situations, there are a few pop-up gun ports on the plane."

"Gun ports?"

"For strictly emergency situations."

"Yes, you said that. The Falcon Express has gun ports on its exterior to shoot people."

"The Falcon Express was built primarily to cater to the elite of our planet. Such measures would be required in case of extreme emergencies."

"Mr. Java, I have no problem with it. I'm sure the Falcon Express isn't the only hoverplane on this planet with such defense systems. What you're telling me is that we had the means to shoot the Wing Nut from the cockpit."

"Wing Nut? You mean the Flying Man."

"Flying Man lacks originality. He landed on the wing of the plane and started banging on it with his arms like a nut. Wing Nut."

"Anyway—"

"Disabled how?" I asked him.

"From within the plane. Deliberately. The person knew exactly what they were doing, and they were quick about it."

I slowly shook my head. Not surprising that the terrorists would have someone on board the plane for an operation as bold as this one.

"Who do you suspect?" I asked him.

"I have no idea," Java said with trembling fear in his voice. "It could be anybody, even one of the passengers."

I sighed heavily. "I'll do it."

"You mean you'll take the case?"

"This is no case, Mr. Java. You've hired me to help find Wing Nut's accomplice. This is survival. Let me ask you one question. Besides the gun I got from the king's chief of security pretending to be the air marshal and the corporate samurai soldiers, what other weapons are aboard the Falcon Express?"

"Just the one, or two in the cockpit for the pilots."

"Nothing else?"

"No."

"Not any of the passengers?"

"No."

"Not even if they paid extra for the privilege."

"Absolutely not, especially with the king aboard."

"Okay. I know what I have to do."

"Thank you, Mr. Cruz." He shook my hand, and I could see he was feeling a bit better.

"Just don't go investigating anything yourself. I don't want to hear on the overheard that one of you was strangled and your dead body was found in one of the bathrooms, where the sentient toilets used to be."

He smiled. "No, Mr. Cruz. We'll leave the detecting to you. I will be seated with a drink. I need to calm my nerves."

* * *

As I opened the door, I was certain the atmosphere within the bathroom was drugged somehow. Don't get me wrong. Any air fragrances pumped into the environment of any bathroom were more than welcome by me, but this fragrance seemed a bit hypnotic. Sentient toilets and doped-up fragrances. The Falcon Express had some "bathroom issues."

"Hold on a minute. My turn," said Deca Punk from the passageway outside the door with a waiting Mr. Apex and Strata.

"What now?" I asked. "Another meeting?"

"Another meeting." She gestured Java out and she marched right in, closing the door. The chief didn't even have time to protest.

"This is ridiculous. The plane does have real meeting rooms."

"But where passengers can see who's coming and going."

"How's the hand?"

"What?" She glanced at her now bandaged hand. "I've forgotten all about it. I'm sure you've been stabbed or shot. Spend much time dwelling on it?"

"No. Well, one time, I was shot point-black in the chest with my body armor on."

"Who did that?"

"My friend or associate, I should say."

"Friend? Those are the friends you have in your world. I thought my life was dangerous. In the interest of time, I'll get right to it. However, you are not to share this conversation with even King Bahamut."

"Why? He's your boss."

"He hides it well, but this whole affair is overwhelming to him. He need not be troubled by anything else. I believe the terrorists have a co-conspirator aboard."

"An accomplice?"

"Yes."

"Why do you say that?"

"Not say. It's a great deal more than that. I am certain of it."

"Why?"

"The king leaves the kingdom very rarely, and flies even more infrequently than that. However, those times that he does, his security detail travels with a full armory."

"Armory? What kind of weapons?"

"The inventory is unimportant. The fact is that the armory is gone."

"Gone? Gone how? Where is this armory kept?"

"In the plane's private cargo hold that can be only accessed from the first-class section. That entire cargo hold was evacuated."

"I don't know what you're saying."

"The hold was opened to the atmosphere, and all the contents within, including the armory, were sucked out into the air. The cargo hold door was manually opened from outside the plane while we were in flight. It was the flying man. He knew of the armory and knew how to open the cargo hold. Its security alarms were disabled. We only learned of it because I do a check on all areas as standard protocol when a trip begins."

"You personally did the check?"

"One of my soldiers, but he called me and others and we saw it for ourselves."

"Not an accident."

"Impossible. Deliberate. Someone knew our detail protocols and the hold's security measures. Also, my soldiers were in different parts of the Falcon. When this discovery happened, they were all immediately summoned back to the king's quarters. We got another message from the terrorists on the king's official but private communication channel, as with the previous ones. The terrorists made mention of the soldiers 'running back to the king like scared rabbits.' How did they know that?"

"Unless someone aboard could tell them."

"Exactly."

"What do you want me to do?"

"I am personally hiring you to be one of my eyes and ears among the passengers. We are among the Falcon's crew and staff, but not the passengers. You have their trust. You can be my operative amongst them."

"Operative."

"You will be paid, of course."

"Of course."

"Then let me get you back to Chief Hub."

"Please do. He's not the patient kind, and I want out of this bathroom."

* * *

I needed to get off this plane. I had barely made it out of first-class but had three new clients. Yes, I was being paid and each one of them gave me more information that made me come to the conclusion that the bad guys were way, way ahead of the good guys. We were stuck in a flying metal rectangular box called the Falcon Express, albeit exquisite and posh, but still grasping around in the dark like drunken blind dead-end dudleys. We didn't know what else the terrorists could throw at us or their full scheme.

The door opened and there were Chief Hub and Kojo with a conspicuously bandaged shoulder and arm in a sling, facing each other and ready to go ten-rounds in a fighting match to the death. Apex, Java, and Strata frantically stayed between them to keep them at bay.

"What's happening here?" Deca asked.

"I need to get Cruz to the cockpit," the chief said.

"I need to speak with him beforehand," Kojo sneered.

"Don't you two see you're causing a spectacle in front of the passengers?" she whispered, but it was one of those loud whispers that was more like yelling.

"Chief, five minutes," I said.

The chief shot Kojo a dirty look.

"Five minutes is all I need," Kojo announced.

It was back in the bathroom for me with Kojo replacing Punk and the door closing.

"You're healing nicely," I said.

"What?"

I pointed to the bandages.

"That is of no importance," he said.

"I thought I was tough."

"It is an expected hazard of my duties. Being wounded in the protection of our king is expected and an honor. Think nothing of it."

These corporate samurai soldiers were hardcore, all right.

"Five minutes isn't long."

"What I am about to say, is between the two of us alone. I am contracting your private investigation services. You are not to speak of this to Mrs. Punk, any of my comrades, or even the king. This arrangement is between the two of us alone."

"Not even Mrs. Punk. She's your boss."

"The king is my boss. She's head of his security detail, but we all serve the king."

"An arrangement between us. You're hiring me?"

"Yes."

"To do what?"

"This terrorism group."

"The U.F.O.?"

"Their name is a joke and a distraction. They are undoubtedly a collection of enemies we have dealt with before. This is an operation that is far beyond their capability."

"How is their name a joke?"

"They appeared not so many years ago. Some called their actions attacks; I would call them stunts. Their operatives execute these stunts offensively dressed and flying by means of jetpacks. Before you ask, I will tell you, but only this once and never again. Wearing private women's undergarments or grotesque body-augmented clothing. We are a traditional nation-state. When the shock-value wore off, they began dressing as mythical monsters from our ancient fables. Distraction is all it is."

"Until now."

"Yes."

When his king told me of this U.F.O. group, it was from a high-level, highbrow perspective. Kojo gave me the real deal, the street-level perspective that I preferred. Their name had nothing to do with "unidentified flying objects." Even to this day, when people heard the phrase U.F.O., they thought of flying saucers. But we had flying saucers. Up-Top had been flying in them for over a century to show off their technological prowess along with their space stations and colonies on Luna and Mars. Flying saucers and Space Men were all real in our time, courtesy of off-worlders. However, we faced a new U.F.O., and there was nothing amusing or interesting about it.   The one word that stuck in my mind from Kojo's description of them: monsters.

"The king may have mentioned in his talk that he has enemies even in the royal court," he said.

"Enemies capable of working with terrorists."

"We are not proud of it, but it occurred in our historical past, and, I believe, such evil has returned to take hold within the monarchy. I believe they are not working with the terrorists but are directing them."

"How does this involve me?"

"The terrorists are dogs of habit. They do not work alone. They work in teams."

I felt my stomach mentally drop to my feet. "Teams?" I asked. "Meaning more than one."

"More than one always. When we dealt with them in the past, their teams ranged from three to as many as a dozen. For something of this magnitude, I cannot even fathom how large the team might be. However, what I can say with utmost certainty, is there are more of them than the flying man outside the hoverplane."

"You're hiring me to do what?"

"If the time should come, the time none of us wish to see come to pass, I will need your help directly. We plan to thwart their attempt to kill the king. That is their ultimate goal. Not money or release of prisoners or for the king and his family to abdicate all claims to the monarchy. Their goal is to kill the king."

"I'm a detective, Mr. Kojo."

"Today, you are more than that. If we thwart their plans, they will strike at everyone on this plane in, any way they can. We could have a battle for our very lives on the aisles and corridors of the Falcon Express. If it should come to that, we will need to neutralize the terrorists, in any way we can."

"You're hiring me to be an assassin?"

"I am hiring you to be what my comrades and I would be to the passengers and personnel aboard the mighty Falcon Express—a savior."

He reached into his jacket and handed me a black leather square bag.

"You have the gun, but these accessories and rounds will be most helpful in your mission."

"Should we be shooting live rounds in a plane?"

"The hull of the Falcon Express is armored and, as I can attest to personally, you know the difference between shooting a person and shooting the wall of a plane."

I was an assassin now. Of course, I didn't tell him that the king had already hired me to do, in essence, the same thing. Same job. Two clients. Double the money. Fine by me because after the Falcon Express, assuming we survived, I didn't think I'd be flying again—ever.

* * *

I had four new clients and still hadn't made it to the cockpit yet.

Chief Hub was pissed. He didn't like to wait. My legs struggled to keep up with his determined march. I realized that I actually had no idea how to get to the Falcon Express's cockpit, which was on purpose. The direct path was the only thing missing from the schematics I studied. It was need-to-know. Now, I needed to know.

We reached the spiral staircase and went down to the lowest passenger deck, marched to its elevators between their regular and first-class sections, with passengers ogling our every move, then inside the elevator. He waved a pass key that looked like a flat piece of metal the size of your pinky, and his thumb pressed the button. We went up, but to a level not indicated on the elevator car's control panel.

"Are the terrorists jamming all outboard calls and signals?" I asked.

"We are, per the terrorists' instructions. But they are too now after the incident with the rescue jets."

"I was told it was a little more involved than you led me to believe."

"I suppose it was, but I wasn't there."

When the door opened, it was eerily quiet. Two corporate samurai soldiers in black suits stepped into view. The chief led me into the long corridor. Ahead of us were more of the samurai soldiers. The two who met us at the elevator followed behind us.

"How many men are on cockpit security?" I asked.

"Ten," Hub answered. "The plane has its own normal security, but for the king's presence, all were upgraded to his own corporate samurai soldiers."

We stopped at the door at the other end of the corridor. "This is where I take my leave."

"To come up with the plan to save all of us."

"We already have the plan. All we need is the window of opportunity. Remember what I said before. Backup. Come running when I call."

"What do I do when I finish here?"

"You'll be escorted back to your passenger section and do what you do."

"Be my cool detective self."

"If you say so. If this all goes sideways and Flying Man attempts to bring this plane down, I'll need more than your juvenile humor."

"Gun-slinging Cruz."

"One-shot, Cruz. One shot for all of us. All of us will have to be that good despite whatever panic and chaos is happening around."

"I hope it doesn't come to that."

"All of us do, but we plan for everything." With that, Chief Hub knocked on the cabin section door.

CHAPTER TWENTY-ONE

Speaking for Captain Pilot

The door looked impenetrable even with its dark mahogany outer skin and embellished with retro-deco iconography around the edges. It opened to an inner darkened corridor. My eyes adjusted and soon made out a group of more corporate samurai soldiers armed with long automatic pistols, laser machine guns strapped over one shoulder, and the hilt of their samurai sword showing from the back of the other. Clad in the same shiny black suits and bright white shirts as the ones protecting the king in the first deck first class, they also wore glowing black shades, but theirs were unique. The white illumination of their eye gear all had golden crescent moons on the lenses. The pilots of the Falcon Express had more than a security detail; they had royal paramilitary guards protecting them.

"We've been expecting you," one said.

"I hope so. I'd hate to get shot by any of you."

"You shot one of our comrades," another reminded me.

"Completely justified at the time, and we've already made up and are the best of friends, life-long friends even." I kept a slight smile on my face and I knew I wasn't in any danger, but entering a corridor with gun-toting, sword-strapped corporate samurai soldiers all around me still made me a bit nervous.

"Don't worry, Mr. Cruz. We only kill those who threaten the life of our king, or if he tells us to. He hasn't made any such request about you—yet."

"What request has been made?"

"To show you to the pilot."

"Yes, Mr. Dash. I'm eager to speak with him."

"That may be quite difficult."

"Why?"

"He was shot in the head."

I stopped in my tracks for a moment. "Shot in the head? Is he dead?" I asked.

"The laser passed through his skull. They are operating on him at this moment. Follow us."

"Laser?" I asked.

The king did tell me I'd be shocked. The corporate samurai soldiers took me to a room—one of two private captain's lounges—but this one had been converted to an actual surgical operating room! I peered through the door window to watch people operating on the man lying on a long table. I'd only seen Dash on the holo-deck, but he wasn't smiling and he wasn't conscious.

I was more than shocked at what I was seeing. The operating garments the three medical professionals—if that's what they were—wore were made of an assortment of ripped clothes in stripes to cover their faces and heads. They had no gloves, so their hands were bathed in blood. The operating tools they were using looked to be kitchen cutlery and a Swiss army knife. Surrounding them were even more civilians, some with bloody hands and another had knitting needles in her hand.

"I think I've seen enough." To say I felt wobbly enough to faint or throw up, or throw up while fainting was an understatement. I truly was in a never-ending horror show.

"A grown man like you, Mr. Cruz. A private detective in Metropolis. You've seen far worse than this," said one of the soldiers.

"I don't do the blood stuff. Blood is nasty. See red, run. That's what ambulances and hospitals are for. But this is a luxury plane—my delicate sensibilities aren't supposed to be exposed to that here. I need to sit down."

"The other room," another said.

The room opposite the lounge-turned-operating room was a reading room and business office. I grabbed a plush chair pod and planted myself in it to get my bearing. What I'd seen was truly nasty. If they could save a man with that severe of a head wound, they would need to be officially recognized as miracle workers. But modern doctors did miracles with machines doing all the work, not kitchen cutlery.

"How can you save the man's life with all that blood? Are those even real doctors? They looked like civilians to me."

The dozen corporate samurai soldiers had encircled me in my chair. They rested their long guns at their sides. I was an amusement to them. More than a few had smirks on their faces.

"They are passengers, Mr. Cruz. On the second passenger deck is a group of doctors who invested in the Falcon Express too. You know their group—Doctors Without Planets. The two men and woman in there are renowned surgeons, famous world-wide and off-world too. They use what are eating utensils to us, but to them, they are tools to exercise their skills."

"I hope you plan to throw all those utensils away when they're done. You can't use them again on this plane after they've been poking around in your pilot's brain. High-powered heat dishwashing isn't going to cut it, you know."

The corporate soldiers didn't answer. They grinned. I continued to amuse them.

"The pilot was shot in the head. Do you have medical staff aboard the Falcon Express?" I asked.

"All our flight attendants are first-responder certified."

"Who can tell me what happened?" I asked.

"None of us saw it directly, but Mr. Hacker can tell you."

"Why did the chief say he was going to have me speak to the pilot then?"

"You were going to speak to the pilot. But he collapsed. The operation began less than an hour ago."

"He was conscious."

"Yes. The doctors have been monitoring him since the incident."

"What incident do you mean? I know of several now."

"The incident when the flying man jumped onto the nose of the plane and shot the pilot with a laser from his arm."

"What," was all I managed to say.

"We called the military jets to shoot him down. He retaliated."

"He shot the pilot in the head," I said to myself. "I'm going to remember that Wing Nut."

"What will you do?" a soldier asked.

"What will we do, is the question. Let me talk to Mr. Hacker. But if the pilot is being operated on, who's Mr. Hacker's co-pilot?"

"We will show you."

It's never a good sign when you ask a simple question and you are told instead: We will show you. I'd had enough shocks for one day. I didn't need any more.

I covered my eyes as the corporate soldiers led me out of the room past the door window of the lounge operating room for the main cockpit.

* * *

The sole corporate samurai soldier in front of the direct cockpit door was far bigger than any of the others, including Kojo. I'd seen ones like him before with ocular implants—the kind where the sunglasses were actually part of your face permanently. The grizzled man with a full dark beard was a cyborg with oversized metal hands to hold his long gun. I'd faced off with some of the worst cyborg criminals around. This corporate cyborg samurai soldier, like them, was not someone you'd ever want to meet in a dark alley, or any alley with full illumination.

At first, I thought he raised his empty hand to pat me down, but his bionic hand was also a body scanner. He waved it over me, side to side, head to toe. I instinctively, and very carefully, took out my gun, or the one I liberated from Punk.

"Put it away," he said dismissively. "You're clean."

"You're going to let me walk into the main cockpit with a gun?"

"Do you plan to shoot the pilot?" he asked.

"Of course not."

"Then what do I care? They have guns too and you won't be going in alone."

"What's your name?" I asked.

"Crescent."

I nodded. "I don't want you to take this the wrong way, because I have a wife, two kids, a classic vehicle, and a cool hat, but on this plane, you're the most beautiful thing I've seen all day."

The laughter rolled out of the man slowly at first, then became a rumble. He put a fist over his mouth to hide his mouth.

"All we have to do is get your hands on Flying Man," I said.

"I'll crush him like a bug," Crescent declared.

"I know you will if you can."

Whatever Wing Nut was, whether human or android, Crescent was the one person aboard the Falcon who could single-handedly neutralize the crazy maniac. No doubt about it.

The door opened and I was let in with two of the other corporate samurai soldiers following me. All the lights were off, and despite the big bay cockpit windows, it was hard to see. The outside sky still looked ominous, but at least it wasn't raining.

I stepped forward to confirm what I was seeing.

"A robot! A robot is flying the Falcon Express," I called out.

The robot wasn't completely humanoid, but it had arms and legs, but no head. Mounted on its neck were finger-like protrusions spread out and pointed at different places: the plane's indicators, controls, and displays, and the main cockpit window. In its case, it truly had an eye on everything.

"A robo-phobe," a voice said from the shadows.

Mr. Glowing Eyes, aka Mr. Jomar Hacker, acting captain of the Falcon Express, had turned on his high-beam eyes.

"Don't shine your lights on me," I said. "It's a legitimate concern, especially with these terrorists about."

"The Turing-5000 Robot is the most advanced automated pilot machine ever created. Despite Earther bigotry against them, robots can fly a plane better than any human."

"Can they? Aren't you an Earther, Mr. Hacker?"

"I was born on Mars."

"Figures. Well, we Earthers prefer people to robots. Nothing wrong with that."

"For one, this robot doesn't have to worry about being shot in the head by laser-wielding, flying terrorists."

I sighed. "Captain, I hope he makes it."

Hacker turned off his eyes. "We all do." Hacker rose from his seat. "I've been told to give you the rundown of what happened here since we took off from Metro International."

"Yes."

"I thought you were only a detective. What will you do with the information?"

"Use it in whatever way I can to help."

Hacker had a tablet in his hand. "We need to step out of the cockpit, since we need to keep our lights off. We won't be giving the flying man any more visible targets again."

"But shouldn't we stay in here?"

"The T–5K has been flying the plane since the attack on the pilot. He doesn't need me. I'm only the babysitter. But the guards will remain."

I turned to look at them. "Can either of you fly a plane? In case it runs out of batteries."

They laughed at me. Both raised their free hands.

"That's what I like. People with multiple skills," I said.

* * *

The Timeline of Terror was what I called it. We sat in the same business lounge across from the "operating room." Hacker flipped from screen to screen of the captain's log. Captain Dash wouldn't have been the one responsible for the log. It was all Captain Hacker's task. Thorough didn't even begin to describe the first officer's detail.

In a matter of moments, I knew everything from the vantage point of the pilots. It all started when they saw a blip in the sky flying toward them at high speed. They even radioed in a "U.F.O. sighting" to International Air Command. Then they saw the Wing Nut for the first time, before any of us, hours before Sym's utterance: "There's a man outside."

Hacker's log entries about his observations of the flying man were of interest. Wing Nut flew in circles around the plane, above and below it, always out of the view of us passengers, but not the cockpit pilots.

Wing Nut then began landing on the moving plane and...dancing.

"He started running along the plane next," Hacker said.

"This was before the jets arrived."

"Yes."

The encounter between the two military jets and Wing Nut took up most of Hacker's entire flight log. I already knew what had happened. Hacker's log added descriptive detail. Clearly, the pilots of the military jets were taken by surprise by Wing Nut's incredible speed, maneuverability, and weaponry.

The only gap in the log was when Flying Man rose above the plane's path and landed on the nose of the plane to shoot his embedded laser gun at Captain Dash.

"Captain, do you believe he's a man or an android of some kind?" I asked.

"Honestly, I can't say. In some of the sightings, I was certain it was a machine, but then in others, I was as sure it could only be a human being in some type of exo-suit."

"There's more than one," I said.

Hacker looked at me and I could see him thinking about my surmise.

"Think about it. One is a machine to do the battle; the other is the man, a man who flies across the passenger windows and waves at us passengers inside."

"He's toying with us, or terrorizing us?" the first officer asked.

"Think of a child with a new toy plane. What do they do? They fly it around until they learn all its capabilities, what it can do, and what they can make it do."

"Flying around the plane over and over."

"Dancing on the plane. Why would he need to do that?"

"An android duplicate that he controls perfectly."

"Yes."

"Then you must take your theory to the next step. Somewhere out there on the hull of the plane must be some kind of base."

"Did you see or hear anything else after you first spotted him?"

Hacker looked up at the ceiling, thinking. "I didn't put it in the log that I thought I heard something."

"When?"

"When we came back into the atmosphere from space."

"What did you see or hear?"

"A scraping sound. I can't be sure. It didn't last long."

"And we don't have any external surveillance cameras."

"No, we don't. But what if we did, and there is something on the plane's hull where the flying man, or men, are held up? What would we do about it, flying at nearly seven hundred miles per hour at our altitude? He may be able to do the things he can out there, but none of us can."

"Well, Captain, we'd better start thinking of a way."

"There isn't. We fly or land. We're not a military jet and he had no trouble with two of them."

"If we can't think of a way, then bring in the passengers. Maybe one of them or a few are smarter than us."

"No, Mr. Cruz, no more bringing in the passengers."

"Mr. Hacker, if this plane goes down, whether passenger or crew, no one is going to be able to tell one corpse from another, assuming there are any pieces of us left. I'd say that's your sales pitch, Captain. You'll have no shortage of volunteers."

"It'll give them something to do."

"Now you're thinking, Captain. Idle hands, idle minds. We don't want either."

"Or another onboard insurrection."

CHAPTER TWENTY-TWO

The Uninvited

"Are you crazy?" Mr. Apex yelled at us.

We had everyone in the captain's private lounge: Apex, Java, Strata, Chief Hub, Mrs. Punk, Kojo, corporate samurai soldiers, and—I don't know why—stewards from the sleeping deck. I half expected the kitchen staff to join the pow-wow.

I slipped out of the room. I didn't need to hear any more to know my idea of involving passengers in coming up with plans was going to be a "no-no." But Hacker was a good advocate and wasn't backing down easily. However, the chief had already told me the plan that he came up with which had the king's approval.

The corporate soldiers in the corridor and Crescent at the cockpit door watched me go but did nothing.

Surprisingly, Captain Dash was still in operation. What could they be doing for so long? But I had to remember he was shot in the head. So Wing Nut could shoot lasers through glass windows without damaging the glass. A very important note to self.

I knew he wasn't on my first deck, so straight to the second deck I went. Passengers watched me closely. They were calm, but they too were in the "calm before the storm" mode. No one was talking, and everyone was visibly nervous. I saw him in their deck's first class. Where else would you find an accomplished, globe-trotting, tournament poker player? He immediately locked eyes on me.

"Detective," he said when I reached him.

"I didn't get your name."

"Everyone calls me Ace."

"Of course, they do," I said with a smile. "Follow me, Ace. I need your assistance."

People watched us leave the first class for the elevators.

"May I know where we're going?"

"Once we step inside and have some privacy."

The elevator arrived and we stepped on. The door closed. Up we went.

"I don't need to tell you that everyone is scared to death and believes we're all going to die on this flight," he said.

"Don't need to be a poker champ to read their faces."

"No, you don't. What do you need assistance with?"

"I need your skills."

The door reached the deck. I gestured for him to follow me to—you guessed it—an unoccupied bathroom. The corporate samurai soldier on watch kept his eye on us as we stepped.

"The flying man outside," I said as I closed the door. The lights were already on.

"What about him?"

"He may have help."

"Help?" Ace showed some emotion with a wrinkled brow.

"He may be working with someone aboard this plane."

"Why are you telling me this?"

"Because you're going to help me find his accomplice."

"Accomplice?" Ace stared at me without blinking. "For argument's sake, say he does have an accomplice, how do you know it's not me?"

"You, Mr. Ace, are one of two people aboard that I know couldn't be working with the terrorists."

"I supposed you mean you know of me."

"Seen you before, on TV."

"Doesn't mean I couldn't be an accomplice."

"I think it's a safe bet you're not."

He grinned. "What do you need me to do?"

"The two of us are going to sit glued to surveillance cameras of all the passengers. There will be an announcement. You and I will see if we can spot the accomplice, or someone who could be."

"Simply acting suspiciously doesn't mean they are an accomplice to terrorists. Some people are naturally suspicious. That's their demeanor."

"Let's see what we can see. It can't hurt."

"No, Mr. Cruz, I don't suppose it could with the circumstances we find ourselves in. But only two of us."

"The two of us. But we're up to the challenge."

"Yes, no pressure. The fate of the Falcon Express in the eyeballs of two guys. Not a bet I'd make."

* * *

For a detective, taking someone into their confidence was a big deal. Things could go well, superbly well, or horribly wrong, or be a wash either way. Chief Hub and Ace were the only ones on the plane that I was certain didn't have any complicity with a bunch of terrorists.

But that left hundreds and hundreds of people. Both the senior staff and Mrs. Punk thought there was. Maybe they were wrong, maybe it was still one of them, trying to misdirect me. But after also speaking with Mr. Hacker, everything told me that there was more than one actor involved in this plot and on this plane.

I was back in the first-class section of my deck. I knew the room existed, but now I saw it for myself and brought a friend, to the very rear of the plane. One of the king's corporate samurai soldiers led us in.

"It's like the setup in New Las Vegas," Ace said with a smile as he sat down at a section of a curved table. "They give mini-tours to high-rollers."

I was seated next to him. The king and three of the corporate samurai soldiers stood quietly behind us. The king was intrigued by my addition to the plan.

Ace didn't need me to tell him what to do. He was a professional. Already he was scanning one display screen after another, studying faces. The exact same thing I was doing. He was Mr. Poker Tournament king. I was the Stake-Out king. Strangely, we were both perfectly suited for the task, and it would take as long as it took, which neither one of us had a problem with.

We heard a noise behind us. Someone had entered the room, but neither Ace nor I took our eyes off our designated display screens.

"Who's your partner in crime?" Chief Hub asked from behind us.

"I'm Ace," my friend answered without turning around but simply raised his hand.

"Cruz, does this have any chance of working?" Hub asked.

"Chief, Ace and I are ready when you are."

"I put a stop to your hair-brained plan to involve the passengers in devising a way to get at Flying Man outside the plane. They're passengers—"

"And Falcon Express investors," I added.

"That too, which is all the more reason not to involve them. We have a plan already worked out."

"Good. After this, let's get to it so we can land this plane."

"Not as simple as that."

"Chief, when is it starting?"

"Have a bit of patience."

"This is a risky proposition, Chief Hub," the king said.

"We have to risk it, sir," the chief said.

* * *

"Is there anyone on the rec deck?" I asked the chief.

"No, we searched every cabin and room. Everyone is in their seats from recreation, the restaurant and bar, and the sleeping cabins. The flight attendants have confirmed after doing a visual headcount. What you see on the screens is everyone."

"You're looking for someone?" Ace asked me.

"Yes, but I don't see him. A little man. He was actually sitting behind my seat."

The overhead announcement began. "Ladies and gentlemen. This is the first officer and co-pilot, Jomar Hacker. I have a very important announcement for you. On board the Falcon Express is the Metropolis Chief of Police. I can only thank the intervention of divine providence that he would be with us in this time of crisis. All this time, he and his team have been working diligently to resolve this situation and get us all safely back on the ground. We kept things from you before, but no more. Here is Chief Hub."

Of course, the chief's announcement was recorded, but the passengers didn't know that. Ace and I noticed that the chief was watching the bank of display monitors, over our shoulders, as intently as we were.

"Thank you, First Officer Hacker. Ladies and gentlemen. All of you know of the flying man outside our plane who has been terrorizing us all. You've all whispered the words to yourselves already, so I will say it out loud. Yes, this is an act of terrorism. We have all been their hostages with the flying man as their watcher. I have good news and better news. The situation will be over soon. My team has located the base of the terrorists and they have all been captured. As for the flying man, a squadron of military jets will arrive soon to deal once and for all with him. But hear this, ladies and gentlemen. One among us, inside this plane, is one of them.

"Now I say this to the accomplice of the terrorists directly. We know who you are. At this moment, the pilot will be landing this plane. When we touch down, you will be arrested and you will answer for your crimes. Not in Metropolis or any of the Americas. You will be tried in the Arabic states, and you know their punishments. That is all I have to say."

I knew that the passengers wanted to yell out and applaud. But, from the screen displays of all three passenger decks, people were wildly looking around at each other, too afraid to even breathe. An accomplice amongst them?

Suddenly, the little man that I'd been searching for popped up out of nowhere on the third deck from the solo passenger business section. Passengers jumped from their seats, as the man ran into the aisle and violently shoved away the flight attendant that tried to tackle him.

"Stop!" we heard another attendant yell.

"Stop that man!" Chief Hub yelled into a communicator in his hand.

"Look!" Ace yelled.

The man dug into his clothes for something as he ran for the elevator.

"Stop!" the flight attendants yelled, converging on him.

The corporate samurai soldiers came into view, sprinting down the aisles.

The man may have been little, but he pushed all three flight attendants away as if he had super-human strength. He was trying to pull out something from his clothes.

All we heard was a blaze of gunfire. Screaming. Passengers diving for cover. It was utter pandemonium, and we could hear the noise even from our own deck, in a closed-off section of first class. The sounds vibrated through the plane.

* * *

HELLO, MY NAME IS NEO. I AM UNABLE TO SPEAK, BUT I CAN READ LIPS. BE PATIENT WITH ME.

The thing the little man was trying to get from his clothes was a palm tablet. Those were the words I read on its screen as I knelt over him. He was dead all right, and I had a sickening feeling in my stomach. Was I responsible for getting an innocent passenger killed?

People cowered in their seats as the corporate samurai soldiers clustered around me over the body. Two of the flight attendants had already checked the body, and had found the now-dead man's tablet. I checked over the body again. Wallet with ID and some money.

I felt like the cop who had a shootout with the bad guys but shot a little kid by mistake. Accidents happen, but how do you recover from that? In hovercar racing code, there was no such thing as accidents. It was always your fault, no one else's. I felt awful. Chief Hub was right to question my plan. My big gamble got someone killed, the wrong someone.

"He was reaching for something. He should have remained seated. We could not take any chances," a corporate soldier said.

"He was scared," a flight attendant said. "He panicked."

"He should have remained seated."

Ace was also in my line of sight with the other passengers. He didn't move as quickly as I did when we saw the shoot-out from the security room, but here he was, joining me. I'm sure he could see in my face the guilt I felt.

"Life happens, Cruz," he said to me. "Even I don't get a royal flush every time."

I looked at the man's face again, then stood to get a better view.

"Do you know this man?" I asked the flight attendants.

The two of them didn't answer me right away. The other deck attendants joined them and they looked down at him.

"Did you see him before?" the female attendant asked her colleague.

"Must be from another deck," he asked.

Deca Punk appeared with Kojo, Apex, Java, and four other corporate samurai soldiers.

"Does anyone here know this man?" I asked them when they reached the body.

Staff and crew conversed amongst themselves. It was clear to everyone watching that no one was certain.

"Do you recognize him?" I asked Kojo.

"Why do you ask me?"

"He was the man sitting behind me. You switched seats with him to watch me."

Kojo stared at the man's face. "Yes, it was him."

"Did you speak to him?"

"No, I was the one," replied another corporate soldier. "We asked him to take another seat and he just left."

From the corner of my eye, I saw passengers looking toward the elevator. I turned, and so did all the corporate soldiers. The king appeared with Chief Hub and an entourage of corporate samurai soldiers.

The king reached the body and stared at the man. "Do we know him?" the king asked.

"We are not certain, sir," Deca replied.

"Is he a passenger?" he asked.

"We're confirming who he is, sir," Kojo replied.

"There's a simply way to find out," one of the attendants said. He pulled out a communicator from his pocket and spoke into it, calling his colleagues from the other decks.

It didn't take long for all the flight attendants from the other decks to join us. A dozen of them stared down at the little man. Mr. Polo knelt down and grabbed the dead man's chin to turn it from one side to the next.

He looked up at us. "This man isn't a passenger."

"What do you mean?" the chief asked.

"He's not a passenger," Polo repeated, standing to his feet.

"He's not any member of the staff either," another attendant said.

"Who is he then?" the chief asked.

None of the attendants could answer him.

"How did he get on the plane, then?" the chief asked.

"What does this mean to you, Deca?" the king asked, getting everyone's attention.

"I am without words, sir," she said, tears in her eyes. "It's not possible."

"What does this mean to you, Kojo?" the king asked.

"Sir, I do not know what to say."

"Chief Hub, my son and my daughter-in-law have completely failed in their duties as chief personal bodyguard and chief of security. Do you have a theory beyond the perfunctory 'I don't know'?"

"He snuck on somehow, sir," the chief answered.

"No, that is quite impossible," the king said. "But they are here, so something else must be possible. Mr. Cruz, do you have a theory?"

"I do, sir," I said. "How well do you know Carnegie Cosmo?"

The king looked at me with a slight smile.

"What does that mean?" the chief asked me.

"The only answer," I said, "is if he didn't sneak aboard the plane, which is impossible—Deca and Kojo are absolutely correct there—then he was already aboard the plane. Long before the king's royal guards took charge of the plane."

"A damn Trojan horse," the chief said, looking around the ceilings and floors of the plane.

CHAPTER TWENTY-THREE

Jumper

We had an actual crime scene on the Falcon Express—a fatal shoot-out on an enclosed plane while in flight. Chief Hub was the leader of the largest police department on Earth but, technically, even he wasn't allowed to shoot a weapon on a plane. Air marshals used specially designed tech-guns that could differentiate between flesh and hard surfaces—the real reason I was sure Deca Punk wasn't a real one from the start.

I couldn't imagine what was going on in the minds of the third deck passengers. Their entire business section was a bonafide crime scene, just without the yellow "POLICE LINE. DO NOT CROSS" tape. Clearly it was an untenable position, so the passengers were split up between the first and second passenger decks. The third deck flight attendants would move their stations too, but a contingent of corporate samurai soldiers would remain on the level on guard.

The dead man's body and clothes were thoroughly searched and scanned. Deca personally checked the area where he was sitting. Corporate soldiers questioned all the passengers sitting with and near him. None of them had any useful information about him. He was simply a fellow passenger.

All our concerns turned to the question: if the terrorists had someone on the third deck, did they have someone on the first and second decks too? If so, who? If not, why not? Why a man on just one deck or, more specifically, why the third deck?

"Seems like you have something to actually investigate then," Deca told me.

I'd never heard the chief's "Trojan horse" term before, but I was more than aware of the concept. The chief brought down a criminal crew who "created" their own bank—fake tellers, fake security guards, and fake bank managers. It was all to get people's bank and credit card account numbers. From there, the criminals could drain scores of people's accounts. Then the criminals "closed" the bank and disappeared—until the Chief's police crew caught up with them.

However, here the Trojan horse term took an even more frightening connotation. Were we inside of it and our captors wouldn't let us go?

"If this is true, this entire plane is a trap," the chief said.

We'd all moved back to the king's quarters to talk. The king sat on his large royal chair while all of us stood around him. Deca and Kojo had the demeanor of being demoted, which in their nation meant far worse things than ours. The rest of the corporate samurai soldiers looked as they always did—unemotional automatons.

"A trap for me," the king said.

"Sir, do you believe Mr. Cosmo is capable of such a thing?" the chief asked him.

"If it is as Mr. Cruz has surmised, then it must be true. These are terrorists, Chief Hub. They have many means to coerce a person to do their bidding. We do have a person aboard who was directly responsible for the construction of the Falcon Express."

"Have one of the flight attendants summon Mr. Strata?" Apex said to Java.

Java left the room.

"I do have an announcement," the king said.

"Our time is up," the chief said.

"Yes. The ransom has been paid and received. But the Monarchy has stalled as long as it could with the other demands. We've run out of time. The calm before the storm is over. That storm will be upon us soon. If this plane is a trap, we need to determine that now."

"If this dead man was an accomplice to the terrorists, what was he going to do? If Cruz's plan got him to panic, where was he running to? If he got to the elevators, where would he go from there?" the chief asked.

"All good questions, Chief. Where?" the king said.

"Sir, we will scan every surface on the plane," Kojo declared. "If there are any secret passages to be found, we will find them."

"Then do it now," the king directed. He looked at all the corporate samurai soldiers. "Everyone searches, everyone. I can defend myself."

"No, sir, I'll be at your side," the chief said.

"Then it's settled. Find it," the king said.

Deca Punk opened the door first, and the corporate soldiers followed her one after the other out of the king's quarters, then the first-class section.

"Mr. Cruz," the king said.

He had noticed that I was leaving the room.

"I need to check something, sir."

Red lights flashed on the ceiling, making everyone stop what they were doing.

"Someone is opening one of the doors!" Mr. Apex yelled.

"Opening the door?" the chief yelled. "We're forty thousand feet up in flight! That'll depressurize the plane!"

"That could break up the plane!" Apex yelled

"The hatch on the third passenger deck," a corporate soldier called out.

* * *

The pandemonium had spread to every deck. We knew what was happening, but none of the passengers were sitting in front of a bank of surveillance screens. All they heard was screaming and saw red flashing lights on the ceiling.

So many things passed through my mind as I bolted out of the private security cabin. But all that would have to wait. There was no way I was going to be killed in a hoverplane crash. The Falcon Express was the Titanic then, but I would not be going down with the ship. I had to stop whoever was trying to open the hatch on the third deck. That's exactly how I phrased it to myself. I had to do it. Maybe Deca or Kobo or one of the corporate samurai soldiers were on their way. Still, I moved as if I was literally the only one who could stop the death of us all. If all of us had the same mindset, one of us would make it there in time.

Fortunately, our deck hadn't gone full madhouse. There was no time for running down stairs. When I reached the spiral staircase, I jumped on the golden pole, then let myself drop down the center. I almost missed it, but my hand grabbed the railing just before the third deck and slung my body over it to land on the carpeted second deck.

I had expected the third deck passengers to be relocated already, but that wasn't so. People were literally everywhere, screaming, running, and cowering. We could hear the mechanic sounds. Instinctively, I knew there were only seconds left before the passage door was opened. I knew the direction of the passage door even if I couldn't physically see it in the dim light with passengers in front of me. The plane would tell me where to shoot. My eyes followed the flashing lights to what I was looking for—a flashing arch over the passage door about to be opened. In one brief moment, I launched my body in its direction and just started firing my gun at the only shadowy figure that could be the offender.

I hit the ground with such a thud because I didn't brace myself in any way. However, the red flashing lights stopped. There was a commotion, and I looked up, lying on my stomach.

Deca Punk was securing the hatch door, and a quartet of corporate samurai soldiers had encircled someone on the ground, with long guns pointed.

One of the passengers helped me up, and I stepped toward them. I wanted to know who it was. When I reached the man on the ground, I stared at his face awhile. The man was elegantly dressed in dark colors with a turtleneck top, flashy pants, and skin-tight boots. "Who the hell are you?" I asked.

I looked at Deca. She shook her head. "I don't know."

"He's not a passenger," I said.

"Another one?" she said.

"This crazy maniac almost killed us all," I said and just kicked him. I was that frustrated.

"Look what he's wearing," one of the soldiers said, flipping the bleeding man from his back to his chest.

The man had a compact parachute on his back.

"He was going to jump from the plane," the soldier said.

"And possibly kill us all," Deca said. "Who are you?" She kicked him too with her combat boots.

"He's not going anywhere," I said.

My shots all hit their target—arm, leg, and upper back. None hit the interior of the plane.

"Good shooting," a soldier said to me.

"And he's alive," Deca said. She turned the man over on his back. "You are going to talk. We come from the part of the world that knows how to make people talk."

"You're going to wish you could bail from this death plane too," he managed to say. From the gurgling sound, one or more of my shots was causing internal bleeding.

"Get him to the doctors," Deca yelled. "He needs to be alive for us to torture him to death."

I was tempted to tell her that maybe she shouldn't have said the last part out loud. The corporate soldiers quickly picked him up from the ground to whisk him away.

Mr. Apex and Java made it through the passengers to us.

"Who is this man?" Deca asked Java.

"I don't know. I've never seen him before."

"Another unknown man on the Falcon Express," Deca said angrily. "The plane is not secure. The king!"

The corporate soldiers were about to drop the would-be jumper. "No! Take him to the doctors and keep him under guard. I'll go."

"The flying man is back!" we heard someone on the second deck yell.

I turned to see the women who said it just in time to see the Wing Nut whoosh by the third deck windows like some kind of evil Superman.

I had an uncontrollable, manic desire to get off the plane. Maybe I could grab the would-be jumper's parachute without anyone seeing me.

CHAPTER TWENTY-FOUR

Incursion of the Body Snatchers

For civilian private detectives, getting traction on solving a case often meant coming up with a theory about how things transpired. Sometimes you were right, sometimes you were completely wrong. Bad detectives stuck to theories even when the facts and evidence said something else; good detectives started with the theory and adjusted as the facts came in. However, it always started with a theory.

If the little man was one of the terrorists, would a threatening announcement on the overhead really make him panic and break cover, running away? What was the jumper's intention—to escape or to bring down the plane? Their behavior seemed off to me, very un-terrorist-like, but what did I know? I'd never dealt with terrorists before on a case. What case? There was no case. I was along for the ride like everyone else, despite having four supposed clients aboard the Falcon Express. I felt like we were being played. Only in this game, people died for real.

Passengers noticed I was running down the aisle. By now, the king and chief would have realized the same thing I did. Mr. Java hadn't returned from finding Mr. Strata. Carnegie Cosmo could be a co-conspirator with the terrorists. But equally plausible was that Mr. Strata was the culprit. Strata, not Cosmo, was directly involved in the building of the Falcon Express. It was only a theory, but it was a good one.

"Did any of you see the plane manager, Mr. Strata?" I asked.

The first deck passengers directed me to the spiral staircase. The second deck passengers said they saw him going down to the third deck. When I reached the third deck, none of the passengers or flight attendants had seen him.

I stood on the spiral staircase between the second and third decks scanning every inch, listening for every sound, with my gun in hand. Normally, it was well-lit, but now the entire length of the staircase was in the dark. Still, I could see well enough. Where did Strata go? The spiral staircase was where he seemed to vanish.

"Maybe I can be of help," a voice called down to me.

Kojo came down the stairs. I signaled to him to be quiet by putting a finger to my lips. He nodded and tip-toed down. The gadget in his hand was no bigger than a player card. We looked around us for where any kind of secret passageway could be. Again, we had no idea if there were any secret passageways. For the moment, the Trojan horse theory was only a figment of our imagination. But so was Sym's flying man until we all saw the Wing Nut for ourselves. Little Man and the jumper came from somewhere, and it wasn't from the luggage or a ladies' handbag.

* * *

Sometimes you wish your theories were wrong.

I wished I could say I knew what happened next. One second, I was watching Kojo wave his scanner over another part of the wall, stretching out his arm as far as he could. The next moment, I was falling over the railing. Someone had pushed me from the shadows—hard. I slammed into the ground, and so did Kojo. He tried to yell, but his sounds were muffled somehow.

The pain I felt was intense. Then I realized it wasn't because of how I fell over the railing and hit the ground. Someone was kneeling on my body!

"Get off of me!" I yelled, but a hand immediately clamped over my mouth so that no one heard me.

Another set of hands grabbed me. But I felt the presence of more than one person. They had my head pinned down so I couldn't see. They were pulling me up the staircase somewhere. They were going to snatch me away, and I'd never be seen or heard from again.

The two unseen men on top of me patted down my clothes. I knew what they wanted. They wouldn't have the satisfaction. Their grubby hands were feeling inside my pockets for it, but my hand got to my gun first. Why bother pulling it out of the holster? I was bound to hit something. Hopefully, it wouldn't be Kojo.

The first man yelled out so loud when I pulled the trigger. He did our work for us by alerting everyone within earshot. Once I started firing, I was not about the stop. The two on top of me had jumped off like kangaroos.

When I got to my feet, I finally saw what we were facing. It wasn't simply two or a few of them. Armed men wearing black masks and dressed in black were jumping out of their secret hidey-hole between the second and third decks. I wasn't about to let them begin firing. I counted five when one rushed me before I could get off another shot.

He yelled as a blade burst through his neck. Kojo was on his feet too. All I heard were his combat yells and the brief, very brief, flash of his sword as the attackers were cut down.

Laser fire erupted from the darkness of their secret hiding place. I returned fire as Kojo finished off the last of the attackers and bolted up the steps for cover.

Then a red ball bounced out of the pitch-black hole of their hiding place.

We knew what it was. I sprinted for the third deck passenger section. Little did I know that studying the schematics of the new Falcon Express would literally save lives, including mine. I slapped a button on the side of the entrance to the section as I dove in. The bomb exploded just as the retractable door extended.

I heard the yells as the terrorists-in-black still conscious were sucked out of the plane.

The hull of the Falcon Express may have been armored, but even its hull couldn't withstand a direct bomb blast. Nothing could prepare you for the frightening reality of a plane depressurizing as the atmosphere was sucked out and emergency air masks dropped from the ceilings.

The plane steeply descended. No one could scream because they were too busy grabbing and fastening their oxygen masks. I may have kept the section passengers from being sucked out of the plane, but now I was the only one on the deck without a seat and a mask. My only lifeline was a floor-mounted hand-hold near one of the seats. If I let go, the retractable door wasn't strong enough for my body. Both door and I would be sucked out to "return to surface," as we said in amateur hovercar racing parlance. As for being without an oxygen mask, all I could do was hold my breath.

The plane leveled off. The terrifying sucking sound had stopped. I didn't fully understand the tech, but the hoverplane could repair any breeches, even in flight. I could understand why they didn't hype this particular feature. Ladies and gentlemen, fly the Falcon Express and even if we suffer an onboard bomb explosion, have no fear, the plane can fix itself.

The explosion had jammed the protective partition just before it was fully closed. I saw a hand appear, then another. At first, I thought it was Kojo and his fellow corporate samurai soldiers. But the four hands that pulled the door open wasn't them. Instead, there stood more of the black-clad terrorists, with black masks that fully covered the entire head of the wearer and obliterated all facial features. Their secret hiding place wasn't some little compartment; it had to be its own deck. Kojo and I had taken out at least six of them—all the bodies were gone from the floor, but several more stood at the entrance with a model of laser rifles I'd never seen before.

Just as I began to sit up to shoot, laser rounds of all colors shot over my head. I lay back down and tilted my head back to see Deca and the corporate samurai soldiers letting loose the barrage from behind me.   I looked back and several terrorists were on the floor.

We then heard gunfire from the deck above. I jumped up and almost crashed into Deca racing down the aisle like a rocket.

"Go!" I yelled to let her get past me.

She began firing her weapon as soon as she stepped past the partition door and reached the spiral staircase. I heard a body fall. The other corporate soldiers ran around me as I stayed put. No need for me to be a fifth wheel on a hovercraft.

* * *

A full-scale gun battle broke out above me. With my gun raised, I stepped into the dark hidey-hole between the second and third deck. I had to step over bodies to get to the steps, and again once I climbed into the darkness of the room.

My eyes saw a crack of light ahead of me. I groped around in the dark until I found the latch to open it. I was right. They did have a deck all to themselves, which meant it was always part of the Falcon Express construction, and so was the plot. The Chief's Trojan horse theory was correct, which was disturbing. The maiden voyage of the Falcon Express had always been meant to be the last voyage of the king, and those unlucky enough to be aboard.

Aiming my gun ahead of me, I went from room to room. They had sleeping cabins, kitchen and cafeteria, bathroom and showers, entertainment, and the control room, which is what I was looking for. Like the one in the first-class section, the terrorists had their own bank of surveillance cameras. They'd been watching us the whole time.

My ears picked up a faint ticking sound. When I sat down in the seat in front of the surveillance table, I saw there were a set of prominent digital numbers in the corner of the console, and it was no clock. The console had one other thing that I hadn't seen anywhere else— a wired phone. I smashed the receiver apart, pulled out every circuit I needed, and stuffed them in my pockets. The camera display feeds blanked out and the entire surveillance bank crackled as every wire, circuit, and component blew out and burned. What remained of the phone was now on fire, but it was going out. Hackers did it all the time when the police found their lair. All their computers and technology self-destructed either automatically or were remote-activated. Why wouldn't terrorists do the same?

"Were you part of the plot from the beginning?" I asked.

I don't know where Mr. Strata was hiding, but I sensed someone behind me and gave a quick glance before I spoke.

"I had no choice," he replied.

"Where's Mr. Java? He came looking for you."

"They...I don't know where they took him."

"Why would they take him at all?"

"I don't know."

"Are you sure? You do have a gun in your hand. Have you used one before?"

"You can't understand the pressure and threats I was under."

"They're terrorists, so I might be able to understand. What now?"

"We can still make this work."

"Make this work? What does that mean exactly?"

"Tell the king to follow his instructions."

"You hear the gun battle going on, don't you?"

"Even if you kill all of them, there's more."

"More where?"

"You've seen him flying around the plane. There are more."

"Outside the plane."

"Yes."

"You will never win. You were doomed the moment you stepped aboard this plane."

"I don't like that word 'doomed.' Do you mind if we at least try to avoid the doom?"

"Tell the king to follow his instructions."

"Then what? You'll allow us to land the plane?"

"Yes."

"But that would be a win. You just said we'll never win."

"I don't have time to play word games with you, Mr. Cruz."

We both noticed that all gunfire had stopped.

"Sounds like your friends have met their Maker."

"More likely they have taken hostages."

"Really?"

"Yes."

"Where's Mr. Java?"

"I told you. I don't know."

"Why would your friends take Mr. Java? Your friends are body snatchers too."

"They're not my friends."

"I need to leave and see if I'm needed upstairs."

"I need you to promise me you'll get the king—"

"To follow his instructions. I heard you the first time."

"Don't bother trying to shoot me."

"Why is that?"

"We're not the only ones in the room, Mr. Cruz. I don't shoot anybody. I'm a plane architect and builder."

"And terrorist."

"Call me whatever you want."

"How do you want this to end, Mr. Strata? You seemed like such a nice man."

"Because I am. I want this nightmare to be over. The plane to be back on the ground. The passengers to go home to their families. Maybe get some semblance of my life back."

"Was this you alone, or was Mr. Cosmo the mastermind of it all?"

"Which Mr. Cosmo?"

"What does that mean?"

"Nevermind. My associate wants you to drop your gun to the floor."

I had been slowly angling my body to see if there was actually anyone behind me, but I saw no one.

"I'm not dropping my gun."

"That's very unfortunate for you."

Actually, he never finished the word "you." It was like we knew each other's thoughts and drew on each other at the same time. But unfortunately for him, I was much faster. Fortunately for him I was in a charitable mood. I shot him in the chest, but not to kill him.

He crashed to the floor and, without hesitation, I scooped up his gun.

I looked up as the door opened. Deca stepped in, but not alone. Kojo and several of the corporate samurai soldiers followed. I was glad to see Kojo. I was almost afraid he was sucked out of the plane in the explosion.

"The other terrorists?" I asked.

"Give us some credit, Mr. Cruz," Deca said. "They've been dealt with."

"Why are you smiling?" Kojo asked the wounded Strata on the floor.

"You have no idea," Strata said to us.

"Then tell us," I said.

Kojo kicked the man in his side. "You were given a position of trust. You took an oath to your company. You will find out what we do with those who betray our trust and threaten the life of our king."

Deca knelt down and thoroughly searched his pockets. She found a tiny remote device.

"So you activated the self-destruct of the console," I said.

"None of you will live past that day," he said to us.

I leaned down over him. "Mr. Strata, shut up. You're a liar. You told me that you had another confederate in this room. A lie. You said Deca and the guards couldn't put your terrorist friends down and likely took hostages. A lie. You hinted that you were coerced to aid the terrorists. Another lie. You're just a habitual liar. Here's the truth. We will live past this day. You will be a guest of the king in his country—permanently. What do you have to say about that?"

He smiled. "We have already beaten you. Long live U.F.O."

"Long live U.F.O.?" I asked. "Do you know how stupid that sounds? What kind of bad guy are you?"

CHAPTER TWENTY-FIVE

These Things Go Down

As we suspected, Strata was up to a lot more than activating the self-destruct of the terrorists' surveillance-communications-computer console, and boring me with his lying conversation. He'd been trying to stall me. Their entire secret hidey-hole was wired with incendiary devices. If they had activated, the Falcon Express would have been a flying ball of fire in the sky. Deca and her men deactivated all of the devices. If we ever got the plane safely on the ground, whatever DNA and clues were left behind would be ours.

But that still left the aftermath of our onboard battle.

Both the chief and I had the distinct displeasure of having been in full-scale riots, out-of-control protests, and every kind of human disturbance there was. We'd already had the conversation about it on that very hoverplane. Panicked people were dangerous people—to themselves and everyone else around them. But all those situations were outside, not trapped in a flying rectangular box where there was no place to run or escape to. No one aboard was singing the praises of the Falcon Express anymore.

I purposely didn't linger on the first deck passenger section because it was mine. We'd spent time together chatting, having laughs, and engaging in plane mutinies. The moment they had the chance, they'd inundate me with questions. Could I blame them? I was where they were—on the outside, without answers. But I had to be on the first deck because that's where the king and chief were, along with the senior plane staff.

It was all too much. Shoot-outs, explosions, a flying man. From their faces, both passengers and crew felt they had been cursed and were trapped on the "flight of the damned." We were the first-ever passengers to fly on the state-of-the-art Falcon Express. We even gave ourselves applause a few times. We were so happy. Now, if we had to do it all again, courtesy of time travel, not one of us would have stepped aboard this hoverplane for all the money in the universe. We would have avoided all of Metro International as if it had contracted an alien plague.

"Land the plane!" The loud chants from the passengers began again. "Land the plane! Land the plane!"

Before, I was part of the insurrection. But now, my peanut gallery warriors were looking at me sideways. I was with "them" now. They were seated for the moment, only chanting, but that wouldn't last long. I didn't want any of the passengers to be "free to move about the plane."

"This place's going to explode if we don't land." It was Ace, standing in the aisle in front of me. I'd taken a position between the business and first class, near—you guessed it—the bathrooms.

"We had one explosion aboard. We don't need another," I said.

"Land the plane! Land the plane!" The passenger chants were louder.

I brushed past Ace as I headed to the passenger section, not first class.

"I need your help," I said to Mr. Sym and Mr. Mortran, who were sitting across from each other.

"Me?" Sym said.

"We can do nothing for you," Mortran said.

"Are you going to ask us too?" It was evolutionary biologist guy and his investor wife.

"Maybe."

"You can count me out," Dog Mom sneered at me, with her rat-dog Muffin in her arms.

"Your dog tried to eat my leg, so I'm counting you out of everything."

Someone grabbed my arm. I turned and I saw my sleeping-pill-dependent investor friend. "Make them land the plane! We know you can."

He might not have realized, but he started the dominoes falling. One after another, passengers were getting up from their seats and making their way to me. The flight attendants were conspicuously nowhere to be seen—again.

I froze in the aisle. Soon everyone was looking at what I was. The "land the plane!" chants began to die down. We all saw the Wing Nut peering at us through a window from outside the plane.

He was smiling.

That's when I shot him.

* * *

Wing Nut should never have shot Captain Dash in the head through the cockpit window. He gave me the idea to do what I did. One clean head shot with Deca's laser gun and Kojo's weapon enhancements. The laser passed through the window and blasted a hole in his forehead. Everyone saw the flying man drop like a stone and "return to surface."

Passengers rushed to the left side of the plane where he'd been hovering at the window. His body was gone, but people still pressed against the windows to see anything at all.

"The detective Cruz killed the flying man!" It didn't become a chant, but I heard the sentence travel throughout the first deck like wildfire. Someone ran to the spiral staircase and yelled it down to the lower decks.

The teenage girl in her mink coat and leather skirt appeared next to me with her teenage friends. "You saved us," she said, smiling.

The partition to the first deck opened, and the king came out with Chief Hub at his side, followed by corporate samurai soldiers. The passengers repeated what I did.

"He did what?" the chief said. He looked at me with his mouth open, in shock. I'd never seen the chief in shock.

They walked to the window where passengers were pointing.

"He shot him right there," one beaming passenger said.

"Shot him right in the head. Gravity did the rest," another said.

The corporate soldiers couldn't believe it either. They clustered around the window, behind passengers.

"You killed him?" one of the soldiers asked.

I didn't say anything. Passengers were now coming up to me, patting me on the shoulder or back, or giving me a hug. Even Dog Mom tried to hug me with her rat-dog in her arm.

"Our terrible affair seems to be at an end," the king said to me.

Apex ran down the aisles with all the flight attendants.

"Cruz killed the flying man," they were told.

Deca appeared, running down the aisle with more corporate samurai soldiers.

"Cruz killed the flying man," a passenger told them, who happened to be Ace.

"What? How?" she asked.

"Shot him in the head through the window," a passenger replied.

"Through the window?"

"Dropped like a rock."

Deca stood next to me with her mouth open, looking at the same window passengers were pointing to. Chief Hub was still standing there with his mouth open.

"I can't believe it," Deca said. "Weren't you afraid you'd blow out the window? No. The flying man shot the chief pilot with his laser weapon from outside the plane and didn't. You knew you could do the same from inside the plane."

I so liked it when a person asked me a question but figured out the answer all on their own.

"Mr. Apex," the king said.

"Yes, sir," Apex said, stepping toward him.

"Land the plane."

The entire first deck erupted in applause.

"The plane is landing!" people cried out, and that spread through the decks even faster than wildfire.

"Yes, sir, immediately," Apex answered. "We can be at Cairo International in forty minutes."

"Make it so," the king said.

Apex ran back to the first deck. The king walked to me and shook my hand. "Thank you, Mr. Cruz. I didn't know you would take my verbal contract so literally. But there is not a complaint from me or anyone else aboard this plane."

"I don't imagine there would be," I said.

The horror show was over. We would be landing the plane on terra firma at last. We were all elated.

So why did we hear gunfire erupt somewhere on the plane?

* * *

I appreciated Deca's loaner gun, but what I needed was my gun, my omega-gun. My associate got it for me from Up-Top, possibly as far as Mars. I also missed my pop-gun, the gadget I wore on my left hand as my backup weapon and sucker-shooter protector. Also, the way things were going aboard the get-the-hell-off-anyway-you-can-Falcon Express, I needed my bullet-proof, laser-resistant vest.

The gunfire we heard could have only come from one place—near the terrorist hidey-hole. I had thought Deca was only the head of the king's security, but she also had to have been the faster sprinter I'd ever seen. We were all fast—Kojo, me, and the other corporate samurai soldiers—but Deca moved down the spiral staircase and was gone like she could fly.

When we finally stepped into the secret passage between the second and third decks, Deca was speaking to a group of the corporate soldiers, with their weapons still smoking. Deca marched to us.

"He was here," she said. "They were shooting at him."

"Who?" Kojo asked.

"The flying man," she replied.

"Cruz killed the flying man."

"Then there's another one, because he was on the plane."

"Where?" Kojo asked.

"He disappeared out of a secret passage in the floor. The same way he got on," she said.

"We must scan every surface of this compartment thoroughly," Kojo said.

"There isn't time," Deca said. "If there's another flying man, then the plane is still in serious danger. We'll station guardsmen there."

"We must have answers," Kojo said. "We have two of them."

"So, how goes the interrogation of Jumper and Mr. Strata?" I asked.

"They may not be talking now, but they will be soon," Kojo told me.

Deca shook her head. "The priority is the flying man, not them."

"We must increase the consequences for not telling us what we need to know," Kojo said.

"Why did he come aboard?" I asked.

They all looked at me. I repeated my question to the corporate samurai soldiers who had the shootout with it.

"We don't know," one of them said.

"If he can get on the plane, why now?" I asked.

"Maybe he's been moving back and forth all this time. Maybe he's been hiding here when not flying around the plane," a soldier answered.

"Maybe he came to avenge the death of his brother," another soldier said to me.

"Mr. Cruz, we don't have time to solve a mystery," Deca said.

"That's why I'm here. You all do what you need to do. If I can shoot another Wing Nut in the head, I will, but do what you need to do."

"We will," Deca said. "We need to make it so if he ever crawls out of where he's hiding, it will be the last thing he ever does in life."

The questions remained for me: Why did he come inside the plane? How many flying men were there?

A corporate samurai solider came down the staircase. "He's out of surgery," he said. "Captain Dash. He'll make it."

"Good," Deca said to him.

Kojo pushed me out of the way, and I hit the wall hard as gunfire exploded around me. When I got up from the floor and turned, covering my ears, I saw him. I killed one, but his twin stood there taking gunfire from Deca and the king's royal guards. He looked identical to what we'd seen before: a dark, bluish, green-ridged skin-tight scuba diving-like suit, with a single-window mask over its eyes. But this one had no mouth.

He had to be an android. Like most Earthers, I was not fond of robots and especially hated androids. In my A.I. Confidential case, I had to deal with not one but a whole zombie apocalypse of them. It was also the case where my formerly-posthumous mentor, Wilford G., who worked the streets of Metropolis as a private detective for seventy-plus years, was killed by one. I hated androids.

Deca and the royal guards fired their guns like robots themselves, but the Wing Nut blocked every round, every laser with his palms and forearms. He was like no other android I'd ever seen. His lightning-fast movements reminded me of an insect. The way his way hands bent over and forearms moved was like a praying mantis. I'd realized that my kill shot of his "brother" must have been pure luck. Deca and the royal guards were running out of rounds.

I threw my hat at it, but just out of reach. It stretched out to block it as I threw one of my spare clips over its head. For a split second, it didn't know what to do.

Androids were programmed machines, programmed to respond to a multitude of variables, but still finite. Behave and do anything outside that variable database, and you could confuse it and cause it to pause functions. My plan was to shoot it.

Suddenly, the Wing Nut flew through us with a speed no human could react to, knocking us all to the floor, and out of the secret section into the rest of the plane. A sickening feeling came over me. Was this how it was going to bring down the plane all this time?

We all tried to run out of the opening at the same time and only knocked ourselves down to the ground again. If we weren't about to die, it might have been funny.

All of us looked at each other, realizing that there was literally nothing we could do to stop the flying man. There was a strange sound, like the combination of a shotgun blast and the loud crackling of electricity. The lights of the plane flicked off, then back on.

"Move!" Deca yelled, and ran out with Kojo and the other corporate samurai soldiers following after her. I let them go.

I got to the first deck farthest from the spiral staircase. In the aisle on the way to the king's quarters was what was left of the second Wing Nut. It lay on its chest with a hole so big that there was nothing left of its head or upper torso. The entire body was charred.

The king stood in the aisle with some contraption in hand that looked like a wizard's wand, not a gun, but I knew the weapon was what ended the second Wing Nut.

"We are even, Mr. Cruz," the king said. "One and one."

"Thankfully, you're a king who believes in being armed at all times."

"Yes, thankfully."

"Was he after you or the plane?" the chief asked.

"Both, I imagine, Chief," the king replied. "Kill me personally and then the plane and all aboard."

Passengers watched, standing or seated in shock.

"But Cruz killed the flying man." It was Sym, the original one of the passengers who'd seen it. "There were two?"

"How many more of them are there?" Mortran asked, standing next to him.

"We must get the external cameras working," I said.

"Why?" the chief asked.

"We need to see what's on top of the plane," I answered.

"On top of the plane? Why do you ask that?"

"Something Strata said, Chief. Let's just get it done."

"Strata," Kojo said with anger. "He'll talk now, or out the plane he goes!"

"Mr. Apex, how much longer until we land?" the king asked.

"No more than thirty minutes away from Cairo now, sir."

I had no doubt in my mind that the terrorists would attack again. This was going to be the longest half hour of our lives, on a day that was the longest of our lives.

* * *

I killed one Wing Nut. The king killed another. Captain Dash would survive. For me, I had to hold onto all the good news I could, or I'd look like the passengers and staff who were in complete shock—again. For them, I had killed THE Wing Nut, but then a second one popped up, flying right into the plane from outside.

The royal guards had turned the steam room on the recreation deck into their interrogation room. The corporate samurai soldiers didn't seem to mind the heat at all, their shirts and jackets stripped off. Strata and Jumper were tied to chairs fully clothed and looked like soaking wet human-sized rats. The bruises showed me that the interrogation was ongoing.

We waltzed in with Deca and Kojo leading the way with a sense of urgency. However, I wasn't interested in seeing a beat-down, no matter how much they deserved it. We only had thirty minutes left. I was convinced there was more to come.

"Before I leave you to my friends to continue your talk, Mr. Strata, help me out with something," I said. "Why won't you tell me where Mr. Java is?"

"No one cares about Java," Kojo said. "We need to know how to fix the plane's external surveillance cameras and gun ports. That's all that matters."

"You do your work. I'll solve my mystery," I said to him. "Where's Java, Mr. Strata? We searched the entire plane, but couldn't find him. No body, nothing. You didn't have time to throw him from the plane. Where is he?"

"We did throw him from the plane," Would-Be Jumping Man said.

"No," I said. "I don't believe you."

"We will do anything for the cause," Would-Be Jumping Man said with a forced smile.

"We should just kill them!" Kojo said.

I ignored the other man and focused on the plane manager. "Mr. Strata, I'm going to find Mr. Java. I think it's important, so I'll take my leave and let you continue your chat with my friends."

Strata glared at me. "You'll never find him. You said yourself that you searched everywhere."

"We did, but there is one place aboard that could shield or fool our scanners."

Strata just glared at me. "I don't believe you," he said.

I touched his face. He jerked his head back.

"What are you doing?" Deca asked me.

I poked Strata's face again and again. He was getting angry.

"Why are you doing that?" Deca yelled.

"Ms. Punk, sorry, Mrs. Punk, this isn't Stephen Strata."

"What!" she said.

Kojo angrily grabbed the man by the collar of his shirt.

* * *

When I stood on the spiral staircase looking for the missing Java and Strata, I realized it was the only place that could have a secret passageway. Studying schematics was both an art and a science. But for a rare breed such as myself, especially one who built his own hovercar in high school, it was a skill I learned early. I poured over the Falcon Express plans for a long time, courtesy of my friend Run-Time. I knew every dead space on the Falcon Express. If there were any more secret rooms or passages aboard the Falcon Express, that's where they would be.

Two of my deck's flight attendants—Ms. Proxie and Mr. Marquee—led the way to the biggest one aboard. We reached the inner cargo hold from the third deck. That's when we heard the screaming above us.

Ms. Proxie lifted her communicator to her mouth. "This is Proxie. What's happening?"

"It's the flying man!" a voice responded. "He's back."

"Another one?" Proxie said. "How many of them are there?"

The corporate soldiers had lent me one of their hand scanners, but I wasn't expecting it to be of much help. The scanner wasn't powerful enough for a hoverplane that seemed to be constructed for the sole purpose of this maiden flight and to kill a king.

"No time to stop," I said and moved ahead of them, scanner in the left hand, gun in the right.

"The cargo hold is closed. If it's opened, staff and crew are alerted by alarm," Marquee said.

"Let's see for ourselves," I said as we reached the entrance.

Proxie scanned her access card and it opened. I gestured for them to stand to the side as the door fully opened on its own.   We stepped inside when the lights automatically came on.

"Is that supposed to be there?" I asked.

The cargo hold was empty except for one massive wooden crate in the corner of the hold.

When the attendants stepped in, they glanced at each other. "There shouldn't be anything in here," Marquee said.

"Who checked it?" I asked.

A look came over their faces. "Mr. Strata," he replied. "Sorry, we didn't realize."

I cautiously walked to the crate. First, I visually expected all around it, then I began scanning it. "Help me find the way to open it."

They joined me and we scanned every inch of the crate and began touching anything that could be a secret release for a door.

The plane descended sharply and we were all weightless for a second. I could see the look on their faces.

"Go!" I said to them. "I'll find my way in. You go to the passengers."

"What about you?" Marquee asked.

"Go! I'll be okay."

The flight attendants ran out of the cargo hold. Of course, I had no idea if I was going to be okay. I had no idea what was in the container. It could take me forever to find the way in. If I had my employee PJ on the plane with me, she'd be able to punch her way in. But the Falcon Express did have a cyborg I could enlist.

The cyborg samurai soldier ripped into the container with his metal hands. The outer wooden crate splintered into pieces and then Crescent yanked out one of the walls like it was paper.

"What were they planning?" Crescent asked.

We stared at a thick glass mobile prison. Metro PD and other major cities had them for transporting high-value prisoners. But why did the terrorists have one on the Falcon Express? At the moment, it held two prisoners, both bound on the ground, unconscious, and hooked up to wires and tubes from the floor—Mr. Java and another man dressed like one of the cabin stewards.

I held my breath. The plane had dropped again, then leveled off. Something was happening, but nothing good.

"I return to my post," Crescent said.

"Rip off the door lock before you go. I'll release them and find the fake cabin steward."

"Do it quickly," Crescent said and didn't bother with the mobile prison's lock. He just ripped off the door, lock and all.

* * *

Before heading back to the king's quarters, I had one pit stop to make. I knocked and the cockpit door opened.

"Mr. Cruz," Hacker said.

"Can your robot co-pilot make copies of files?" I asked.

He let me in with the two corporate soldiers watching me. "The T-5K can fly a plane and many other things. Copying files would be on the easy list of those many things it can do," Hacker said.

"I have some circuit files for him to copy. Put it on a hard data stick for me."

"You can tell him yourself. He understands English along with every other language on Earth and off-world."

I approached the robot. "Mr. Robot, I have a job for you to do muy rapido." I looked at Hacker. "I'm a language virtuoso."

"Yes, Mr. Cruz, I can tell. You can leave it with him," Hacker said as he sat back in his co-pilot seat.

"No, I'll wait."

* * *

Doctors Without Planets had a new patient—Mr. Java. He was unconscious because of the tubes and wires attached to his body. If they could save a man's life doing skull surgery with kitchen utensils, then getting Java back on his feet would be a stroll around a megatower rooftop park in the sunshine.

The cabin steward prisoner revived as soon as we unplugged him. We stormed the sleeping deck, or the corporate samurai soldiers did the storming, and the freed cabin steward and I did the following. We found our impostor and Deca, Kobo, and company had a third onboard terrorist for their sauna interrogation room.

I stood outside the room with Deca and Kobo.

"A mobile prisoner," Deca said to me. "The terrorists' plan was to capture the king and crash the plane with all of us aboard."

"We haven't landed yet," I said.

"The terrorists' plan has failed."

"We are ready for them," Kojo said.

"You are not convinced?" Deca said. "Still looking for a mystery to solve?"

"Did the man calling himself Strata not want us to find Java, not want us to find the cabin steward, or not want us to find the mobile prison?"

"Mr. Java will be able to talk soon," Deca said. "The guardsmen are thoroughly inspecting the cargo hold and the mobile prison."

"Whatever plot they had with their cabin steward impostor will be uncovered," Kojo said.

"Good. That's your mystery to solve. But we need those external surveillance cams," I said.

"We know," Deca said.

"Is there a way to get to the roof of the plane?" I asked.

"We aren't these flying men," she said. They all stared at me, as if I wasn't serious.

"What is your plan?" I asked.

"We have many plans, Mr. Cruz," she replied.

"To protect the king, yes, but do the plans involve saving everyone aboard too?"

"Of course, they do," Deca said. "We are not barbarians."

"Deca!" a voice yelled from her wrist communicator. "We have outside communications restored. The king speaks with Mr. Cosmo."

* * *

When we returned to the first deck, all I saw were corporate samurai soldiers stationed at specific locations armed with laser rifles or laser-tipped swords, and the nervous faces of passengers and attendants. The suit soldiers almost weren't going to let me back to the first-class section, but Deca appeared and they let us through.

Carnegie Cosmo was already speaking when we stepped into the king's business. The room was filled with the king, the chief, Mr. Apex, and suit soldiers. The uber-wealthy president and CEO's big head was on the wall screen phone. After this whole fiasco, assuming we survived, he'd probably have to think up a new venture for his Fortress Enterprises.

"This is the man, Mr. Cosmo," the king said, looking at me.

"I see. Mr. Cruz, is it?"

"Yes, it is, sir."

"Then was fortunate that both Chief Hub and you are aboard to help us through this crisis. My entire organization is now mobilized to see everyone aboard the Falcon Express safely back on the ground and to their homes and families."

"We will hunt down all those involved and this U.F.O. will never be seen or spoken of ever again," the king said.

"Sir, can you tell me who this man is?" I held up a tablet of the picture of Mr. Strata I had taken before.

Cosmo stared at it for a bit. "That's Mr. Strata's brother, I believe. I don't remember his first name. I haven't seen him for many years."

I turned the tablet so everyone else could see. "Who's this man?"

Mr. Apex's face turned as red as a cherry.

Chief Hub stepped and took the tablet from my hand. "This is Stephen Strata, the plane manager. Isn't it?"

"No, that isn't, Chief Hub," Mr. Cosmo replied. "What are you telling me?"

The Chief looked at Apex. "What are you saying? Is this or isn't it the man you know as Stephen Strata?"

"I—we all know him as Stephen," Apex replied.

"How long have you known him?"

"I've worked with that man for over ten years," Apex said, his body trembling.

"How is that possible?" the chief asked. "Two different people. I know Fortress Enterprises is an immense megacorp, but how could you not know the real Strata from someone else?"

The king raised his hands. "We can deal with this later. Mr. Cosmo, have you notified Cairo? We are less than thirty minutes out."

"Yes, the airport will be ready for your landing with all emergency and security services standing by."

"We need air support," the chief called out. "Another flying man is outside the plane. He's trying to pull apart one of our wings."

The revelation made me queasy. Cosmo's face looked like how I felt. "How can this flying man do this? I don't understand this."

"Sir, we need that air support," the chief said.

"The last time this flying man destroyed a military jet and the other retreated. Is this thing going to destroy my plane? I can't have hovercraft firing at the Falcon Express," Cosmo said with weepy eyes. "I was opposed to the action the last time. They could miss and blow you out of the sky. Isn't that what the terrorists want?"

"No, sir. Distract the flying man until we can land," the chief said.

"Mr. Cosmo, all our external surveillance and defense systems were disabled," the king said. "We need those systems."

Cosmo nodded on the screen. "Yes, I understand. I can re-enable all the systems without disrupting the main plane's systems."

"No!" Deca and I yelled, startling everyone.

"It must be what they want, why the terrorists have allowed our communications," Deca said. I could see that Kojo and all the corporate soldiers thought the same thing as me.

"Sir, get one of the planes you're in touch with to do a visual fly-over of us and..." I began, but the screen went black.

"Damn!" Chief Hub yelled.

"The terrorists allowed us to speak to him," Deca said.

All our ongoing communications were jammed again. We'd been thrown back into the darkness, flying blind, deaf, and cut off from the world.

"Why then? If our external cameras and defense systems were re-enabled, what would have happened?" the chief asked.

"We have to remember one thing here, Chief," I said.

"The terrorists built this damn plane," the chief said. "Probably use the plane's defensive systems against us."

"The terrorists built the Falcon Express, indeed," the king said. "Hopefully, Mr. Cosmo understood Mr. Cruz's message and will act accordingly."

"Assuming he's not part of the terrorists' plot too, sir," Kojo said.

Just then corporate samurai soldiers entered the room, escorting a newly conscious Mr. Java, the deck manager.

CHAPTER TWENTY-SIX

Lone Flyer

The cockpit of the Falcon Express had the greatest panoramic view. With the inner lights off, we stood in the near-dark watching. Their T-5K robot was still piloting, with Captain Hacker in the co-pilot seat. All those gathered before in the king's onboard office were in the cockpit now and, because of the spaciousness, we were by no means cramped.

"Mr. Java," I said.

"Yes."

"Tell us a story while we wait."

"Story?"

"Yes. What happened that made the terrorists try to disappear you?"

"Disappear him?" Deca asked.

"Yes, Deca, we Metropolitans don't know our nouns from our verbs, but that's how we talk. Well, Mr. Java?"

"Something made me suspicious of him from the very start of the day. He was acting very strange, nervous and secretive. Then all this happened, and our defense systems were disabled. Then the terrorist demands."

"You suspected he might be involved?"

"I had no proof. That's why we hired you."

"He was there with you and Mr. Apex."

"He suggested the same thing too. Mr. Apex and I thought he only did that because he knew we suspected him. We've known him forever. He'd never do what he suspected him of."

"Only he's not the real Stephen Strata," I reminded him.

"That makes no sense. I've worked with him for seven years in the same headquarters."

"You went looking for him?"

"I saw him. He was speaking to someone on a small mobile phone. It was so small I thought he was talking to his hand. He saw me watching and ran off. I followed him. When I came down the spiral staircase, everything went black. I felt myself being pulled away."

Deca looked at a couple of the corporate samurai soldiers. "I don't care what you have to do. Find that mini-mobile."

The men nodded and left the cockpit.

"Hopefully, he didn't destroy it," the chief said.

"If they can find that phone, we can call out," Apex said.

"We can call the national authorities, in case Cosmo didn't do so," the chief said.

"We can call the Monarchy, sir," Kojo said. "Begin the round-up of everyone involved with this U.F.O."

"We can call our military, sir," Deca said. "Send ten military jets or more."

"We can trace the call logs and maybe it'll lead to a terrorist or two," I said.

The king glanced at me and smiled.

"Yes, Cruz," the chief said. "That too."

"Don't look at me like that, Chief. You did hire me to be your backup. I'm backing you up by thinking like a detective."

"I meant shooting-wise."

"I already killed one of the flying men, what more do you want? The king vaporized the other."

"Let's get the third," the chief said. "How many of them are there?"

"Identified craft approaching," the robot announced.

Personally, I didn't want any robot talking to me. Do your task but no talking.

"Identification?" Hacker asked.

"Small two-seater hovercraft approaching," the robot replied.

"A two-seater?" the chief asked. "Can they fly this high and this fast?"

"They can, Chief," Hacker said, "if that's what they're designed to do. I see it now."

We all looked to the left and saw the approaching craft in the dim sky. We had a fifty-fifty chance of having good news or bad news. The bad news was that it was more terrorists coming for us. The good news was that Mr. Cosmo understood my directive before our communications were cut off and contacted another party to do that fly-over.

The small red hoverplane reminded me of my own Ford Pony classic hover vehicle. It was one of those ancient models retrofitted with newer hover-engine wings. There was no telling how long the craft had been airworthy—possibly as long as centuries, but with its lightweight and good maintenance, they could be in use for a millennium.

I told everyone that I recognized the symbol on the sides of the plane. "He's a stunt pilot."

"Then Cosmo is with us," the chief said. "But if he can see anything, how will we know?"

"Falcon Express, this is the Red Baron. Do you read me?" The message came over the cockpit speaker.

"Craft-to-craft communication can't be jammed like phones and communication," Hacker said. He picked up the receiver. "Falcon Express here, Red Baron."

"Falcon Express, making my first pass over your craft. Oh no!" the Red Baron said.

We were confused as to what had panicked him until we saw him too. The Wing Nut came into view, flying straight for the small red plane. Finally Flying Man had meant his match. The Red Baron spiraled away as he dove his plane. The flying man shot past the craft.

"Is there anything we can do?" the king asked our pilot.

"T-5K, alter course and back west," Hacker said to the robot.

"Complying with instructions now," it answered.

"I'll try to put us between it and that plane, sir," Hacker said. "We can't maneuver like him, but we can keep him off balance."

"Falcon Express, making my pass now," the Red Baron's voice came overhead. "What is that?" the pilot yelled. "Recording and sending..."

The red hoverplane shot over and dove. At that very moment, the flying man hit its midsection like a missile. It all happened so fast, but I was certain that the flying man was no more. However, its metal body wasn't crashing to Earth alone. The Red Baron broke apart in mid-air, crashing below.

"He killed him," Kojo said.

Hacker stood from his chair and his bionic eyes flicked on for a moment. He pointed it out the window. "I see a high-altitude parachute. Good, it opened. I think the pilot made it."

An indicator light flashed on the cockpit dashboard.

Hub and I didn't know what it was, but everyone else in the cockpit did. Hacker pushed a button. "We have a download," he said. "T-5K, describe the file."

"Media file," the robot said.

The Red Baron, hoverplane stunt pilot, lost his craft getting us the file, but went beyond the call of duty by taking out another flying man.

"Play the file," Hacker directed.

"Playing file."

Of course, the Falcon Express cockpit had its own dedicated big-screen display, which flipped down from the ceiling. But we should've never watched that video file. We all learned what caused that noise Captain Hacker told me about—the scraping sound he heard when the Falcon returned into our atmosphere from our space trip.

The horror show was far from over.

On the top of the Falcon Express was another craft, but one like we'd never seen before. We stared at the screen, speechless at what looked like a sickly green giant mantis—one with a human head, the head of the Wing Nut. The third flying Wing Nut was gone, but then a fourth one flew out of the mantis craft. It flew straight up into the sky and out of view. The next moment I was being pushed to the floor as the cockpit was showered with laser fire through the window.

CHAPTER TWENTY-SEVEN

Crescent

The laser barrage ended as quickly as it began when the flying man darted away. Crescent burst into the cockpit with more suit soldiers. Deca fully briefed him on what had transpired and showed him the video.

"Silver City," I said to the chief.

Only another lifelong Metropolis resident would know the reference.

"What is this reference, Silver City?" Kojo asked.

"Silver City is the center of robotic production in Metropolis," the chief replied.

"Are you saying the craft on top of the Falcon Express is its own android construction facility?" the king asked.

"There isn't an army of these flying men. It's constructing them as needed," the chief said.

The flying man whipped past our cockpit window. Then another.

"Is that the same flying man, or are there two of them?" one of the royal guards asked.

The entire plane violently jolted, almost knocking some of us in the cockpit off our feet.

Hacker got up off the floor and took his co-pilot seat. "We're losing power!"

"Why?" the king asked.

Hacker looked at the displays. "We've lost one of the sky-walker engines!"

Apex touched the console behind the pilot stations. We could hear the audio from each of the decks. I immediately recognized the two little kids from my deck.

"BEM, mommie! It's BEM, mommie! It's here to kill us!" they screamed, unnerving us all.

"What are they seeing?" the chief asked.

"One," a royal guard's voice came over Deca's communicator.

"Yes," she answered.

"They're on the wings!"

"What? Repeat!"

"There's more of them! They're on the wings, the flying men! They're trying to destroy the wings!"

"How many of them?" Deca asked.

"We count four, no, five!"

"How far are we from Cairo?" the king asked.

"Fifteen minutes," Hacker said. "But if we lose another engine, we won't make it."

"We need a solution now!" the king yelled. "Anyone!"

"Shoot them from the passenger windows!" Kojo yelled.

"Do it!" the king yelled.

Kojo ran out of the cockpit with almost all of the corporate samurai soldiers following. Crescent stepped directly in front of the king. "This must end, sir."

"Kojo and the guardsmen will attempt to shoot them from the wings of the plane," the king said to him.

"We need to be direct, sir. We have sat idly as the wolves have attacked us in the night. We must take the fight to them. Find the wolves in their lair and kill the dogs where they lie," Crescent said, brimming with anger.

"Yes, the time has come," the king said. "What do you suggest?"

"I'll go outside the plane," he said.

"No, Crescent. You can't do that," Deca said.

"I will leave this plane and get to the top of the Falcon Express if I have to claw my way to it."

"It's madness," Deca said.

"I go, sir."

"Mr. Hacker, what happens if we lose another engine?" the king asked.

"We had four. Now we have three. We lose another, and all our lives become far more complicated. We can get there on two engines, but we won't be fifteen minutes away anymore. It'll take us well over an hour with the diminished power. Another our weight will crash us."

The king looked at the big corporate cyborg soldier. "Those are the stakes, Mr. Crescent."

"Mr. Kojo and his men will fight from within. I will fight the battlefield outside. We will be in Cairo soon victorious, sir."

"Yes, Crescent. It will be so."

Crescent marched out of the cockpit alone. For the first time, I clearly saw the sword strapped to his back—a golden scimitar.

* * *

When the king left the cockpit with Deca, the remaining corporate soldiers, Apex, and the senior plane staff, the chief didn't follow.

"What will you do?" I asked him.

"I'm staying right here with our remaining pilot."

"Staying in the shooting gallery."

"Not the first time I've been shot at. Don't worry. I'll shoot back. What about you?"

"I'll be back up for Crescent."

"That cyborg doesn't need backup from us."

"I don't expect to do anything, but someone has to have his back."

"He'll have corporate soldiers to do that."

"I'll be an extra gun."

"Just don't get sucked out of the plane."

"They're going to throw everything at us now to make sure we don't land," I said.

"I know. We all know it."

"Don't get shot, Chief," I said as I left the cockpit.

"Don't get sucked out of the plane, Cruz. And good luck."

"Good luck, Mr. Cruz," Captain Hacker said to me. His bionic eyes had a faint glow in the dim cockpit.

∗ ∗ ∗

What Crescent was about to do was beyond crazy. Not even the best stunt people on the planet would do what he planned. The roof hatch was used by maintenance, not to be used when the hoverplane was in flight at forty thousand feet and traveling at seven hundred miles an hour. The cyborg pulled the ladder down. He had a big, black backpack, which I assumed was a parachute, in case it all went wrong. But with this height, any parachute would likely not be effective at all.

I'd met every kind of cyborg imaginable on the street—from pathetic to extremely dangerous. Some of them thought that being a big cyborg made them king of the hill, but being extremely musclebound or grossly obese negated any big bionic arm, bionic hand with retractable claws, bionic forearms with a pop-out rifle, or a steel-armored upper torso. What good did it do you if you couldn't move without passing out from exhaustion? Cyborgism didn't replace eating a healthy diet and doing basic exercise on a frequent basis.

One the other end of the spectrum were those cyborgs who had parts bigger or heavier than their natural bodies. If one had the body type of a walking toothpick, having big bionic arms wasn't going to intimidate anyone. All it would get you was constant ridicule in the "nice" parts of town, or a laser shot to the head in the "bad" parts where they'd remove those bionic parts from your corpse with a knife or sword for "reuse."

Crescent wasn't any of that at all. He was solid, toned, and trained, muscle and metal. Who knew how many decades of martial arts and tactical training? The king didn't hire any slackers for his royal guards and only the best of them would be stationed outside the cockpit in this crisis.

Before he climbed up, he looked at the two corporate samurai soldiers and me. All of us had portable oxygen masks on our faces, and we had upgraded our weapons to high-powered, rapid-fire hybrid laser/steel round slug-throwing machine guns.

"You sure you want to be here?" he asked me.
"The king and I are even in the shot count. I want a chance to beat him."

The cyborg chuckled. "Stay close together. When the hatch opens, the siren will be deafening, and the emergency containment will engage."

Emergency containment? What the hell was that?
I almost forgot. I removed my tan fedora and set it on a wall hook.

Laser gunfire had erupted on the passenger decks. We could hear the chaos. Kojo was doing his part. I'd hoped that it would distract the terrorists above in their creature craft on our plane. I thought to myself that I was a detective, not an aerial commando, but there I was.

Crescent was at the top of the step ladder and pulled the latch. The siren was so loud I thought my eardrums would explode. A circular wall shot up around all of us and hit the ceiling. Crescent pushed the hatch open, and suddenly the two corporate soldiers and I were sucked up and toward the open hatch. Crescent was gone.

The hatch closed and we all crashed to the floor. We all looked at each other. Without external surveillance, we might as well be blind. The two suit soldiers climbed up the step ladder and pushed the hatch open with all their might.

One laser blast and I was on my back on the floor with a dead corporate soldier on top of me. I pushed him off of me as the second pushed open the hatch again, and, in a blind rage, climbed out of the plane. All I saw was his one hand holding on, his body obviously airborne. But he steadied himself on something and was gone, the hatch closed.

Did I really want to do this?

Up the step ladder I went. I glanced down at the one dead corporate samurai soldier. His chest had a nasty laser blast. I pushed at the hatch, and it wouldn't budge. With all my leg and shoulder strength, I slowly pushed the hatch open. Then the hatch flipped open, and I was sucked out of the plane!

* * *

Sometimes people do stupid things not because they were trying to be brave, but because they're stupid and didn't think things through. I, more than most people, had a working knowledge of flying aerodynamics—I built a classic hovercar that not only worked but competed in the illegal amateur hovercar circuit. Maybe Crescent could do what we planned, and the Wing Nuts obviously could do this, since they could fly, but we mere unmodified humans were just asking for death.

I held on to the handle of the hatch for dear life as my body was pulled out and slammed on the top of the plane. When I finally was able to calm myself, my head turned to see the second corporate soldier's face. Even with the oxygen mask around his mouth and nose, I could see the terror. One hand held onto hand-holds on the plane's roof, while he fired wildly.

When I turned my head the other way to see what he was firing at, the media file we viewed in the cockpit by no means represented the reality of the thing. I literally almost had a heart attack. I hated bugs in general. On the plane's roof was a giant green mantis-like creature extended from behind the plane's cockpit section to the fuselage, reaching the plane's first set of wings. From my position at the hatch, it towered above me, about fifteen feet away. Its great big bug eyes stared down at us. This was the children's BEM—bug-eyed monster for real—and it had Crescent in its forearm claws! I knew it was really a hovercraft of some kind, but the uninformed would have sworn it was a real giant, monstrous insect.

A blur flew by and I snapped out of my fear-induced trance. It was a flying man. The second corporate soldier tried to hit him but the Wing Nut was too fast.

Another flying man flew straight at the second corporate soldier with such force that he was knocked off the plane. He was gone—his body disappeared over the side into the dark clouds. I could only assume a second corporate soldier was dead. The flying man who did it rose up in the sky, looking at me. In the blink of an eye, its body was blown apart by multiple laser fire from the passenger deck windows. Thank you, Kojo and company!

I didn't move or fire. The corporate samurai soldiers were dead because they forgot the mission. We were here to back up Crescent, not join the fight. This was his show.

Another flying man rose in the air from below the plane. It saw me and I saw the smile on its mouth. Well, I'd move if they attacked me too. I whipped around, firing my weapon. The Wing Nut trying to sneak up on me was about two feet away and about to yank me from my perch to send me into the sky to my death. Instead, I blasted the android apart, and all the debris was sucked away.

Thud!

Did Crescent weigh a ton or two? He landed on the roof with such force. I looked up and the cyborg had ripped off both claws of the mantis craft that held him. Crescent yelled out in triumphant rage as he let the nasty-looking insect claws drop away.

The creature craft tried to swat him from the plane with one of its giant middle legs. Crescent grabbed it with both of his brawny arms. I saw his clenched teeth. Watching his feet, the only explanation as to how he was able to remain standing on the plane's roof was his feet or legs were magnetized. Crescent ripped off the leg and then broke it in half. He did say he'd rip it apart, and he was doing it.

The giant mantis hit Crescent with its wing with such force and speed that the cyborg was knocked from the plane, taking parts of the fuselage magnetized to his feet with him. All I heard was the cyborg samurai yell as he disappeared into the same dark cloud the Falcon Express was bordering.

I let loose with my trigger finger, firing at the head of the giant mantis. My shots weren't missing, and without its giant forearm claws, the creature couldn't block them.

One. Two. Five of the flying men launched at me. I pulled myself back into the plane through the hatch opening, then let myself fall to the ground. The first corporate soldier's body was still on the floor. It was like the plane was hit by five missiles at once. The entire section above me exploded.

* * *

Officially, our plan was a very, very bad one. The flying men weren't Wing Nuts, dancing or trying to pull apart the wings of planes. They were part android, part missile, and all it would take was one to bring down the plane. We were focused on the sky-walker engines. But I knew of ten spots they could hit with a missile to crash the Falcon Express, even with the sky-walker engines, I'm sure the terrorists knew of fifty.

I held onto the step ladder for dear life because I was in the plane but with the gaping hole outside of the cockpit section, I might as well have been outside the plane. The emergency containment section was still intact for me, which was the only thing that saved me, but outside of it was exposed to the elements. The corporate soldier's body was gone. Above me, I could see the giant mantis's ugly head looking down at me. For the moment, there was little I could do as the explosion had blown my weapon out of my hands and out of the plane.

The cockpit door opened and there was Chief Hub in an oxygen mask. The section of the emergency containment barrier lowered and he grabbed me. When he pulled me in, the door slammed shut.

"Cruz, I told you not to get sucked out of the plane," he said.

I slid down into one of the extra seats in the cockpit, pulling off my oxygen mask. "I need another weapon, Chief."

"What happened to the other one?"

"It got sucked out of the plane."

Something tapped me on the arm. Hacker handed me another gun. "I want it back."

"I wish I could say it had an effect," I said.

"I think you should stay here. We all should," the chief said.

"One corporate soldier shot dead. Another was thrown from the plane. Crescent too. I think they're all dead, Chief. Not much of a plan so far."

"Have some faith, Mr. Cruz," Hacker said from his seat.

"Do you know something I don't?" I asked.

"Yes, Crescent isn't dead."

"How do you know that?"

"Because he's outside the plane, flying."

The chief was as surprised as I was and we moved to where Hacker sat. Outside the cockpit window was a man in the sky flying by means of a rocketpack. His backpack wasn't a parachute. With his bionic eyes, if Hacker said it was Crescent, then it was.

"What's he going to do?" the chief asked.

"Oh no," Hacker called out.

A flying man streaked toward him. Even with our normal eyes, we saw Crescent punch the flying man. The android dropped like a stone.

"If only the plane had its defensive systems," Hacker said.

"If only we had more powerful weapons ourselves," the chief said.

"Systems are coming back online," the T–5K announced.

"What systems?" Hacker asked the robot.

"External surveillance has been restored," the robot answered.

"Yes! Thank you, Mr. Java!"

"Mr. Java?" I asked.

"Mr. Java is only acting deck manager. He's actually one of our chief engineers for the Falcon."

"That's why they took him," I said.

The display screen showing the external vantage points of the plane began to blink on. We could see for ourselves the damaged mantis ship attached to the top of the Falcon Express. The creature craft kept spitting out flying men.

"Those flying men are missiles too," I said.

"We have to destroy that craft!" the chief yelled. "Where are they going?"

The flying men, now a dozen or so, flew higher into the sky, out of the view of our external cameras and view from the cockpit.

"This, Chief, is the end," Hacker said. "They're going to fly up and dive down into the plane."

"Then we have to dive first!" the chief said.

"What?"

"Dive!" he yelled.

"We're not faster than them. We won't make it," Hacker said.

"Through the clouds and down into the sea," I added.

"Captain, we don't have many options," the chief said.

Hacker flicked a switch in controls above his head. "Ladies and gentlemen, prepare for an emergency dive!"

"Look!" I yelled.

Crescent jetted across the sky at us. Our eyes darted from the cockpit window to the external camera screens. The cyborg soldier hit the mantis craft center-mass like his own living missile. As the Falcon Express steeply descended, the mantis craft violently broke apart, with every piece of it—arms, wings, body—flying off the top of the plane. But the visible head of the craft flew away on its own power by its own independent hover engine. A smaller hovercraft.

"There's a person in that," I said.

"How do you know?" the chief asked.

"Androids don't smile and taunt people. There's a real human being in there."

"Who's flying away and escaping," the chief said. "But Mr. Crescent did it. That mantis ship won't be making any more androids."

"Thank you, Crescent," I said. None of us saw any trace of the cyborg's body after it made impact with the terrorist's mantis craft.

"Gentlemen, the flying men are gaining on us," Hacker said.

CHAPTER TWENTY-EIGHT

Phishy

"Captain Hacker, we have communications back!" Apex's voice came over the cockpit audio.

He touched a button on the cockpit console. "Message received, Mr. Apex! Thank you."

I could see the chief's eyes light up. He fished his mobile phone out of his pocket and already had the number dialed when the receiver touched his ear. "It's Chief Hub. Yes, it's me. Who's the duty officer? Get him on the line right now, and have Interpol standing by."

Hacker was also on his phone. The little I heard before I left the cockpit was he was talking to his family. Was he diving the plane, or was it the robot? I didn't have time to worry about it. The flying men were on our tail.

I had retrieved my hat from the outer corridor so my head didn't feel naked anymore. With my own phone up to my face, I looked at its screen. There were so many messages. I felt sick. It meant that the ill-fated, maiden voyage of the Falcon Express was known to the world, which meant my family and everyone else knew.

"Phishy!" I said to myself as I scrolled through my messages and realized that almost all of them were from him. And there was the one from Mrs. Cruz. I could only call one.

"Phishy."

"Cruz! It's you!"

If PJ was my sole employee, Phishy was my main associate. If you were wondering about his name, Phishy always wore a dark-colored vest and pants, with some off-white, long-sleeved shirt extravaganza with colored fish all over it. His day job was street hustling—courier work, information, finding things, and he was a fully licensed gun dealer. Also, he was the one who acquired my omega-gun.

"Phishy, I don't have a lot of time to talk like we usually do."

"I know, Cruz. Everybody knows."

"Knows? Phishy, our plane has been hijacked by terrorists."

"We know, Cruz. They're saying they damaged the plane. You're on the news. They're saying a lot."

"What are they saying now?"

"The pilots can't land your plane. A mechanical failure with the new sky-walker engines."

"No, Phishy. The problem isn't the engines or landing. It's crashing."

"What do you need me to do, Cruz?"

"Phishy, if we were back in Metropolis, or I was, there'd be a ton of things you could do, like getting my hands on my gun. But then, I'd never be anywhere without it."

"I got it."

"What?"

"I picked it up from PJ."

"Why?"

"To get it to you, Cruz."

"Phishy, you lost me."

"We know where the plane is."

"Phishy, I'm completely lost."

"You know those U.F.O. freaks, I know?"

"No, Phishy. I don't know the U.F.O. freaks you know, and I don't like that phrase U.F.O. anymore. What about your freak friends?"

"There's a whole planet-wide network of them. They watch for any spaceship that enters Earth's atmosphere. Some of them also watch for real U.F.O.s, you know, like from another galaxy."

"Phishy, focus! What are you trying to tell me? I called you before even calling my wife, Phishy."

"Oh, sorry, Cruz."

"What about your U.F.O. freak friends?"

"They've been watching your plane. They know exactly where you all are."

"Where are we then, Phishy?"

"Just outside Cairo International."

"Okay, Phishy, you have my attention, but what does that do for me?"

"Your weapon is on its way."

"What does that mean, Phishy?"

"The monarchy—"

"How do you know about that?"

"They sent a military jet, Cruz, filled to the brim with weapons."

"Weapons?"

"Lots of them, Cruz. The kind you'd like, and your omega-gun is with the package."

"Phishy, to translate: the Monarchy is sending a military jet filled with weapons and my omega-gun to our plane. But the Monarchy wouldn't need your U.F.O. freak friends to locate our plane. They can do that themselves, so I don't know why you told me about them."

"No, Cruz, China Doll got your gun to their jet."

"What? Why? How?"

"She marched right to Police Central and spoke to the person in charge with the police chief on the plane with you. They're working with the Monarchy. This is big stuff, Cruz. Everyone's involved."

"How is my omega-gun on a military jet to me?"

"They're sending stuff to the chief and you too."

"How, Phishy? You're all in Metropolis. We're here up in the air with terrorists flying around us."

"Cruz, they left yesterday."

"Yesterday?"

"I told you, Cruz. Everybody knows. You're all on the news. The weapons jet isn't for you. It's for that king you have on the plane and his men. Your gun is just hitching a ride."

"Where's the jet, Phishy?"

"It's there with you. It's following you."

If the jet was sent by the Monarchy, it was under the king's command. He'd know how to signal it. In fact, I was sure he already had.

CHAPTER TWENTY-NINE

Attack of the Flying Men

I double-timed up the spiral staircase and almost ran smack into Deca and several corporate soldiers.

"I was coming for you," she said.

"I need to see the king immediately," I said.

"Yes, he sent for you," she said.

The plane was on a steep incline down, which made moving through the aisle difficult. We had to move slowly and hold onto a seat every step of the way. Every passenger was strapped in their seat pods and most of them were on their phones. Some made eye contact with me. Some looked like they were on the verge of a mental collapse.

We reached the first-class section on the first deck and the king and his royal guards waited at the entrance to his private section.

"Sir, I got through—"

He stopped me in mid-sentence by simply raising a hand. "The Monarchy has sent a jet."

"Yes, a weapons plane."

He nodded. "I suppose that is what it is."

"You were able to call them before then, sir."

"It is standard protocol. If communications are cut between myself and the Monarchy, a military jet with national soldiers, weapons, ammunition, and supplies is dispatched immediately. The terrorists may have known of the protocol, but they would not have been able to locate it on their own radar."

"May I know who Mr. Phishy is?"

This time I managed a smile. "He's a good associate of mine. He had my weapon on the jet."

"It is," the king said. "Though this might be taking sentimentality toward one's own weapon a bit too far."

"Once I get my omega-gun in my hand and you see what we can do, you'll see sentimentality has nothing to do with it."

"Americans and their guns," Deca said to me.

"Did Kojo destroy any more flying men?" I asked.

"Yes, Kojo and his detail did what they needed to do," the king said. "But the flying men were able to shoot back."

I did not like what he was implying.

"Two royal soldiers dead, Kojo wounded, three royal guards wounded, and two passengers wounded," Deca revealed.

"What about Mr. Crescent?" I asked.

The king gestured for me to follow him to his security room with the surveillance display screens. We all followed him. If external surveillance was re-established, then his would be too.

"He's alive!" I said, seeing the big cyborg holding on to the rudder of the Falcon Express. "We need to help him."

"It's being attended to, Mr. Cruz," the king said.

"He has another task."

I hadn't even paid attention to my surroundings when I first entered the room. I had shot Kojo in one shoulder already. Seemed like the flying men shot him in the other, but the wound was far worse. Then I saw the bodies, covered over by sheets or blankets. There were two dead bodies and the other wounded royal guards were sitting on the floor with Kojo. The other three corporate soldiers' wounds to the chest, stomach, and neck were very serious too.

"Where's the weapon's plane, sir?" I asked. "These terrorists need to be put down now, and for good."

"And so they shall," the king said.

* * *

The Falcon Express was diving through the sky toward the Mediterranean Sea. Well, they had promised us passengers an underwater flight too. Though they hadn't promised us that we'd be "running" from flying men.

I pulled my phone from my pocket again. "Phishy," I said. "I have a job for you and your U.F.O. freaky friends."

Everyone in the business office looked at me.

"Freaky friends?" Deca said.

"My friend Phishy has his own eclectic array of associates," I said, then turned to the king. "Sir, can I assume the Falcon Express still has its own self-contained, enclosed, mini-landing pad?"

"How do you know about that?" Deca asked.

"You do know this craft well. You can more than assume, Mr. Cruz. My private craft sits in its hanger."

The king sat at the external surveillance displays and for the first time we saw our salvation, but on another screen, we saw our destruction. The military jet from the Monarchy was a huge jet, but its design made it look like a flying saucer with a pointed beak. The craft was due east of us and stayed with us on our descent.

The display feed of the rear of the Falcon Express showed the ominous figures of seven flying men gaining on us. We thought there were only five, but the other two came from somewhere. Likely they were seeking out the Monarchy jet. However, their only mission was to destroy our hoverplane.

The king touched the console's communicator. "Mr. Apex, are you ready?"

"Yes, sir. We are," his face replied over the receiver.

"You and Mr. Java will take charge of the passengers. I do not envy your task, but do let them know that a full rescue detail is already en-route to them."

"Yes, sir. Good luck, sir."

"You as well, Mr. Apex. Mr. Java too."

"What are you going to do, sir?" I asked.

"We're going to eject all the passengers the moment before we dive into the sea," the king replied.

"Eject, sir?"

"Yes, Mr. Cruz. Another feature of the Falcon Express. One that you probably wouldn't be aware of is the plane needs no escape rafts or escape pods. The entire hoverplane is an escape pod. The passenger decks will break apart into eighteen self-contained section pods and be ejected out of the plane's main body. Once in the sea, they will dive to a safe distance and await rescue. The terrorists will no longer have the passengers. They will have to choose, and they will choose me aboard the Falcon Express. We will give them me and the Falcon Express, but not much more."

"Give me one second, sir." I ran from the room and out of the first class into the passenger section.

Passengers, the flight attendants of our deck, and cabin stewards were all not just strapped in their seat pods, but protected by a leather-padded metal like a roller coaster. No one was expecting to see anyone, let alone me.

I found my fellow passenger, the ex-military pilot. Sitting next to him was his mental sherpa friend, who looked like he'd need his own mental sherpa or full-blown intense psychotherapy after all this madness.

"Interested in helping shoot down one of the terrorists responsible for all this?" I asked the ex-military pilot.

The man said nothing. A devilish grin came over his face, and in two seconds, he was out of his seat belts and restraints, following me to the king's quarters.

"How far, Mr. Hacker?" the king asked over the communicator.

"Three minutes, sir," Hacker's voice came over the receiver.

The entire hoverplane shuddered.

"That was another engine," Deca announced. "We only have two left."

On the screen, we saw only six of the flying men trailing us.

"They can overtake us now," the king said. He pushed the button for the communicator. "Abandon ship, now, Mr. Apex!"

"Good luck, sir."

Wailing sirens screamed out. The soft white ceiling lights turned to flashing red. The sounds that followed reminded me of massive artillery fire, like the guns the size of a small skyscraper. I assumed our nearly two thousand passengers and flight staff were no longer aboard the Falcon Express.

* * *

"We need every man and woman for this," the chief's voice said over the receiver. He said he wasn't leaving the pilot's side, and he meant it. "What about our terrorist prisoners?" he asked.

"Don't worry about them, sir," Kojo said from the floor. "We may be wounded, but we will manage them while you deal with the final assault on these dogs."

Kojo and his men could be armless, legless, blind, and deaf, and they'd be capable enough to watch our Strata impostor, would-be jumper, and fake cabin steward.

All the time, I was wondering how we'd get our weapons cache from the Monarchy jet and save Crescent from outside the plane. Even Crescent couldn't hold onto the rudder of our plane forever. I got my answer by watching the external surveillance feeds.

The Monarchy military jet blasted off from where it held its position and when it was almost above us, did its own ejection. A giant black container dropped from its cargo hold area, then the jet streaked away at hypersonic speed just as two of the flying men were nearing it.

Crescent let go of the rudder and did his own "superman" maneuver flying after the black container. He grabbed it and followed it down.

The Falcon Express dove into the Mediterranean Sea.

Kojo and the three wounded royal guardsmen had already left the room for the rec area. We ran from the king's quarters.

The passenger section looked like a hollowed-out shell. No passengers, no attendants, no seats. The red lights and empty plane, except for us, gave it all an eerie feeling.

"Pike. Montgomery Pike," my fellow passenger introduced himself and shook my hand.

"Let's get some weapons and then do what we have to do," I said.

"You do the shooting. I'll do the flying."

"Deal."

We were all back in the corridor outside the main cockpit. I was amazed by the repairing technology of the Falcon Express. When I last saw it, the explosion had exposed most of the section to the air, but mechanical arms had reconstructed the outer fuselage. It wasn't as thick and sturdy, but solid enough to repressurize the section. The plane's self-repair systems had also repaired the ceiling hatch above us.

We heard something hit the plane, then a click. Yellow sparks shot out from the ceiling, showering us. A large square was cut around the hatch, then it was pulled up into the darkness.

"King Bahamut," a voice called out.

A new corporate samurai soldier jumped down through the opening. But he was far from alone. We had ourselves a small army of the suit soldiers. All I thought to myself as I studied them was: "Nice guns."

"Colonel Sandman, sir," the first man said.

"Thank you, Colonel."

A final thud landed on the deck. I'd know that sound of thunder anywhere now. Crescent stood there. He looked at me with a grin.

"I told you I'd rip that mantis from our plane," he said.

"Yeah, I don't like insects with big bug eyes either," I said.

The new corporate soldiers were speaking Arabic a mile a minute as the weapons were lowered into the plane.

"Who is Cruz?" Colonel Sandman asked.

"That's me."

I grabbed the black suitcase and set it on the floor. I opened the case like a kid on Christmas. When I saw its contents, I had a smile as wide as the Falcon Express. My omega-gun glistened in the light. Also, it looked like Phishy included some new attachments for me.

Up-Top called the omega-gun the gun to end all private guns. At least that's what the user's manual it came with said. On Earth, it was illegal, but the police never hassled me. After all, I knew the chief, and the head of the police union, and saved all police personnel from the Spacemen. (Okay, I was a bit giddy at the moment. My omega-gun had that effect on me.)

The royal guards already had some high-powered, rapid-fire hybrid laser/steel round machine guns. The new guards replaced those weapons with bigger, bad versions, complete with bayonet attachments on the muzzles.

I walked to the colonel. "Do you have an extra pair of magnetized boots by any chance?"

"Of course."

"What about explosives?"

"Are you kidding?" he said.

Chief Hub also had a delivery when he popped out of the cockpit. The colonel handed him two suitcases. My chief of police had a foldable hand-cannon in one, with an assortment of attachments, and a full portable communications system in the other. He'd be able to securely speak with Metropolis Police Central, the Feds, Interpol, the Monarchy, and the military or civilian authorities in every country around us with crystal clarity. He barely got back in the cockpit and he was on a call with someone, barking orders at them.

Now I knew why the royal guards wore their fancy combat boots. They were much more than boots. The wearer not only had automatic magnetization, which meant you could walk up a metal wall, but they were also hoverboots, which meant you could float above the ground. No matter how much shaking the plane did, you'd be fine. I stood up with my new footwear with a feeling of contentment. I had my omega-gun, with attachments, my bag of explosives, and my own rocketpack strapped to my back.

Pike looked at me and shook his head. "Do you have enough weapons there?" he asked.

"You can never have too much," I replied.

Old and new guardsmen, fully armed and fitted with rocketpacks, stood in a casual formation as Deca stood before them at the king's side.

"Make every shot count," Deca said. "We want all those flying men dead before they have a chance to act or escape. We have only the two engines left."

"Sir," I said as I stepped forward. "Hold on to this." I handed him a sturdy gray data stick.

"What is this?" he asked.

"Let's just say if the terrorists were dumb enough to call their confederates or their boss on the phone in their secret hiding place on the plane, we should be able to trace those numbers."

"I thought their console was booby-trapped and self-destructed, burning out anything usable."

"I grabbed the communication storage and log files before that."

"How did you know to do that?" Deca asked.

"I'm used to it. I've worked on many hacker and corporate espionage cases. They all do the same thing. First thing I do with computers nowadays is remove all the disks and files, just in case."

The king started to chuckle. "You are quite a resourceful man, Mr. Cruz."

The chief was already at the king's side, listening to the conversation. "Cruz is a continuous source of surprises, and trouble."

"Don't worry, Chief. I didn't forget you." I handed him a duplicate data stick. "The hunt will continue."

"Yes, it shall, Mr. Cruz," the king said.

He looked at his mini-army of royal guards around him and raised his communicator to his mouth. "Captain Hacker, execute the plan."

"Yes, sir. Hold on," Hacker's voice came through.

The Falcon Express went from a fast-level velocity to a sharp ascent.

I looked at Pike. "Let's execute our plan." He nodded, ready to follow me.

"Mr. Cruz," the king said. "Good luck to us both."

* * *

I led the way as we ran down the same secret third-deck corridor to the rear of the plane. The door to the secret onboard landing pad hangar was not visible to the human eye, even a bionic one. However, I knew exactly where it was, and Deca's access card opened it right away.

We both felt the plane not just rising at a steep incline, but beginning to rotate as well.

Pike was an accomplished pilot all right. The small hovercraft was called an escape pod, but it was really made to be an added VIP perk, or in emergencies to fly injured or sick passengers to a hospital. No more than a dozen could fit on it, and it had the same high-end, retro-vintage design as the rest of the Falcon Express—before, of course, we ejected all the passenger sections, had two explosions aboard, and the plane became a giant silver target for a team of terrorist-created flying androids.

Again, we were doing something that not even an experienced stunt pilot would do, but Pike was an ex-military pilot.

"I should never have told you I used to be a military pilot," he said as he engaged the hoverengines.

"How do you think I feel? This was supposed to be a once-in-a-lifetime vacation flight for me."

"They got the once-in-a-lifetime part right."

A hidden door in the roof of the mini-hangar retracted into the plane. The sky raced by the opening. A figure shot by.

"You'd better be ready to fire, or this will be a very short flight," Pike said.

I placed my oxygen mask on my face, with my omega-gun in hand. "Let's do it."

We shot out of the Falcon Express—not up, as normal people would do on a normal flight, but vertically, as the plane had made a ninety-degree rotation in its sharp ascent.

I had the side bay door opened a crack.

"Don't worry about me," I said. "You floor it."

"This is a plane, not a hovercar, but I know what you mean. Hold on," Pike said.

We shot away moments before a flying blur of a projectile streaked by—a flying man—missing us by only a few feet.

I did get to see the Falcon Express fly up toward the stars. The black container that fastened itself to the top of the plane, ironically where the mantis ship had been, wasn't just a transport for our royal guard army, weapons, and my omega-gun. It was also a military multi-gun turret, and those big guns rapid-fired a dizzying barrage of lasers. The flying men were fast, but not fast enough. The Falcon Express was blowing them out of the sky.

CHAPTER THIRTY

The Flying Head, The REAL Crazy Maniac #1

The contrast of the sky was breathtaking. On one side, the sun hung there, as if smiling at us. It reminded me for a moment that all this mayhem started out as a simple vacation flight of VIP passengers. On the other side were ominous clouds. Guess which way we were flying? I could already write the media headlines. "The Falcon Express to Hell." "Nightmare at Forty-Thousand Feet." "The Horror Express." We'd ponder that later. Pike and I had work to do.

Just as the monarch's military jet stayed out of range of the mantis craft and the flying men, I suspected the remaining mini-mantis craft would do the same. The flying men had a puppet master and he was human. He was on that mini-mantis craft and he wasn't going anywhere. A criminal would have retreated, but he was a terrorist criminal. He'd want to watch the end of the Falcon Express. I intended to take full advantage and make him regret that fatal flaw.

I also had my ace in the hole, or my Phishy in the hole. His U.F.O. freaks were the ones who gave me the craft's coordinates. He was out of our craft's radar range, but not orbital satellites. How Phishy's U.F.O. freak friends knew how to tap into government and megacorp satellites, I didn't want to know, because it was so obviously illegal. But intel was intel, and without it, we would have never found the mantis craft on our own.

"He's seen us," Pike said.

I looked at the craft's radar console. The same stationary dot we first saw was moving away.

"Do you think he has guns?" Pike asked.

"In the private detective business, you assume everyone is armed. Assumptions like that keep you alive and kicking."

"Your morality lesson for the day is that his plane is armed?"

"Yes."

"Maybe he isn't running at all."

"What do you mean?"

"Maybe he wants us to think he's running."

"You're more suspicious than me," I said. "Good."

Pike noticed something on the radar. "He's increasing speed."

"Are we faster?"

"Much faster. We're streamlined. He's a flying bobblehead in the sky. But we'd better catch him before he gets to land."

"Why?"

"He gets to land. He'll likely lose us. This is his domain, Cruz. We're just passengers playing at terrorist chasers. He's not playing at being a terrorist."

"Pike, we should move to Plan B."

"Cruz, that plan is so insane that I wouldn't know where to begin."

"Pike, I didn't ask you to join this hunt to get you killed."

"I don't think Mrs. Cruz would think much of your Plan B either, since it could easily get you killed."

"Well, you're not going to tell her. I'm already in trouble if we're already on the news and she's making visits to Police Central in Metropolis. We're doing Plan B, and you're getting as far away from here as possible."

"Cruz, I'm not leaving you over the ocean."

"I can fly too, just like the flying men. The Falcon Express promised me two countries, remember? Technically, I didn't get to see the first one, Fiji. I stayed on the plane."

"Your plan won't work, Cruz."

"It'll work exactly because the plan's so insane and absurd that not even a terrorist will see it coming."

* * *

Our craft dove into the sea before we were in visual line of sight of the mantis craft. But we'd both be visible on each other's radar.

Pike flipped a switch. "He can't see us anymore," he said.

"But we can't see him."

"I calculated his trajectory. Have your associate track him and give me the exact coordinates when we're ready to make our move."

I was already dialing Phishy from our craft's phone.

Our craft was much faster than the mantis craft. We emerged from the sea into the sky like a rocket and saw the mantis craft with our own eyes for the first time. It was a flying bobblehead—a sickly, bugged–eyed insect head on a stalk. That's what we were chasing.

Pike caught up to the craft at its rear, jumped directly above it, and then gunned the engines. I wish I'd been aboard to feel what Mach 5 felt like. Not the fastest hypersonic speed on Earth, which was greater than 10, but for the average commuter, Mach 1 at just over 767 miles an hour would be the fastest we'd ever travel in our lives. The Falcon Express's normal cruising speed was close at 700 mph, but it never broke the sound barrier.

Pike piloted the craft away, turning toward the Falcon Express and Cairo.

It was up to me now, thirty thousand feet in the sky and alone.

* * *

Chief Hub wouldn't have allowed most of his own police detectives to do what I was doing. He definitely wouldn't have allowed any civilian to chase after a terrorist. But I wasn't any civilian. It wasn't that I was expendable to the chief, or the king. It was because I could actually succeed in this little operation of mine, bring in Pike for an assist. I'd done this kind of craziness before, actually many times in my oh-so-brief career as a Metropolis detective. Maybe I did have a knack for attracting trouble. But I also had a knack for dealing with criminals, no matter how tough they were, how clever they thought they were, or how crazy their actions showed them to be.

"I can see you," a voice boomed overhead.

"Can you hear me too?" I asked, climbing up the inner ladder of the mantis craft's stalk-like neck section.

"How could I miss that tan hat?"

"Fedora," I said. "It's called a fedora."

"Are you all that the king sent to arrest me?"

"Arrest? Who said anything about arresting anyone? I'm doing to you what you planned to do to us. Shoot you dead and crash your craft into the sea."

All I heard was laughter.

"Do you feel your plot worked out the way you intended?" I asked.

"No plot works as intended," his voice echoed.

"If you're any good, it does. How long did you plan it?"

"Many years."

"And all that's left is you. The king's alive. The passengers are alive. Your men are dead. Your flying androids are destroyed. Your main mantis ship is gone. What did you accomplish again? I forget."

"A direct blow against the monarchy is a great accomplishment."

"A blow? You mean like a little blow through two little child lips. I prefer the fill-up-your-entire-belly-with-so-much-air-that-you-double-in-size-and-when-you-exhale-you-can-blow-someone's-house-down approach myself."

"U.F.O. will triumph in the end."

"Did you come up with that name? How is that even a terrorist organization's name? It's stupid."

"We are everywhere and will never stop."

"Do you know what a crazy maniac is? That's what you are. Your craziness puts you in a class all by yourself. You know, I'm going to name this my U.F.O. case."

"What case?"

"You're just the hired help. I want the mastermind."

"I am the mastermind."

"No, you're not. Masterminds don't dirty their hands and pretend to be bugs and hide in hovercraft shaped like bugs. They lounge in fancy rooms sipping expensive drinks half-naked with half-naked 'companions' around them. Sorry, that's not you. How do I get to the real mastermind?"

"You're almost there."

"Am I? I have a lot of questions for you, and I'm expecting answers."

I reached the top of the ladder and went into the cockpit compartment. There he was. The final Wing Nut. The real one. In a dark, bluish, greenish-ridged skin-tight scuba suit. Instead of a single-window mask over his eyes with a silver reflective lining, he had two perfect round monocle-like eyes.

"You're very insulting, man with the fedora."

"I see you made your flying men in your own image," I said.

"I did."

The beauty of my omega-gun was that I could switch its setting with a flick of a thumb. Sometimes you keep the criminal talking, especially if you think they're armed and they plan to draw on you. Sometimes you take no chances at all. This situation was the latter, and I shot him between the "I" and "did" of the last sentence he'd ever utter.

Unfortunately for me, my kill-shot didn't kill him. It blew a hole through the face of yet another android that crashed to the floor.

All I heard was laughter from the overhead. A screen flicked on, and there was a man's face—dark, bluish, greenish skin and wearing silver-coated spectacles.

"You are a crazy maniac and a coward."

"You'll never get to me. I'm in the belly of this craft in a compartment that's impenetrable to any weapon you can carry."

"Okay," I said.

I fired up my rocketpack, stepped back to the entrance of the ladder, and simply let myself fall through the vertical tunnel I came through. I emerged from the exit, did the "spin" maneuver—that I learned on the street as a kid—and flew away.

The mantis craft had circled around to fly after me. A second later, explosives cascaded throughout the craft—very large explosions. All that debris fell into the dark sea and was gone.

CHAPTER THIRTY-ONE

Thank You For Flying the Falcon Express

I had to make him think I sincerely wanted to get answers or something silly like wanting to understand his motives. I could care less. Would I have liked to have captured the real Wing Nut puppet master? Have Deca and Kojo "interrogate" him for days until he talked, and maybe have Crescent crush a rib or two as an added incentive? Of course. But as Pike said, we were in his domain. It was far too dangerous to take the chance, even with my weapons and oversized bravery. I had no backup. It was the terrorist and me, and on his ship. The only play I had was to blast him out of the sky and bring his evil, terrorist career to an abrupt end. But I already knew he wasn't the mastermind of it all. That person was still out there.

But finally, I was flying through the sky into the proverbial sunlight, thanks to my royal rocketpack. Every racer alive loved the feel of the wind across their face and the speed. I'd never been to Cairo International before, but all I had to do was look where all the hoverplanes were flying to or from. It wasn't as big as Metro International, but it was still one of the largest air and spaceports on Earth.

I wished I was there for the final battle. With the multi-barrel laser port, the royal army and their weapons, Chief Hub's and his, and, of course, the cyborg soldier, Crescent, with the scimitar sword, the remaining flying men would be deader than dead. The king and I had killed one each. I'd have to know if anyone passed us on the kill count, or if the king himself dispatched any more androids.

I'd arrive, say my hellos, get all the details about the last stand of the flying men, do my own debrief, then I could relax and call my wife and family. That was going to be a multi-hour phone call. After that, catch the first flight back home. I'd already decided to call the client who planned to hire me and put a fat retainer in my hand and tell him, after this ordeal, I'd have to pass. That was the plan.

Ahead of me, a single golden military jet dropped from above and followed alongside me. Its pilot gestured to me, then took off. I was getting my own personal military escort into Cairo International. All I had to do was not get sucked into its wake and crash into the sea.

* * *

Free-flying was illegal in every nation on the planet. Civilian hovercar traffic was bad enough, and student hovercar drivers definitely needed to be banned. But imagine the sky filled with wayward kids on jetpacks and hyper-hormonal teenagers on rocketpacks. Yeah, I'd outlaw that too. However, this time I had the full consent of the national authorities.

As with every major airport hub on Earth, the sky traffic could be seen from miles away. In the distance, I could even see the pyramids. But no time for play, the work of the day was far from over for me. I followed my royal military jet escort in at a safe distance. In this region of the world, the military were the main police, and the streets around the airport and at the terminal were swarming with them.

Rocketpacks were not jetpacks, and people killed themselves everyday thinking the two were the same. With jetpacks you could stop and softly land on the ground. Rocketpacks were...rockets. The whole purpose of strapping the piece of tech to your back was for speed, not landing nicely on your tippy-toes. But there was a trick to it. The maneuver was called the "nose-up, drop" on the street. You came to the slowest speed possible, which still meant you were going pretty fast, came close to the ground, and when you came to approximately where you wanted to land, jerked up, and shut off the pack's engine. If you did it right, you'd drop to the ground with style. I did it right and the crowds of people on the street, watching my every move, applauded. I guess they saw plenty of people who didn't do it right.

Immediately before I could pull my crumbled hat from within my jacket, attempt to pull it out to its original shape, and place it where it belonged, I was inundated by military soldiers in gold uniforms.

I had no idea what they were saying. It was a Middle Eastern language, but not Arabic. But "hey fellow, follow us," was clear enough to me as they led me into the grand terminal.

Oh my God! I'd seen hordes of media before, but never on the scale racing to me. My hand instinctively wanted to hit the "on" switch of my rocketpack to jet away. The soldiers knew what I was thinking from my facial expression, said something amongst themselves, and started laughing.

"Mr. Cruz will not be making any statements," one of the soldiers said to them.

The soldiers made a circle around me as we pushed through the zombie-like hordes of reporters snapping pictures and yelling questions at me in multiple languages.

"No hables espanol," I said.

I got the reporters laughing, which was a good thing. When they went on air, they'd at least say things like: "soldiers prevented us from asking Mr. Cruz questions at this time" rather than "Mr. Cruz used soldiers to brazenly prevent us from asking him questions. The people have a right to know!"

I was so thankful for my armed military soldier chaperones. If it weren't for them, I'd still be at the terminal entrance with no chance of escaping the media jackals. Of course, that meant that the wife and kids would see me on the news. But it would be a live shot, not a photo of me along with all the Falcon Express with some stupid reporter asking aloud: "Are they dead yet?"

"The king will see you," one of the soldiers said as we were waved past the airport security checkpoints for the restricted offices.

With the media hordes of hell behind me, I could now look around the airport. The interior didn't look much different from Metro International.

We met up with more soldiers and they joined us as we beelined for a set of double doors guarded by a lot more soldiers. Doors opened, my entourage led me through, and I was taken to an empty conference room.

"You wait here," one said to me.

I'd been sitting for more than twenty minutes at a large center table when a man came in. His dress was identical to Apex and Java, which meant he was a Falcon Express employee.

He walked up to me and extended a hand. "Stephen Strata," he said.

"You mean the real Stephen Strata," I said, shaking his hand.

"Yes."

He looked very similar to the fake Strata—same height, hair and eye color.

"I'd like to speak with you later."

"I've been speaking to one person after another for hours."

"I bet. Are you okay?"

"Yes, surprisingly. This terrorist attack is beyond shocking. We have a lot of answers, but far more questions."

"The man pretending to be you. Do you know him?"

"I do."

"Who is he?"

"Maybe we'll talk later. I'm not going anywhere."

A familiar voice rang out. "Mr. Cruz."

The king entered the room with a mini-army of new corporate samurai soldiers.

I smiled as I approached him. "You made it too, sir."

"I was about to say the same," he said. He looked at the real Strata. "You can return to your offices, Mr. Strata."

"Yes, sir." Strata left the room.

"The real Mr. Strata," I said.

"Yes. Today is the first time I've met him."

"I'm sure there is a whole story behind how the real Mr. Strata wasn't known by anyone aboard the Falcon Express, but the fake one was—for a decade."

"Undoubtedly, Mr. Cruz. A very intriguing story, but the matter is in the capable hands of our military police to resolve."

"Yes, sir, of course. But I did manage to do what you hired me for."

"Yes, Mr. Cruz. We were able to watch the explosion of the last terrorist craft from aerial surveillance drones."

"I didn't see them, but I figured I was under someone's watchful eye somehow."

"We were very happy to see you escape unscathed."

"Wish I could have seen the final battle with the last flying men, sir."

"It, Mr. Cruz, was a very short battle."

"I'm sure, sir."

"It was also recorded by aerial surveillance drones. I'll have one of my men ensure you receive a copy of the file."

"Thank you very much, sir. I'd like that."

"The Monarchy has launched a full investigation, so, unfortunately, the passengers, crew, and staff will have to remain in the airport until questioned and cleared."

"Of course, sir."

"Cairo International has all the amenities, so your wait will not be an unpleasant one. I'll have my men show you to the VIP lounge where everyone is resting."

"Thank you, sir. Am I able to make calls?"

"Yes, of course. I'm sure your family would welcome your voice."

I simply nodded. At that moment, it hit me. We had survived.

"May I ask one thing, Mr. Cruz?"

"Yes, sir."

"The pilot of the craft you destroyed—"

"He was not the mastermind, sir."

"Mastermind? Curious term. You are saying he was not the one in charge of the attack."

"He might have been the one leading the attack and controlling the flying man, but the one who directed him and put this whole plot together from the start? No. That person or those persons are still out there."

"Agreed, Mr. Cruz. The security forces of the Monarchy owe you a great debt for your quick retrieval of those data disks from the terrorists' communication systems."

"Have some phone numbers to trace, sir?"

"Already traced. Arrest warrants are being served at this very moment."

"Good, sir. Glad I was of service."

"You were integral to the safe return of the Falcon Express. Let me not keep you. You have family to call."

"Yes, sir."

The king shook my hand a final time. Two of his men led me out of the conference room.

* * *

The new Shangri-La Lounge at Metro International may have been the most amazing airport VIP lounge I'd ever seen, but the one I was led to was the largest I'd seen. Filled with only the passengers of the Falcon Express, it was practically empty.

Most of the faces I didn't recognize, but then, other than Ace, I didn't spend any real time with any of the second and third-deck passengers. But I did recognize the smiling teenage girl in a mink coat and leather skirt with her two teenage friends.

"You're back," she said.

"I am. So what was it like being shot out of a diving hoverplane over the sea? Must have been fun."

Was I kidding? I wouldn't be surprised if, while all the adults were trying hard not to take a bathroom break in their pants, the teenage trio were hysterically laughing all the way down. They told me the whole story in less than five minutes. Their passenger escape pod crashed into the sea and dove underwater. No one had to wait long as royal aquatic hovercraft arrived to rescue everyone and shuttle them to the main airport.

Passengers began to come up to me. I was happy to see them, and they were glad I survived too. The teen girl's parents greeted me along with other first-deck passengers: my sleeping pill-popping investor friend, the evolutionary biologist and his wife, the professional bodybuilder with his juggling pecs, and the celebrated classical musician.

Then I passed by Dog Mom with her rat dog, Muffin the Great, in a bag on her lap. They sat next to the laser tattoo artist, recruiter, and the family of realtors.

"We were wondering when you'd get here," Dog Mom said to me. "From Falcon Express passengers to prisoners."

"Prisoners?" I asked.

"We can't leave."

"This is all routine. We're witnesses. Don't go starting rumors. We've been through enough."

"Yes, we have. I'm not going to forget what you did to Muffin."

"I won't forget that your Muffin tried to eat my foot, but I'm over it. Forgive and forget. Our feet are on the ground, and the terrorists were killed or captured. Not the best time of our lives, but we're all alive."

"That we are, Mr. Cruz. Maybe we misjudged you. Forgive and forget."

"Or at least, forget," I said.

"What's next?" the laser tattoo artist asked. "They question us and we go home?"

"We go home," I said.

I continued moving through the lounge. The mother with the two kids waved at me as she kept an eye on her screaming little kids chasing each other.

"Mr. Cruz returns." It was Mortran with Sym also seated next to him.

"I have, and Mr. Sym, if you see anything weird, please don't tell us."

Sym laughed. "I learned my lesson."

"How do you think I feel? I wasn't even supposed to be on the plane," I said.

"Then we're glad you were." I turned to see Mr. Professional Poker Player. He was a hugger, and he gave me a bear hug.

"I wouldn't have bet on our chances otherwise," he said.

Then I heard my name again, and there were the Movie-Town guys.

"How long do we have to wait for the movie-of-the-year adaptation?" I asked.

"Funny, you should say," one of them said.

"The Taking of the Falcon Express," the former studio producer announced.

"What's that?" I asked.

"The name of this case," he said.

"Case? What case?"

"Whatever this is."

"That's exactly what I'd call this—whatever. There's no case."

"Isn't there?"

"Isn't there a supervillain for you to catch?"

Now, I laughed. "The authorities from at least three countries, the international police, and the Monarchy are hot on his trail. Besides, a detective needs a client, a paying one. We don't work for free."

* * *

Finally, I got my chance to sit and talk with Mr. Pike.

"You know, Cruz, after meeting you, I've decided that I'll never tell anyone I was a pilot ever again."

"Then I'm happy to know that I was your last passenger. And what a mission it was."

"Yes, it was. They showed me the recording of you rocketing out of there just before the craft exploded. Did he confess?"

"No confession, but I learned what I needed."

"Where's your mental sherpa friend?"

"Sleeping, like I should be doing. I'm plum tired. Don't think I'll be doing any more flying."

"Well, there's always sailing."

"That I could do. Stay close to terra firma, and I can swim."

"Too bad we didn't get to see the last of the flying men crash into the sea."

"We saw our part of the battle. That's what matters. Looks like it's happening."

I turned around in my seat to see the military police begin to enter the lounge.

347.

"Cruz, what's really going on here?" Pike asked me. "The Falcon Express had some of the wealthiest people aboard on the planet, including the ruling king of a sovereign country. How do terrorists do this? That plane would have had more security than an ultra-top-secret military base. The terrorists didn't just breach our security. To get all their people aboard under the noses of the king's and airport security means this was their game from the start. The Falcon Express was their plane, never ours."

"There's no shortage of questions," I said, "but I'm certain every last one of them will be answered."

"I'd say they should hire you to help them. Can't say I have all that much confidence in them, since the only way this could have happened was if it was an inside job at the highest levels."

"We're not the only ones who've figured that out."

"Who then? Sounds like a job for a detective not affiliated with any of this bunch."

"Give them the benefit of the doubt to do the right thing, for now."

"As long as these military soldiers don't try to use this questioning of us to cast blame on the passengers. It's bad enough that we've lost every digital penny of our Falcon Express investment. The Turkey Express, is more like it. A picture of a turkey falling from the sky in flames, riddled with laser blasts, and wings blown off."

"Pike, our feet are on the ground and we're alive. Glass half full, please. Positive thinking. We're about to be questioned by military police."

"Yeah, I guess."

* * *

The gold-uniformed military soldiers marched into the VIP lounge. People instinctively began to stand to their feet. We were safe, but people were still nervous. No matter how wonderful the accommodations were, we did feel like prisoners of a sort. Soldiers randomly pointed to various passengers, seemingly picking families and couples first. After hours of waiting, the questioning began.

I was back to one of my favorite pastimes—people-watching. Pike rose from his seat next to me and approached one of the soldiers. Most of the Falcon Express passengers had already pushed the horror of our flight to the back of their minds, but not everyone was doing okay. Pike wanted some English-speaking medics sent in to talk to them, including, of all people, Mr. Mental Sherpa. There was no shame in it. I expected that most of the passengers in the lounge wouldn't be getting a good night's sleep anytime this week, or for a long time to come.

Sets of passengers were escorted from the lounge by soldiers. We were going to be here a long time still. When we Falcon Express insurrectionists were chanting, we forgot to add the other part. Not simply "Land the plane!" "Land the plane and let us go home immediately!"

I gestured to the closest military soldier who passed by me. "Sir, can I ask a question?"

He stopped. "Yes."

"Is Chief Hub available?"

"Who is he?"

"American consultant to the king and chief of police for Metropolis."

"Ah, yes. He's in meetings. Not available."

"If you can, sir. Let him know that a Mr. Cruz wants to speak to him when's he free."

"Ah, Mr. Cruz. Yes, we know you. Yes, I will tell him."

"Thank you."

In this region, name-dropping the king opened all the doors. I sat quietly in my seat. The first bit of real quiet time I had in a while, and I planned to use it to reflect on everything we endured. The investigation was in the hands of many, many other people. I had to remember that I was simply a passenger, nothing more.

There was no case, but there was a bad guy out there. However, I had to let it go. My formerly posthumous-now-posthumous-again mentor, Wilford G., who worked the streets of Metropolis as a private detective for seventy-plus years, said simply: "Don't expect closure in every case. It doesn't always happen in life, so why should it be any different in a detective's life."

I wanted to make sure I wasn't going to be dragged away before getting on the phone with the family. My eyes locked on two men in dark suits who entered the lounge and were obviously looking for me.

"Mr. Cruz," one of them said in a British accent when they reached me.

"Yes."

"Interpol," he said, showing me his ID. I knew a real one from a fake, but did the average Joe and Jane? I doubted it.

"Interrogation time?"

"No interrogation, Mr. Cruz," said the other in some European accent. I think it was Swedish. "Some questions. We hear you played a pivotal role against the terrorists."

"I don't know about all that."

"Killed a couple of them, and blew their escaping hovercraft out of the sky by personally delivering an explosive device. We consider that pivotal."

"Well, if you put it that way. Let's go," I said as I stood to follow.

"Chief Hub will talk to you afterwards."

Great! I thought negatively. Who knew when this week I'd get to call my family?

I had dealt with Interpol before. People still called them the International Police, which was back when cars drove on wheels on the ground. They were actually the Interspace Police, or the police from Up-Top. Their authority included not only off-world, but superseded the city police and the Feds on Earth. But only if they were invited in by the nation.

"Are you running the investigation?" I asked, as they led me to a small conference room. I noticed that my fellow passengers were in all the rooms on either side of the corridor.

"We're guests of the nation, Mr. Cruz. They're running the investigation. We're simply helping question passengers," one said. "But please, Mr. Cruz. Let us ask the questions."

"I'm all yours, gentlemen."

I was in that conference room for almost two hours. No living human beings were as thorough as these two agents. They literally knew everything I did from the time I stepped into Metro International to the time I got my royal military jet escort to Cairo International.

"King Bahamut had a lot of good things to say about you, Mr. Cruz," one of them said. "Though your Interpol file is not as complimentary."

"I have a file?" I said with a smile. "Cool."

"We have everything we need, Mr. Cruz. Anything else you'd like to add? Anything you've thought of? Chief Hub gave us a copy of the data file you retrieved. Good work, by the way."

"Thank you. No, nothing else. I told everything to Chief Hub."

"You believe the terrorist you and Mr. Pike chased was not their ultimate ringleader."

"I'm certain of it."

"Certain based on what? Did you talk to him and he told you that?"

"I talked to him but only to distract him before I blew him up."

"Not so good work then."

"It was his ship. We beat them, but they were slightly more intelligent than the average dumb criminal. I wasn't going to take any chances walking on there alone, no matter what fancy weapons I had."

"Then it was good work. You got the last terrorist."

"I got the last terrorist that tried to take down the Falcon Express. What about the rest of the U.F.O. terrorists?"

"Who told you about the group?"

"The king."

"Again, thank you for your time, Mr. Cruz. I'm sure you're eager to get back home to your family."

"I am. But in the meantime, a call will do. Can I speak with the chief?"

"We'll see if he's available."

Chief Hub wasn't available. So, I was released, and that meant I could finally call my family.

* * *

I could have used my own mobile phone and linked it to the airport's net, but I didn't want to see my family on a tiny screen. I kicked myself when I came out of the conference room because I wouldn't be the only passenger thinking the same thing. Every VR phone booth I could find was already occupied. There might have been other booths I could have found, but that would have meant leaving the restricted section of the airport and going back out into the general terminal crawling with reporters. I had to wait. But not long. I'd lucked out. The family of realtors stepped out and I stepped in, but not before the patriarch handed me his card.

"Call us. After all the fame coming your way, you're going to be in the market for a new home. On the way up, you have to keep up appearances," he said.

Soliciting so soon after surviving a terrorist hijacking aboard the Falcon Express. As for fame, I didn't need any more. I was a Metropolis detective. I didn't need the planet and Up-Top knowing about me.

As for my residential accommodation, I loved living at Concrete Mama in Rabbit City. My megatower apartment was handed down to me by my grandfather. We weren't living in some super upscale part of Metropolis, but it was a solid working-class neighborhood and it was home. Neither the family nor I were leaving. There's comfort in knowing every neighbor and store for a ten-mile radius for many years. It's called community.

"Cruz!"

At that very moment it hit me again. The Falcon Express. We beat the terrorists, but it could've easily gone the other way. In the next split-second, I was overcome by the emotion of seeing my family on the video-screen. I leaned forward in the booth's seat with the biggest smile in the world.

My wife, the consummate fashionista, was in a trendy yellow outfit. I always wore my hat. She always wore a colored neck scarf—today was shiny white. Like most days, every finger had a colored ring, and each wrist had multiple bracelets. My son was on one side and my daughter was sitting in her lap, giggling and swaying back and forth.

"Daddie!" said Cruz Jr., sporting his little black fedora.

"Da-da!" said adorable little Kat, in an outfit very similar to my wife's.

"There you all are," I said.

"Cruz, I'm mad at you," Dot said. "But we'll forgive you for now."

"Forgive and forget," I said and kissed the video-screen. "There you go, wifey."

The kids laughed.

"Stopped that, Cruz. Aren't you the recovering germophobe?"

"One for you," I said and kissed the screen where Cruz Jr.'s face was, then Kat's.

Cruz Jr. and Kat were in full-blown laughing mode. Of course, it was contagious, and Dot and I were laughing too.

"Kids, say it with me. Mommie, kiss the screen! Kiss the screen!"

She laughed and gave me a big kiss on the screen.

"Yeah!" the kids screamed, or Cruz Jr. did and Kat followed along.

I sat in the video booth for a good hour or more. I gave the family the antiseptic, Hallmark, sweet violence version of events, but they were spellbound nonetheless. Cruz Jr. was asking me a ton of questions.

"Didn't you shoot anybody, Daddy?" he asked.

"We don't have to go into that, Cruz-control," I said and tried to continue my story.

"But you did shoot somebody, Daddy. How many bad guys?"

"It all happened so fast, Cruzie. I can barely remember all the details," I said, trying to continue my detailed story.

"You are in so much trouble when you get home," Dot said to me. "Oh, before I forget."

"Forget?"

"PJ said to tell you that you already collected the retainer."

"Retainer? Oh, the client I was going to be meeting with at the end of this flight."

"Not him. PJ said you'd know who when the time came."

"What does that mean? I have a secret client who hired me without him meeting me? PJ knows better than that."

"Not a secret, a client," Dot said. "But I can't tell you who."

"Why?"

Then it came over the airport overhead: "Will a Mr. Cruz please see the Information Desk. Paging, Mr. Cruz. You have a call waiting."

I would have ignored the announcement, but Dot had a devilish grin on her face. My curiosity got the best of me too. I had my call with the family, so I was re-energized for the rest of the day until I got my flight back home. I bid the family loves, kisses, and byes and exited the video phone booth. The line of Falcon Express passengers in the hallway had quadrupled in size, which meant military police questioning was moving at a quicker pace.

I so didn't want to venture back into the general terminal where the crowd of media vultures had also quadrupled in size. Fortunately, I was led by airport staff to enter the Information Desk from the rear employee entrance. More than a few of the reporters saw me and sprinted to the counter.

"Mr. Cruz, can we have a few words?" one yelled.

"No hables espanol," I said to them.

The chuckling counter attendant pointed to a free wired phone. I picked it up. "Who's this?" I asked.

"Mr. Cruz! I found you! Hiring you as my inside man was the smartest and luckiest move I've made in my life."

I could not believe it! I was speaking to the Queen of the Media Vultures—Holly Live!

* * *

I never liked the phrase "win-win," especially coming from Holly Live.

"The station will pay you for the interview, Cruz," she said over the phone. "In fact, we've already dropped off the money with your office manager."

"Isn't paying for interviews unethical or something?" I asked.

"You're joking. This is the high-stakes, cutthroat world of prime-time journalism. You don't pay, you don't play."

I'd gone from the flying horror express to the madhouse at Cairo International. I let Holly Live ramble on about how my prime-time interview with her would catapult us into greater fame and fortune. Not really an incentive for me. The bottom line: Terrorists tried to kill two thousand innocent people, and I was one of them.

I made up an excuse to get off the call because I was focused on one and only one thing—sleep. I planned to book my flight home, and for the rest of this day, I'd do nothing but sleep. I'd leave the terror-hunting to the professionals next time.

The good news was that I'd been officially released, and, courtesy of Carnegie Cosmo, all Falcon Express passengers were put up in one of the swankiest hotels in the city, not too far from the airport. I'd heard some of the passengers had already caught flights back home aboard private jets. When you had the money to buy a private hoverjet outright, then such things weren't surprising. However, most were doing the same thing I was doing—rest and sleep.

The bad news was that the hotel was a virtual fortress with military police stationed in and around the building. I didn't even see the name of the hotel but was driven there in a military hover-jeep by two soldiers. When I stepped into the massive lobby, a staffer was waiting for me and handed me my key card to my room. The soldiers escorted me from the lobby to the elevator to my room. The question in my mind was: Are they my bodyguards, or am I their prisoner?   I didn't care. I fell asleep the moment my body crashed on a circular bed big enough for a full-grown elephant to sleep on its side with plenty of room left over.

Since I never looked at the clock when I went to sleep, I had no idea how long I'd been sleeping when a knock at the door woke me. The room was dark except for the faint glow of the lighting system lining the edge of the ceiling and various appliances in the room.

I so didn't want to get out of that bed. I was like a baby kangaroo inside momma's pouch—nice and warm. Why would I ever move? The only thing I had done when I first entered the room was remove my hat to toss it on the bed beside me. But the knocks on the door continued.

Mrs. Deca Punk and several corporate samurai soldiers stood in the hallway when I finally opened the door.

"Mr. Cruz," she greeted.

"I was sleeping."

"I see that, but enough of that. We must speak with you."

Why bother to protest? I let them in. One of the corporate soldiers turned on the lights. I had no idea where it was.

"I must advise you not to talk to the media," she said, sitting down on one of the chairs in the room's sitting area. All the corporate soldiers remained standing.

"I don't like the media, so there's no problem with that."

"When do you fly out?" she asked.

"Ten o'clock in the morning. But I'll be there at eight." I had slumped down in the chair across from her, still half-asleep.

"Yes, that's what we needed to speak to you about."

"What does that mean?" I asked.

"Your services are needed."

"The king hired me to kill the Wing Nut when the time came. Done. Chief Hub hired me to be a backup officer on the plane. Done. Java hired me to find a possible terrorist accomplice aboard. Done. Found two. You hired me to be eyes and ears among passengers. Done. Mr. Kojo hired me to deal with the terrorists when the battle began. Done. I think I'm done with any more services. Besides, no one has paid me."

"Yes, you have been quite busy when all you were supposed to be was a passenger on the Falcon Express to enjoy its maiden flight."

"Where is Mr. Kojo? Is he all right?"

"He's in the hospital with all the guardsmen who were injured."

"I should go visit him."

"No need."

"I'll do it anyway."

"If you insist, we can take you there. But we still need your services."

"Why would you need any services from me? National police, international police, Metropolis police, you and the king's police. Why would any of you need me for anything?"

"The king was very impressed with you. Very few people warrant his attention, let alone his respect. Let's speak frankly, Mr. Cruz. This plot was an inside job."

"Of course, but you would be the person best qualified to find that person or persons, not me."

"The king has his own plot in mind."

"Which is?"

"All the many authorities you listed will conduct their investigations, thoroughly and far and wide. But you will conduct your investigation secretly. The conspirators will be watching us, but they will not know about you."

"I don't know the players, the country, the language, should I go on?"

"Has that ever been a real obstacle to you before?"

I hesitated in answering, because she already knew my response before she asked the question. "No."

"This U.F.O. terrorist group could never have done what they did without the help of insiders."

"You're talking about the Monarchy."

"Yes. This fact limits how far I can go, even as the king's head of security. It would not limit where an outsider could go, who they could question, what stones they needed to overturn."

I couldn't believe I was seriously considering her offer, but I wanted to find the real mastermind, who I knew was still out there.

"Am I actually going to be paid this time?" I asked.

Deca reached into her jacket, and out came a golden envelope.

* * *

I had a bona fide paying client, but I had to wonder. Who was the real crazy maniac in this case? I was starting to believe it was me for not running back home immediately rather than starting a new case in a foreign country. But that golden envelope was really fat, and I wasn't giving it back. So Liquid Cool's primary private detective was on a real case.

Though I was still the stake-out king, I realized that, in fact, I had some worthy competition—a lot of them. When a big city reporter smelled the human blood of a source in the news waters, nothing could wave them off. Even the most sophisticated of people could freeze or wet their pants from nervousness in the face of a stampede of reporters. My shield against them was that I really didn't care. I'd used them before, as they were using me, so with my new client and payment in my pocket, it was time to begin the games. My impromptu nighttime press conference in the hotel's lobby didn't take long to organize.

I'd noticed that Chief Hub was in the crowd at the back. He seemed satisfied with my answers, giving them juicy stuff but nothing that would compromise a serious investigation.   All I caught was the back of his head when I had to answer another question and looked back at him. He left through the lobby doors for outside.

"Thank you for your questions," I said to the media crowd in closing. I told them I'd answer questions for thirty minutes, and that's what I did. "I'll be on the next flight back to Metropolis, first thing in the morning," I added.

"Will you be helping the authorities with their inquiries?" a reporter asked.

"No, sir. They have everything well in hand. It's back to my family for me. Otherwise, they'll have me arrested and put on the plane."

The media liked jokes. That one was going to be played ad nauseam on their B-roll clips. The beauty of my performance was that the clips would play on the news for the night and all the next day.

I had to make good on my pronouncement of only thirty minutes, otherwise the questions would never stop. I waved and headed back to the elevators to my room, restricted for guests only, where Deca and her corporate soldiers waited for me.

Instead, we bypassed the elevators for the corridor to the restricted rear exits. It seemed like we were walking forever.

"How's the real Mr. Strata?" I asked.

"He was not part of the plot," Deca answered. "He was a victim of it."

"Sounds like you're making good progress on your investigation."

"We've hunted down and captured most of the U.F.O. organization. Other nations are helping us find the rest."

I was going to say "except for any directly connected to or part of the Monarchy," but didn't. We said the term "monarchy" in confidence but what we were really saying was direct family members of the king. What a life to live when your own family members might have orchestrated and launched a terrorist attack against you. I wouldn't complain about the Hell-Spawn (my parents-in-law) ever again.

We finally reached the exits where other corporate samurai soldiers waited. They opened the doors for us, and there floating just above the ground, was our golden hoverlimo transport.

* * *

"How's Mr. Crescent?" I asked as the hoverlimo began its descent from sky-traffic.

"He's back at his post, at the king's side," Deca replied.

In this nation, there were private and public hospitals. Since I was now in a country where all the signs were in Arabic or other languages I didn't speak, I made no attempt to remember names. The hospital lobby looked like a luxury hotel, but with nurses instead of attendants. We were waved through all security and the elevator capsules took us all the way to the penthouse level on the two-hundredth floor.

Kojo was in a hospital bed sipping some colored drink in a glass, not sure if it was fruit juice or alcohol. He lay there in a gown and slippers in a spacious room all to himself.

"Mr. Cruz," he said, putting his drink down on the bedside table. He was genuinely glad to see me.

"Mr. Kojo," I said as I shook his hand. "Why are you in bed? You've had worse wounds than these."

"The king told me that I was to rest for at least a day, so that's what I do."

"Why are you really here?" Deca asked me. She had entered the room, but the corporate soldiers remained in the hallway outside the door.

"The prisoners, of course," I said. "Fake Strata, Jumper, and fake cabin steward."

"You think they said anything to us?"

"If you made them, yes. Just curious."

"We had no time. Too much going on with the plane spinning around."

"Yes, we saw that."

"I was standing on the floor inside. I was standing on the ceiling inside. We were watching them too closely to do anything else. But they are in the hands of our best interrogators."

"They likely don't know anything," I said.

"I tend to agree, but we are very thorough in these things."

"Well, this is me being thorough. I asked the question directly. I have one more request from both of you, but I need paper to write on."

"Paper? Who uses writing paper anymore?" Kojo asked.

"Peasants and people in Metropolis. We're an analog town," I said with pride.

"Quaint," Deca said and yelled out something in Arabic to the corporate soldiers outside the hospital room.

It didn't take long for them to enter with an old notebook with some blank pages. The thing looked like it was centuries old and was caked with dust.

"I told you no one uses paper anymore," she said. "That's what computers and tablets are for."

"Yes, but paper can't be hacked."

I had terrible penmanship, so I pretended to be a five-year-old and printed out my question on the page. I gave Kojo a blank page, then Deca one. I held up my page to her and then to him. They looked at each other, then stared at me for a bit.

Deca literally walked to the other side of the room to write her answers. Kojo started scribbling, and I thought the man was writing an entire five-hundred-page novel.

"I need more paper," he said.

In the end, he took four more sheets from me. What I thought was going to be a quick exercise turned into a not-so-short task for both of them. They handed me their "homework" as if they didn't want each other to see it.

My written question: Who in the Monarchy is capable of this plot?

It would be hours later before I learned what names they had given me.

Deca wrote all the names of the senior royal family, including all of the king's six brothers and two sisters. Kojo wrote what amounted to all the senior royal family, all the king's nephews and nieces, endless cousins, all major business moguls, and all the generals of his military. When they told me the monarchy—the Saud's form of government going back millennia, they meant the Monarchy—the true ruling elite of the nation, a single megacorporation run by the royal family, and ruling an entire region beyond its nation's borders.

Deca's golden envelope was starting to feel a bit light in my hidden jacket pocket. What had I gotten myself into, when I should have been hopping on the first flight—without terrorists and flying men—back home?

* * *

Deca had her corporate soldiers drop me off back at my hotel in the hoverlimo. The security was tight and outside swarmed with press and onlookers. When I got through the lobby checkpoints, I noticed the chief waiting in the lobby. He sat alone at a chair facing the entrance, so he could see all who came in.

I walked straight to him. He had stood and gestured me to the elevator. So, it would be another hotel room meeting. At least I'd moved up from meeting in hoverplane restrooms.

The chief sat where Deca had sat before, and I sat in my same seat.

"I'll be heading back to Metropolis tonight," he said.

"You're not helping with the investigation?"

"I've contributed all I could. On a case when you have one chief of police from out-of-country and a chief of police in-country—"

"First flight out tonight."

"Yes. I did my part, but I'm surprised, or not surprised, to see you're still here."

"I'm leaving in the morning."

"Cruz, you can't play me like you played those reporters."

"I don't know what you mean, Chief."

"Be very careful, Cruz, here. This is a cruel country, even by Metropolis standards. Even though the authorities in charge did their best to keep the full intel files from me on this U.F.O. group, I still got my hands on them. No way possible these terrorists could have pulled this off without serious help."

"The Monarchy."

"You do know then. This is not a case, Cruz. This is a possible civil war. They're overdue for one. Whatever you're doing, you'd better get out."

"Thanks for the warning, Chief, but I have one more thing to do. I have a case, and a mastermind to find."

"They officially hired you."

"Official channels and unofficial channels."

"A private detective poking around 'unofficially' means you're on your own. We're outsiders, Cruz. If they don't know exactly who the person is, you'll never smoke them out on your own. Unless you plan to live here permanently."

"Not on my own, Chief. I'll do the same as I'd do in Metropolis, or I did on the Lunar Colony, or anywhere else. Every supercity has the street. I'm a street detective."

"But do you speak the language of this street?"

"No hables espanol."

The chief grinned as he stood. "You saw what they sent after us on the Falcon Express. This investigation is a long way off, no matter what the king says to the press. You won't make a bit of a difference. This is more politics and palace intrigue than street detective work."

"I won't stay long. I'll do what I can and then go back to where I belong in Metropolis."

"Don't get a dagger or laser blast in the back, Cruz, while you're not staying long," the chief said.

* * *

The areas around big hotels were for tourists and foreigners—very Euro-American. Not where you hung out for real street intel. I took a hovertaxi out and had myself dropped off at least twenty miles away from where native residents actually lived. Usually taxi drivers were great sources of information and conversation, but it was just my luck that I had an American college student new to the country, which meant he was less than useless for my purposes. None of the languages I heard around me, I had any clue about. I should have had a portable translator device, but I'd never used one before and over a thousand languages were spoken in Metropolis.

Supercities like Metropolis had their sidewalk johnnies—our on-the-street community of non-violent street hustlers, scamming and scheming for cash, which the police completely ignored. Violent crime was their priority, not those hanging around, watching trouble, causing mischief, hustling, looking for a hustle, but doing little of anything meaningful. They congregated, watched, chatted it up, sat around, smoked, joked, disappeared to the johns when needed, or disappeared to their sleep shack for a few hours—and repeat. But they were harmless. For a detective like me, they were my main source of straight street intel. I even had Phishy create our own Sidewalk Johnny Brigade, which was a loose organization to keep me informed of what was happening on the streets.

But everywhere on the planet had its own version of them, and so did this country. Their version wore casual suits and those Middle Eastern headdresses, which I'd later learned were called kaffiyehs. It was a rich country, so even its poor would be wearing some very stylish hand-me-downs. All sidewalk johnnies and sallies had their "turf," which was often a street, street corner, or alleyway.

I found myself near a market square. Lots of average people, but no police, military, or a visible criminal presence to be seen. I began chatting it up with three sidewalk johnnies on one of the main corners. Different countries and regions had their own style of dress. Suits were universal, but the variations were endless. The Japanese liked shiny, slick, and silk. The Americas liked basic. This region liked retro-suits with pinstripes and vests. These three were the best dressed, and their corner was free of the clutter of all the others around. Even though I was useless when it came to languages, at least most of the world could speak English. Theirs wasn't the best but good enough. If I spoke to them long enough, I'd soon know the entire history of the region and everyone I needed to know about—from the lowest person on the totem pole to the most powerful—the Monarchy.

"Who could an overseas detective talk to, to get real information?" I asked.

"You should talk to Arabic detective," one of the johnnies said.

"Is he related to you?"

"Possibly," he said, grinning.

"I need a driver first of all. One who can be a guide too."

All of their hands went up. "We can drive," one said.

"Where's the hovercar?"

They laughed. "You have to buy it," another said.

Getting frustrated with sidewalk johnnies gained you nothing. You had to keep talking, coaxing, haggling, joking, bribing, and promising to get what you wanted, or close to it. I had found three johnnies, and by the time the day was done, I'd know fifty of them. One of those fifty would get me what I wanted and be able to answer my questions.

Another day passed, and I talked to lots of people, always starting out with the same question: "Tell me about the monarchy. Who doesn't like who?" You start with the basics and work outward. You start with the theory and either confirm or disprove it. But you must always roll up your sleeves and start somewhere to get some place.

As I had told the chief, I wasn't going to be working this case alone, and I wouldn't be staying long. There were a million people and dozens of agencies working on this case, but the mastermind would have prepared for that. I had to find the angle that no one else would think of, let alone pursue. I had to find the vulnerability that not even the mastermind would have realized he had, let alone thought of in one of the boldest attacks on the Monarchy's supreme ruler in recent history.

I was still on the street with the johnnies as the sun set. Then I realized that all us Falcon Express passengers had left the grand airport but never got our final "Thank you for flying with us. Hope to see you next time soon" message. Yep, probably highly inappropriate given the circumstances.

CHAPTER THIRTY-TWO

The Blood Red Sea Hotel

Three giant crystal pyramids stood in the distance outside the main city. They were twenty feet tall and arranged at three points of an imaginary triangle in the sand. At night they lit up and flashed in different neon colors, becoming the sight for nightly outdoor partying. Even after a century, they remained a big attraction for both tourists and natives. The same megacorp architectural firm had constructed the pyramids on Mars too.

I had to pay extra—a lot extra—to have my hovertaxi driver fly by them. Apparently, I wasn't the first foreigner to make the request. To him they were boring glass structures, but to me, they were amazing since I saw them for the first time. He was born in the neighborhood next to them and had seen them every day of his forty-year life.

Metropolitans always complained about how bad our hover-traffic was, but what I was trapped in was utter madness. The hover-traffic lanes weren't straight and orderly; they were all over the place. Drivers could disengage their virtual lane guidance and fly wherever they wanted. That was what my hovertaxi driver had done. I was an experienced former hovercar racer, but I was scared. To survive a terrorist attack but then be killed in hovertraffic in a foreign country. That wouldn't be fun.

Finally, he dove out of the swarm of traffic and coasted about fifteen feet from the ground along a very wide avenue to our destination. I'd never heard of the place before, but wondered why not. The structure looked like it was made of orange-red sand. I'd never seen anything like it.

"That was made by my people," the driver said with pride. "The crystal pyramids were made by your people."

"I've never seen it advertised," I said.

"You would not. Foreigners can't stay there. It is a private hotel. Dignitaries stay there temporarily when they are in the country for business or pleasure."

"I can see the security from here."

"Yes. Much security. If you have business there, I'd recommend eating at the restaurant. They serve only the local delicacies prepared and cooked by the best cooks on the planet. Won many, many awards."

"I can't wait," I said, smiling, but I wasn't there for any meals.

The adjacent landing lot was also packed with armed security in suits, but hovertaxis were waved by to their own spot.

"That is a strange case you have," my driver said as I exited the hovercab with it. It did look a bit strange, like a brown egg with a handle.

"Yes, but it's very light."

"Enjoy your visit at the Red Sea Hotel. And do eat in the restaurant."

"Thank you for the ride, and for getting me here in one piece."

He laughed. "Tourists are always frightened, but I've been a hovertaxi driver for twenty years and never had one accident."

"Because you're the best. That's why I hired you."

"Allah hired me. He just let you borrow me for a short trip."

"Then I was lucky."

"Lucky is good. Skill is better. Bye–bye," he said, and his hovercab shot back into the sky.

* * *

"I am here to see Mr. Jinn," I said to the female counter attendant in a sharp shiny orange-red suit.

"I will call up to the office."

"Thank you."

While she did, I looked around the giant lobby. It was a beehive of activity with a sitting section in the center where people read tablets while having coffee, and small groups conversed or played chess. People were going to and fro. Security was at every one of the multiple revolving doors of the lobby.

"You can go up, Mr. Cruz," she returned and said to me. "The gentleman will escort you."

By "gentleman," she meant a big, gruff, unfriendly man in an orange-red suit. He led me to the elevator capsule, and in we went. We arrived on the one-hundredth floor and he held the door as I stepped out. He didn't follow.

Right near the elevator was a reception desk with two female employees.

"Mr. Cruz," one greeted.

I stepped to the counter. "Yes."

"Please have a seat. Mr. Jinn will be with you shortly."

"Thank you."

My own detective offices had a client waiting area complete with chairs, a center table, and magazines. That was me, but I wasn't the Monarchy. Their waiting area had super plush chairs, golden side and center tables, and entertainment center screens attached to every chair, complete with headphones. I sat quietly and let the time pass by.

"Shortly" turned out to be forty minutes. I actually had arrived thirty minutes early for my appointment so, though I didn't show it, I wasn't all that happy. One of the receptionists led me back and around a hallway. A sole security guard opened a door and she led me into a giant office absolutely fit for royalty. Expensive-looking paintings on the wall, golden furniture, an actual geyser in the center, and a golden statue of the king stood prominently on one side of the room.

"That will be all," I heard a voice call out from one of the dim sections of the room. The sunlight was right in my eyes, so I moved to the side.

The receptionist had left as a man in a sleek golden suit with a white vest and pocket handkerchief approached me.

"Mr. Cruz, at last," he said.

"Mr. Jinn. Thank you for seeing me."

He shook my hand firmly and then led me to his main desk. He pointed to a chair in front of it and he sat behind the desk as I did.

"Of course, I would see you, Mr. Cruz. The king has spoken very highly of you many times. Some might say you were instrumental in saving our king's life."

"It was a group effort, sir."

"Modest too." Jinn made no eye contact with me after he shook my hand. Before that he had stared at me with an angry gaze; now, it was as if I was not worthy of his consideration despite his friendly tone. "What can I do for you, Mr. Cruz? I must say I was quite surprised to get your call. I thought you had returned to your home in Metropolis."

"Matters kept me here for a bit longer."

"Matters such as?"

"The king asked me to help with inquiries."

"Curious. He said nothing to me about it. All inquiries into the Falcon Express affair are being handled by our own authorities. Not sure how a single foreign private investigator could assist with a matter of terrorists."

"I did tell the king the same thing, Mr. Jinn."

"And what was the king's response?"

"He wanted me to act in an unofficial capacity to see if I uncovered anything."

"Unofficial capacity. What have you uncovered unofficially? We have captured or killed all those involved in the terrorist plot."

"Not everyone. May I show you my case?" I asked.

His eyes locked in on me. "By all means. The desk is made of solid gold. I don't think whatever you have in your case will damage it."

"Thank you." I stood up and placed my egg case on the front of the desk. I opened it to show him the head of the person those of us on the Falcon Express called a flying man. Dark, bluish, greenish-ridged mask with silver, single-window goggles over the eyes. The mask was fitted over the plastic bust I had created.

"Do you know who he is?"

Jinn stared at me with contempt. "I am the chief of staff for King Bahamut of the Saud Monarchy. I do not have the time or disposition for games."

"Unless the king instructs you," I said.

His eyes looked down again and his friendly demeanor returned. "That is a likeness of the flying men who attacked the Falcon Express. They were androids, remotely controlled by a final terrorist who you killed."

"Yes, but it's not a likeness. This is one of them that we retrieved from the sea. I was told at one point, there were over a thousand aquatic hovercraft combing the sea for any debris of the flying men or their mantis craft, and bodies, or their parts. I still can't believe that. They created a hovercraft to look like a real giant mantis."

"This U.F.O. terrorist group was quite creative. But alas, they no longer exist. Why are you here, Mr. Cruz? I am not one for melodramatics. Is your presence here meant to rattle me? Are you trying to accuse me of something?"

"What does a praying mantis mean to you?"

"Nothing at all, Mr. Cruz." He slowly rose from his chair. "I believe this meeting has concluded."

"Why did you have me wait in the lobby for forty minutes?"

"I had another meeting to conclude, if you must know."

"Yet you conclude my meeting in ten minutes and I'm not done."

"I will not be accused."

"Mr. Jinn, you're jumping ahead. I haven't accused you of anything, but if you want me to, then I will."

I stood from my chair. "Criminals always slip up in the end."

"No, they don't," he sneered at me.

"You think you got away. No evidence at all for us to find."

"There's no evidence to find, because there is no evidence, and I was not involved."

"I have to thank Deca. She was the one who figured it out. Very thorough she was. We found this head in the sea. There wasn't much left of what we could find. Ironically, this is the one I found. I shot it in the head. We patched that up, though. Do you know this head was made from the mold of a real person? Of course, you do. Because that mold is you, isn't it? Why would terrorists make an army of flying men with heads modeled from yours? Deca and Kojo wanted to come in here and throw you off the roof. But the king saved your life. Do you want to know why?"

Jinn glared at me. Despite my calm, I made sure to keep track of his hands.

"The king wanted to know why? He hired me to find out why. He refused to believe a man who was like another son to him would do this. So I found out why. The terrorist attack gave me the clue, specifically Stephen Strata, or the two Stephen Stratas.

"Ten years ago, it began with the construction of the Falcon Express. The real Strata began it all, while the fake one attended the meetings to be known by all the senior staff. Everything was done in parallel from the start. The fake Strata had the modifications made to the Falcon Express; the real one never knew. They both had access to everything, but the real Strata didn't know about the fake one.

"And there was Mr. Carnegie Cosmo—he spent years speaking to people who were not real at all. Probably many of them were the terrorists from the start. The legitimate contractors all thought they were coordinating and taking orders from the real Mr. Cosmo, but they weren't. There were taking orders from a fake Cosmo.

"I know what you're thinking. That's just a story. You're not the only one in the Monarchy who could have made such a thing possible. Anyone could have."

"Yes, like Ms. Deca or Mr. Kojo, among a hundred others," Jinn said to me.

"You're absolutely right. No evidence at all. Even this mold of the flying men's head could have been taken without your knowledge. Don't even need to touch your skin to take a mold these days. A computer could create a mold based on photos of you. Such a story would get laughed out of court in my country. Besides, a mold isn't a fingerprint or DNA."

"Then your country isn't without wisdom despite its lack of true history," Jinn said.

"Will you tell me why?"

"Excuse me, Mr. Cruz."

"Will you tell me why you put this terrorist plot in motion?"

"You want me to confess?" Jinn started laughing. "To what? Confess to what? Because you ask? Because of a flimsy story and a head of an android? Get out of my office!"

"I can't do that."

"I will have you thrown out."

"You have no authority."

"I have the authority of the Monarchy."

"No, you don't."

"You feel the king's good graces give you power over me."

"No, because you're not Mr. Jinn."

* * *

"In my business, there is no such thing as coincidences. This was a case of doubles. More than one Strata. More than one cabin steward. More than one Cosmo. There was even more than one flying man. I wondered who else out there in the Monarchy might have a double, or be one. That would be my line of investigation.

"While the authorities went through everyone's background with a nano-microscope, I took that different approach. They started with your lives from today, going back as far as they could. I started with the day all in the Monarchy were born and worked forward, including you. Why?

"A mantis hovercraft," I said, "and these flying men. We had a firefight aboard the Falcon Express, and one of the flying men blocked the bullets and lasers with its arms like a praying mantis. I never forgot that. It actually reminded me of the cartoons my son likes. The mantis men. He'd love that as a show.

"Do you know you can pull videos from the net going back centuries? If you know where to look. I also did a search of all the enemies of the Monarchy from a century ago until now. I wanted to become an amateur historian of the Monarchy. Wasn't I so surprised to find a video of a little boy who made a video of himself as this super hero who dressed as a human mantis wearing a scuba mask with single-window goggles. He attached these antennae on the top of his head. He could fly—special effects. He could block bullets and lasers fired at him, just like our flying men did when Deca and the royal guardsmen fired their machine guns at it. The boy was obsessed with mantis. Had models, pictures, and drawings around him, everywhere. I learned everything about this boy and the man he grew up to be. He was an accomplished terrorist by his twenties. One battle I was particularly interested in, was led by Mr. Jinn. Mr. Jinn killed this boy turned terrorist. But then, that's not the true story. Mr. Jinn was killed, and you took his place. You're the mastermind, and you've been the mastermind, not for ten years, but for thirty years."

The man smiled. All his pretense was washing away. "Jinn wasn't like a son to the king. Jinn was one of the king's sons. One of his illegitimate sons. It wasn't my plan. It was an accident. Everyone was taken to the hospital, and in the chaos, one of the nurses or doctors mixed up our names. So I became Jinn. The king came to see me. He kissed and gushed over me. He said he'd make me a top man on his staff for my bravery. The king. The fool couldn't even tell his own son from the man who killed him. I became Jinn because he said I was."

"I can only imagine all the mischief you've been creating since then."

"None of you will ever know."

"We'll know all that matters."

"You should have gone, Mr. Cruz. You should have left for Metropolis the moment you arrived in Cairo. You will never see your family again. You will never be seen again."

"I don't like when criminals threaten me. I tend to shoot them."

"I'm not a criminal. I am a freedom fighter—"

"Please spare me the terrorist speeches."

"Terrorist? Then yours is a country founded by terrorists."

"If you can't tell the difference between breaking away from your home country whose tyrants lived three thousand miles away for independence, and you trying to blow up or crash a hoverplane of innocent people, I can't help you. I was an A student in high school history, pal, along with Chemistry, Mechanics, and Computer Tech. I'll admit that I wasn't so sharp in the other subjects, and barely passed English."

"The Red Sea Hotel is a fortress. This room has every sensor known to man. Enough to tell me you have no weapons at all. You won't be shooting anybody."

"No, I won't. You're right. But Deca will." All I had to do was touch my right ear to reveal to him I was wired.

He realized it too late as a laser blast ripped through the side of his chest through the window.

However, we soon found out why he had me wait for forty minutes in the lobby.

* * *

Fake Jinn threw himself to ground out of my line of sight. I probably couldn't call him "fake Jinn" because, in reality, he'd been Jinn for the last thirty years. The real Jinn and his former life were a distant memory.

The glass of the main bay window exploded, showering us with fragments. That's when Crescent, with his rocketpack, flew into the room and landed on the ground. His rocketpack assembly had a front chest nozzle, so he could stop his forward velocity quickly. He tossed me a packet and out came his high-tech machine gun. Most idiots didn't know that the windows of the modern megatower were more like clear steel. Plenty tried to do the "superman through the glass" routine only to break their necks, splat on the window and "return to surface," or bounce off and "return to surface." Those who did manage to crash through broke most of the bones in their face and body, or did the same by crashing into any wall inside. Crescent wasn't any of those idiots, even though his cyborg body probably could punch through a window. He smartly blew the glass before he flew in.

I was so glad he did because a hidden door opened in the wall and Jinn's personal corporate soldiers ran into the room, already firing their machine guns. Outside the window was an explosion of gunfire too. Jinn had his army; I had mine. However, we were in Jinn's domain.

My omega-gun was in my hand before the pack hit the floor. I never liked statues. In Metropolis, gangs liked to use them for surveillance cameras, cameras with remote-activated guns, or all kinds of things. Whether real or not, I didn't like them. One shot, and I blew off the king's head. But the now headless golden statue didn't fall. It jumped forward as its arms raised to point at me.

"Oh snaps!" I said to myself. Another android!

Even without its head, it blocked the barrage of gunfire I sent its way in those same mantis-like arm movements that the flying men of the Falcon Express used to defend themselves. Crescent had his own hands full with the corporate soldiers trying to storm the room. I was on my own against the golden android, and not one of my shots, steel round or laser, had hit its mark. My gut told me that no matter what I did, I couldn't allow the android to fire at us. I slapped in another bullet magazine as I kept firing lasers at it.

From the corner of my eye, I saw Jinn on the ground peek out. He pulled back his head out of view. I knew he was up to something. Likely, he planned to sucker-shoot me to allow his android to fire on Crescent and me. From the sounds of insane gunfire outside the window, Deca and her men wouldn't be coming to our aid in time.

I may have been firing my weapon with two hands, but I didn't need both of them. Jinn sat up with his own gun in hand, aimed at me. I jerked my gun toward him once without directly looking at him to fire, then returned to my onslaught against his android. I hit him in the neck, but he still managed to fire as he fell. The weapon fired a single laser beam. I managed to dive.

"Crescent, hit the ground!" I yelled.

Without having to defend against my gunfire, the android was free to fire, and it did. Its explosive round blew a quarter of the room apart. Jinn's laser hit the android and sliced the thing apart. The upper part of the android fired as its body fell and the round shot at the ceiling above Jinn, then again. I heard the yells from Jinn's corporate soldiers.

Then all we heard was things falling, and Jinn screaming.

Black smoke filled the room. Thankfully, the room didn't have a window anymore, so the wind dissipated it all fairly quickly so we could see again. The corporate soldiers were dead—their entire section was blown apart. The round that came close to hitting me blew apart half the room, and I could see into the hallway since the entire wall was gone. The round that hit the ceiling blew a massive hole into the floor of the above level. All its furniture rained down on Jinn.

"Crescent," I called out.

"Here," he answered back and I saw him stand to his feet. His clothing was blackened by the explosive round.

Corporate soldiers with jetpacks flew into the room, one after another. I recognized Kojo. "Get this off of the traitor!" he yelled at them.

The guardsmen did and Jinn was still alive at the bottom of the rubble. Neck wound, explosion blast wounds, furniture, and rubble on top of him, but he was still alive. His eyes looked glassy and he seemed to be drifting away.

Deca flew into the room with more corporate soldiers. She marched to the fallen imposter and pulled a metal baton from her belt. A giant needle popped out from the end. "Sorry, you won't be dying today. But soon." She stabbed him in the chest with it, and Jinn's body shook as his eyes and mouth popped open. He was back to fully conscious.

"Secure the floor!" Deca yelled.

More monarchy corporate soldiers flew in through the window from the sky.

I knelt down above Jinn. He stared at me without any emotion.

"You were the chief of staff to the king of the monarchy. You had a royal position for most of your adult life. You had real power. You could have done so much good for your people. Instead, you remained driven by hate. You said the king couldn't recognize you from the real Jinn. Really? You were offended? All this because you were offended? Maybe he didn't recognize either of you because you were too common for him to notice. Or maybe, he didn't notice because he meets a hundred people every day and can't commit all those names and faces to instant memory recall. You really are a crazy maniac. You wasted your life for nothing. All you will be remembered for is this. Your failed terrorist plot. You'll never be remembered for what good you could have accomplished."

"We are what we are," Jinn managed to say.

"That's nonsense. I was a laborer and a hovercar racer on the amateur circuit. I wanted more, so I became more. A foreign private detective helped bring you down. I'm sure you'll have a long time to reflect on it."

"He will have time to reflect on a great many things," Kojo said angrily, "but not any of that."

"If only you weren't on the Falcon Express," Jinn said to me from the floor.

"You're right, Mr. Jinn. Thank you. I thought I was the unlucky one, when it was actually you who was the unlucky one. I wonder how many masterminds like you were foiled because of a simple accident in life. I wasn't supposed to be on the Falcon Express, but I was."

He gave me a bloody smile. "What is it in fiction? Parallel universes? In one of them, I did kill you."

"Keep dreaming, you crazy maniac with the mantis fetish," I said.

* * *

I met the king one last time. They flew me to his palace. I'd never been in a palace before. Like on the Falcon Express, he walked right to me and extended a hand, but this time in front of the monarchy. The term had almost taken a sinister connotation but they were people—the youngest was five, and the oldest was one hundred and one. They were King Bahamut's family.

No one ever spoke of Jinn again. It was like he never existed. No one spoke of the U.F.O. organization ever again, so the acronym went back to meaning "unidentified flying object" alone and describing supposed government and megacorp secret test hovercrafts of Earth or Up-Top, maybe even extraterrestrials from Jinn's parallel universe.

I was treated like royalty myself that one night by the entire Saud Monarchy. I knew the hunt for any real or imagined U.F.O. co-conspirators was far from over. But my part was.

Should I have called this a bona fide horror mystery? There weren't buckets of blood, but there was blood. There weren't real-life monsters but there were real human monsters. A plane of two thousand was taken over by tech-terrorists willing to kill everyone aboard to get one man. A king had to be at peace with the notion that possibly a member of his own family would hate him so much that they might hire such craven psychos. A mastermind so consumed with hate that not even the passage of thirty years diminished the rage and blinded him to the real power he possessed to make the very changes for his people he desired. Yes, I'd call all of the above a horror show in my book. But for now, I'd put this file away. Case closed. My only task now was to cherish my own fortune in life that went beyond the fat fees received for services rendered for the Monarchy. I had something that a king would give away everything he owned to possess—a loving family.

I slept the entire flight back to Metropolis International because I wasn't taking any chances. If I heard anyone yell, "there's a man outside," I might have had a heart attack and died on the spot.

I did wake up as the hoverplane was making its final approach. From my window seat, I smiled at the sight of my Metro International and Interspace Airport and my supercity of Metropolis. When it touched down, I was officially home.

But I had a surprise waiting for me—a good one. I stepped out of the terminal into a light drizzle and there was a Let It Ride Enterprises hovertaxi cab. Its driver was none other than the boss himself, my best friend Run-Time. He wore his slim-fit business suits with slim ties everywhere. His trademark attire also included a flat hat.

"I should be mad at you," I said before he gave me a hug.

"Welcome back, Cruz."

I was so happy when I passed into my home neighborhood, Rabbit City. Then there was the Concrete Mama. My residential megatower that looked like a sparkling blue oasis in a vast desert to me.

Through the door I walked into my one-hundred-and-fiftieth-floor apartment with my single black suitcase on wheels.

"Honey, I'm home!"

I heard Cruz Jr.'s feet pitter-pattering on the floor. He came running first, and then came my wife, Dot, with Kat in her arms. I never knew how to catalog my U.F.O. case. Was it really a case, since I was a victim of the crime along with two thousand other people? I had the same rule as lawyers until then: lawyers don't represent themselves in court; private detectives don't investigate cases they're a victim in. It was a first and last, a one-off. I did identify its chief crazy maniac. I did get paid—many times, in fact, and a lot from many people besides the king for my time. Likely I'd put this case with my Classic Cyborg and Digital Samurai files. For now, I was home with my family. The universe, and anything relating to a case, would have to wait. I was on vacation at home (since the two we tried outside the home didn't work out so well) and would be unreachable for an indefinite period of time.

REVIEW REQUEST

Dear Reader,

I hope you enjoyed *The U.F.O. Case*.

<u>Can You Write Me a Review?</u>

If you enjoyed *The U.F.O. Case (Liquid Cool Series: From The Crazy Maniac Files, Book 3)*, I'd greatly appreciate an honest review on one or more of the following sites:

Reviews are the best way for readers to discover good books. My writer's motto is simple: "Readers Rule!" Thanks so much.

Always writing,

Austin Dragon

CONTINUE THE ADVENTURE

Get Your Next *Liquid Cool* Books!

These Mean Streets, Darkly (Liquid Cool Prequel Short)
Liquid Cool (Liquid Cool: The Cyberpunk Detective Series, Book 1)
Blade Gunner (Liquid Cool, Book 2)
NeuroDancer (Liquid Cool, Book 3)
The Electric Sheep Massacre (Liquid Cool, Book 4)
I, Alien Hunter (Liquid Cool, Book 5)
A.I. Confidential (Liquid Cool, Book 6)
Biopunk Blues (Liquid Cool, Book 7)
The Moon Is A Good Place to Die (Liquid Cool, Book 8)
Write Me a Murder on Jules Verne's Island: A Liquid Cool Cozy Murder Mystery (Book 9)
You'll Never See Starlight Again (Liquid Cool, Book 10) Coming 2023

Liquid Cool Box Set (Liquid Cool Prequel and Books 1-3)
Liquid Cool Box Set 2 (Liquid Cool: Books 4-6)
Liquid Cool Box Set 3 (Liquid Cool: Books 7-9)

***Liquid Cool: From the Crazy Maniac Files* mini-series**

Classic Cyborg (Book One)
Digital Samurai (Book Two)
The U.F.O. Case: A Liquid Cool Sci-Fi "Horror" Mystery (Book Three)

<u>Liquid Cool Box Set 4</u> (*Liquid Cool: From the Crazy Maniac Files Mini-Series: Books 1-3*)

<u>Also by Austin Dragon</u>

See all my books in science fiction, epic fantasy, and classic horror at: <u>http://www.austindragon.com/books</u>

ABOUT THE AUTHOR

Austin Dragon is the author of over 20 books in science fiction, fantasy, and classic horror. His works include the sci-fi detective *LIQUID COOL* series, the epic fantasy *FABLED QUEST CHRONICLES*, the international futuristic epic *AFTER EDEN* Series, the classic *SLEEPY HOLLOW HORRORS*, and the new *PLANET TAMERS* military sci-fi series. He is a native New Yorker but has called Los Angeles, California home for more than twenty years. Words to describe him, in no particular order: U.S. Army, English teacher, one-time resident of Paris, ex-political junkie, movie buff, Fortune 500 corporate recruiter, renaissance man, futurist, and dreamer.

He is currently working on new books and series in science fiction, epic fantasy, and classic horror!

http://www.austindragon.com/books

* * *